Lucy
Checks In

ALSO BY DEE ERNST

Maggie Finds Her Muse

Lucy Checks In

DEE ERNST

ST. MARTIN'S
GRIFFIN
NEW YORK

First published in the United States by St. Martin's Griffin, an imprint of St. Martin's Publishing Group

LUCY CHECKS IN. Copyright © 2022 by Elizabeth Ernst. All rights reserved. Printed in the United States of America. For information, address St. Martin's Publishing Group, 120 Broadway, New York, NY 10271.

www.stmartins.com

Designed by Jen Edwards

Library of Congress Cataloging-in-Publication Data

Names: Ernst, Dee, author.
Title: Lucy checks in / Dee Ernst.
Description: First edition. | New York : St. Martin's Griffin, 2022.
Identifiers: LCCN 2022005928 | ISBN 9781250844583 (trade paperback) | ISBN 9781250844590 (ebook)
Classification: LCC PS3605.R75 L83 2022 | DDC 813/.6—dc23
LC record available at https://lccn.loc.gov/2022005928

Our books may be purchased in bulk for promotional, educational, or business use. Please contact your local bookseller or the Macmillan Corporate and Premium Sales Department at 1-800-221-7945, extension 5442, or by email at MacmillanSpecialMarkets@macmillan.com.

First Edition: 2022

10 9 8 7 6 5 4 3 2 1

For the Parsippany–Troy Hills Public Library System

Jeanmarie knows why

Lucy
Checks In

Chapter One

Arriving in Paris was a big deal.

Well, of course it was. After all, it was friggin' *Paris*. More than that, I was almost to my final destination. As much as I would have liked to have spent days—weeks—exploring Paris and every single thing I'd read and heard and dreamed about it, I had a life to get to, and that life was beyond Paris.

So I boarded the train to Rennes, rested my head against the seat, and waited for my second act to begin.

We were famous for that, weren't we? Women, I mean. We believed in the second act, the next great thing, the moment when fortunes would change for the better. We reinvented ourselves all the time. I *myself* hadn't done it before, but that didn't mean that I didn't believe it was all possible and that I couldn't start over with a new life right now. And I wasn't actually reinventing my *whole* life. I was more or less scaling back. A less responsible job, a smaller place to call home, a more removed set of acquaintances.

Lucia Gianetti *Lite*.

I'd spent weeks thinking about these next few hours, and I had pretty much perfected the entire scenario in my mind. They were sending a car to meet me at the train station. Something sleek and shiny, no doubt. Or maybe a classic Bentley. That would be a nice touch. I would roll through the summer countryside, past fields of lavender—wait, that was Provence, never mind—until pulling into the shaded drive leading to Hotel Paradis.

I couldn't decide if the hotel was going to be a Disney-esque building with turrets and balconies, or something squarer and more substantial, like Highclere Castle, but smaller. Either way, the devoted staff would greet me, and I'd walk through the high-ceilinged front hallway, past priceless antiques and life-size portraits of a family who had run Hotel Paradis for over two hundred years, and into my new domain.

My next big adventure.

I jerked my eyes open. I didn't want to sleep away the train ride. I didn't want to miss a single bit of the exquisite scenery, especially not the rather delicious-looking gentleman across the aisle from me, wearing perfectly snug jeans and reading a battered paperback.

Did people still read books here? Paradise indeed.

I pulled out my phone and answered a flurry of texts that had come in since deplaning.

To my father: Yes, arrived safe on my way now.

I was touched by his concern, but let's face it, that was his job.

To my best friend: On the train to Rennes. Hot Frenchman alert already. I cannot WAIT until you visit.

Julia and I had been to England, Spain, and Greece together. We had somehow missed France entirely, although she had been numerous times, but now . . .

To my obnoxious brother Frank: Of course the FBI knows I left—I needed their permission you idiot.

Oh my God. Frank knew every sordid detail of the whole scandal. More than I did, I was sure. He was the kind of guy who reveled in other people's misfortunes, and to have such a glorious takedown involving his own sister was probably something he would cling to for the rest of his life.

To my less obnoxious brother Joe: Yes, I'm safe. Tell Mimi and Cara I'll send pictures.

Mimi was my nine-year-old niece, Camille. Cara was her twin sister, Caroline, and they were the only members of my family I was really going to miss.

It wasn't that I didn't love my family. I did. But I had been focused on a career that they had never approved of, and the more successful *I* became, the larger and higher the disapproval rating became. I'd lived at The Fielding Hotel for eight years, working twelve hours a day, often seven days a week. That kind of commitment to a job didn't leave much room for a commitment to anything else. Since my family never expressed anything but disapproval at my life choices, it became easy for me to distance myself from them.

I glanced at my watch. I'd taken the fast train to Rennes and had napped away the first half hour. Just a bit over an hour left . . . Maybe time for a drink?

I walked through a few train cars to the bar car. Yes, just like in the movies, there was a smiling man behind a miniature bar setup. I spoke slowly because my French was rusty. I'd studied the language in high school and, later, college. Before I'd been at The Fielding, I spent three years in Quebec at the Saint-Michel Hotel, where I spoke French every day. But that had been over ten years ago. I must have said the right thing, though, because he poured a glass of white wine, scanned my card, and thanked me with a smile.

I sat on the bench that ran across the length of the car and gazed out the window. Rolling countryside. Scattered farms. Wind turbines spinning in the golden French sunshine. I felt a sense of peace, and I finally let myself breathe. The past was past. I was on a new path. I even had a contract, signed and safely stashed in my carry-on, promising a monthly salary, a place to live, and the guarantee of six months' employment as manager of the centuries-old, family-owned Hotel Paradis beginning today, March 1.

I'd been homeless and unemployed for almost two years. Well, not technically homeless. I'd been living with my parents, and it had not been a happy arrangement. My mother never approved of my having a career that kept me from being happily married with lots of children, and she'd voiced her displeasure every time I'd paid a visit home. Having me live full-time in the same house allowed her to voice that same displeasure at least once a week.

I could see her point. Having to move back into my childhood bedroom—still remarkably unchanged after almost thirty years—while in career disgrace and financial ruin was not what any parent wanted for their child. They were both over seventy and had been quietly living out their golden years growing tomatoes and coddling the granddaughters their sons had so graciously given them. The last thing they wanted was a broke and depressed fortysomething moping around every day, only leaving the house to give depositions and appear in court.

The Fielding Hotel scandal had been huge. How often does a handsome and famous owner of a glamorous hotel make off with several million dollars of mostly other people's money and drop off the face of the earth? As the general manager of the hotel, the one left holding the bag, so to speak, my name appeared in newspapers, online, even on the nightly news for months on end. The fact that I had eventually been found entirely blameless had been mentioned once, in passing, and then ignored by pretty much the entire world.

The neighborhood where I grew up had not changed so much that my moving back had gone unnoticed. Old familiar names and faces shook their heads as I passed. Poor Lucy—not only unmarried and forced to live back with aging Sophia and Bruno, but probably going to prison for the rest of her life to boot.

But I didn't go to prison. My lawyers took every single penny I'd managed to save throughout my entire life, but the FBI finally dropped its case against me. Tony Fielding had also left millions in debt, but my lawyers took care of those lawsuits as well, and I was completely exonerated in the end. Although my name was mud in the hotel industry in the US, France had not had the same attitude. And here I was.

I knew how lucky I was. I was not going to take this gift lightly.

I finished my wine, thought about a second glass, decided no, and went back to my seat. The book-reading gentleman did not even glance up as I sat back down. Well, I'd gotten used to that. Once upon a time, I turned heads every time I entered a room. The Fielding had a small but very high-tech fitness center, and I ran nine miles on the treadmill every day for eight years. I had also had a standing weekly appointment for a mani-pedi and a monthly hair cut-and-color at the very chichi salon three blocks away.

But that had been a lifetime ago, when I had the money and the time and inclination. For the past two years, my only motivation for leaving my bedroom had been to appear in court or for yet *another* interview with one of the many law enforcement agencies that had become so intensely involved in my life. Then there were all those Italian cookies from the neighborhood bakery that I became very fond of, to the tune of three or four boxes a week. God knows I didn't have much money, but what I did have, I spent wisely.

I checked my watch again. Just twenty more minutes.

I was going to love this new life.

Emerging from the train with three large suitcases, a carry-on, and a purse required assistance from two porters and a complete stranger. Everything was piled onto a cart and rolled out of the station to the sidewalk where, I assumed, the driver of the limo/town car/Bentley would take things from there.

But there wasn't a limo/town car/Bentley. There was, instead, a shabby Volvo with a hand-drawn sign that read *Hotel Paradis* in the front window. The driver was slouched in the front seat, a cigarette dangling from his mustached lip, reading a newspaper.

"Hello," I called in English, waving.

He didn't look up.

I went over to the Volvo, rapped on the window, and switched to French. "Are you from Hotel Paradis?" He looked up from his newspaper, lifted his shoulders in a visible sigh, and got out. He took a look at my luggage and began to mumble under his breath. I couldn't hear him but easily understood his mood. He was not pleased. He threw all my suitcases into the trunk and slammed it shut, then walked back to the driver's side of the car and got in.

Oh.

I opened the back car door and slid in. The car smelled of cigarettes, evergreen, and cheese. I saw the familiar pine-tree-shaped air freshener hanging from the rearview mirror. It appeared to be very old, faded to gray, but obviously still pumping out an obnoxious, not-quite-pine-tree scent.

"*Merci,*" I said to him.

He grunted, started the car, and pulled away from the curb.

We drove away from the station, and I looked out onto the city. It was modern, with tall, sleek buildings of gray stone next to equally impressive structures that dated back centuries.

"Is the hotel far?" I asked. I spoke again in French. Did he speak English? It didn't matter. I needed to get back to speed, and quickly.

He shrugged and answered in French, "No. Just in the Old City."

Ah. I had assumed it to be *out* of the city, nestled in the countryside, but it certainly made more sense for a hotel to be close to the center of things. The château in my mind was quickly replaced by something more resembling the Plaza in New York—grand front doors opening onto a bustling sidewalk—but on a much more modest scale.

I could live with that. After all, The Fielding Hotel had been right in the heart of the city, all two hundred and twelve rooms of it, along with the bar, two restaurants, and four meeting rooms, which, once opened up, could handle any lavish event with up to four hundred guests.

Hotel Paradis could only accommodate up to forty guests. There was no bar, but breakfast would be served in the salon. A step down, to be sure, but a tiny, boutique hotel deserved the same level of service, and I was up to the task.

We turned a corner, and I knew immediately I was in the Old City. Modern buildings of gray and glass and smooth pavement were replaced by timber frames and cobblestones. The streets were narrow, and café tables crowded the uneven sidewalks. Everything was so *old*. I could feel it and stared in wonder at a Tommy Hilfiger shop displaying its clothes in windows set into a storefront that dated back centuries.

I had never driven a car in New York City in all the years I had lived there. I could tell that I'd probably never drive a car in Rennes, either. If there was a speed limit, my driver ignored it. If pedestrians had the right of way, they had to fight for it. And where, exactly, were the stop signs?

He suddenly made a sharp turn, pulled up onto the curb just at the corner, threw the Volvo into Park, and got out. I cautiously opened the door.

The street was narrow with tall trees shading the cobblestones. Stone and timber-framed buildings hugged the street as it curved away to the left. A café across from me had a bright red awning and tables crowded against the tall windows, and the smell of garlic and roasted meat made me suddenly remember I hadn't eaten in hours. The driver had stacked my suitcases on the sidewalk and slammed the trunk. I hurried over to fumble in my purse for money, but he waved me away. He went up to a set of iron gates with a keypad set into the wall. He hit a few numbers, and I heard a distinctive click. He gave me a quick salute, got in his car, and drove off.

I looked up at the iron gates in front of me. They were set into a high stone wall that stretched from the corner, where we had turned in, to around the curve in the road. Above the gates, in rusted letters, were the words *Hotel Paradis*.

I slowly pushed the gate open and stepped forward.

I was standing in a large courtyard, surrounded by the wall. Directly in front of me was the hotel, large and quite grand, three stories high, and made of gray stone. The front doors were arched and elaborately carved. The facade was perfectly symmetrical, with six tall windows on either side of the entrance, the pattern repeated on the second floor. The attic was slate, peppered with dormers and chimney stacks. There were large cast-iron planters lined up between the windows, but they were empty of any flowers or greenery.

On both the left and right sides of the courtyard were low buildings that looked like they had once been stables. The stone was neatly cut, and on the left, the stable row looked more carefully tended, with multipaned doors and windows where the doors to the stalls once had been. The wooden doors were painted blue, and behind the large windows, I could see pale curtains. The building on the right looked rougher, without modern doors and windows, but instead with the original wide stable doors, padlocked shut.

I walked slowly forward. I felt just like Julie Andrews in *The Sound of Music,* alone in front of the von Trapp mansion for the first time. The place was as big as I'd imagined. I'd googled "French hotels" and "French hotel history" and found whole Pinterest boards devoted to drawings and floor plans. I had, of course, pictured them in a different setting, but the building itself did not disappoint. Its condition, though . . . Were people even *living* here? Should I just walk in? Was there some sort of doorbell?

The closer I got, the more obvious the neglect became. Ripped fabric hung behind cracked glass, the paint around the windows and doors was chipped and faded, dirt and leaves piled up against the foundation. There was a white cat curled up, asleep, in one of the cast-iron planters. The place was silent.

The double front doors were at least ten feet tall, and there was a large door knocker in the center of each, a fleur-de-lis of pitted brass. Did I knock? And if I did, who would answer? A silent hunchback? A tall, sneering woman dressed in black? An ancient retainer with a limp?

As I stood there, trying to decide if I should just turn around and get the hell outta Dodge, I heard a man's voice.

"Can I help you?" He came out of one of the doors along the stable row. His voice was low-pitched, and he sounded British. Very British. Hugh Grant British.

"I'm looking for the owner. Claudine Capuçon?" I said. "Is she here?" I glanced over my shoulder, unsure about all my earthly possessions sitting on the sidewalk on the other side of the wall.

"Are you Lucia? We've been waiting for you." He was tall and rather thin, in wrinkled khaki pants and a denim shirt. "Did Georges just drop you here? Where's your luggage? God, he's so rude."

He hurried out onto the street. It took him three trips to bring my suitcases into the courtyard. Obviously, he wasn't as used to throwing luggage around as Georges had been.

"Where's Claudine?" I asked. My throat was suddenly closed as all my high hopes and great expectations began to slip away. I had envisioned a luxury boutique hotel that just needed a few nudges to bring it full swing into the high-tech, find-on-the-internet world of hospitality in the twenty-first century. This place looked like it hadn't made it much past the 1800s.

"I'm Colin, by the way. Colin Harding. I live here." He held out his hand, and I shook it, numb.

"Live here? Do you work at the hotel?"

"What? Oh, no. I just live here. Full-time. Six of us do, not counting Claudine. You'll meet everyone soon enough, I expect. Well, let's get your things into your *appart*."

He grabbed the handle of the largest suitcase and began to drag it across the courtyard, down toward the stable row.

"*Appart*?" I took hold of another suitcase and followed him. "I was told I'd have the manager's apartment."

"Yes, well, apartment. Here it's an *appartement*. *Appart* for short. You can call it that." He stopped at a closed door in the middle of the row and pushed it open with his foot. "You must have packed up your entire life in this suitcase. It weighs a ton. Did you have to pay the airline extra? I bet you did." He dropped it with a flourish. "Well, here you are. Look around, and I'll be back with the rest of your stuff."

The space was narrow and deep, the only light coming in from the glass panes of the doorway. I dropped the suitcase and carry-on to the floor and clutched my purse to my chest. The room was about ten feet wide and maybe twice as deep, with smooth plaster walls that had been painted a creamy white. The floor was wide-plank, very dark and very old wood, the ceiling low with blackened, exposed beams. At the far end, small paned windows were set high on the wall, and below them was what I assumed to be a kitchen: a white farmer's sink propped up on four elaborately carved legs and a tiny stove with an oven that looked just about right for baking one small cake. A single light fixture, possibly brass, hung over the sink. The room was empty of furniture except for a table pushed against the wall and two wooden chairs. I realized it was probably my imagination, but I could have sworn the place smelled of horse.

I took a few steps in. There was an open archway cut through the foot-thick walls to the next room, the bedroom. There was an iron bedstead near the floor-to-ceiling windows piled high with pillows, folded sheets, and a faded quilt. There was also a tall wardrobe, and when I opened it, I saw that this was my closet space. There was a standing lamp by the bed, but no dresser. The bathroom was tucked into the back, with the same row of high-set windows, a claw-foot tub, a toilet, and a sink, all scrubbed clean and smelling faintly of lemon.

At The Fielding, I'd had a suite of rooms on the top floor. We never called it the *penthouse*. That term had been reserved for the *guest* suites on the top floor. Two rooms and a bath, just like this, but overlooking Fifty-second Street. If I'd faced north, I could see Central Park. Floor-to-ceiling windows let in the view, the bathroom had a walk-in shower the size of most people's cars, and someone came in every day to clean the place up and refresh the vases of cut flowers.

I had, in the eight years I'd lived at The Fielding, replaced most of the standard-issue hotel furniture (not that it was in any way shabby—oh, no, they were top-of-line furnishings) with my own, preferred style of decoration: antiques in soft woods, watercolors on the walls, gleaming brass and copper reflecting the glow of neon coming from the street below. When the FBI closed in, every single item in the hotel was considered evidence, and after eighteen months in court, the only things I could claim as my possessions were the clothes in the closet and personal photographs I could prove were of family members.

Note to self: Save the receipts for *everything*.

So, when Colin had joked about my entire life being in my suitcases, he'd been right.

As he came through the front with the other suitcase full of the only things I legally owned in the world, I turned to him, trying to keep the panic out of my voice. "This is where I'm supposed to *live*?"

I didn't do a very good job in the quelling-panic department, because his face twisted.

"Oh, now, really. It's not too terrible. It's very comfortable in the summer. The thick walls keep the place cool, and it's easy to heat in the winter. I know it looks a bit small, but you really won't be spending much time here, right? You'll be at the hotel most of the time, tending to the rooms, and—"

"What? What do you mean?" I asked slowly. "*Tending to the rooms?* I'm the *manager*. Where's Claudine? I think there's been something of a misunderstanding somewhere."

"Claudine is at work. She'll be home around six. That's . . ." He glanced at his watch. "Three hours. Listen, would you like something to eat? Stavros across the street has excellent food, and I should, well, maybe I should explain a few things to you."

I stepped out into the courtyard and looked up at the hotel. "How many guests right now?"

"Now? Well, just the six of us."

"You mean the six of you who live here? Are there no paying guests?"

He drew himself up. "We are all paying guests."

"Yes. Of course. I meant . . . transient guests?"

"None. We couldn't accommodate a stray cat right now. Besides, no one knows who we are yet. You can't even google us. That's why you're here, right? To put us on the tourist map?"

"But this *is* a hotel?"

"Yes. For over two hundred years, but since the war, it's just been, well, this."

"Since . . . the *war*? You mean, like, since the forties?"

"The late thirties. Lucia, how about some food? And wine. I bet you could really use a glass of wine. It will make you feel so much better."

"Yes. And it's Lucy. Please." I followed him across the courtyard, through the large metal gate, and across the cobblestones, thinking there was not enough wine in the world.

Sitting down at the window, the sun blocked by the bright red awning with a glass of wine in front of me, I did feel so much better. It was possible that, somehow, I had gotten the wrong idea of what the Hotel Paradis was and where it wanted to go, but I was sure everything was just a slight misunderstanding. I sipped the wine while Colin spoke to the smiling waiter. His French was fluent, but even to my untutored ear, his accent was atrocious.

The wine slid down my throat like honey, smooth and soothing. I closed my eyes and took a bigger sip. Well, gulp. When I opened my eyes, Colin was looking at me intently.

"Makes all the difference in the world, doesn't it?" He was an attractive man with a thin face, wrinkles around his bright blue eyes, and fair hair that flopped across his forehead.

I nodded. "Yes. Thank you. You seem to know an awful lot about what's supposed to be going on with me and Claudine."

"Well, yes. I did all the correspondence, you see. Claudine doesn't speak English."

I tilted my head. "She doesn't speak English? At all?"

He nodded. "She understands a bit. Well, she understands a *lot,* but as for actually speaking, not to mention reading and writing, no. English is a very complicated language."

"But I thought that in Europe, everyone spoke everything. Or almost."

He spoke reasonably. "She speaks Spanish, Russian, Croatian, and Portuguese. She understands a bit of Italian and English. How many languages do you speak?"

Touché. "Italian. French. And a little Spanish." Italian because that was what my parents spoke at home. My very little Spanish was a hybrid learned over the years from my Central American housekeeping staff and Cuban kitchen workers. "She speaks no English. Well. So, you wrote all the emails? And the contract?"

"Not the contract. She had the lawyer do that. But as for the emails . . . yes, I sent them. Claudine's words, of course." He shrugged again and smiled.

"But . . ." Those emails had sold me on taking the job. True, it had been the only offer of employment I'd gotten since my rather abrupt and disgraceful departure from Fielding Hospitality Enterprises Inc. "This is not what I expected."

"And what did you expect?"

Should I mention the château and Bentley? My mind circled

back to that very first email introducing me to Hotel Paradis and the city of Rennes. "Has it really been family-owned for centuries?"

He nodded. "Yes. The Perrot family. A fire wiped out half the city in the 1720s, and the estate burned to the ground. The house was rebuilt around 1740. In the early 1800s, it was decided to convert the place to a hotel. The remodel took almost five years, I believe. The stables were built about the same time. They were converted to flats in the twenties. For the staff."

"Is that where you all live now? You full-timers?"

He nodded. "Yes. And we'll continue to stay there. The only rooms that are going to be rented out are in the hotel proper. I hope you have lots of ideas."

I *did* have ideas. Tons of them. Most of them were about noodling around on a brand-new website and uploading photographs of grand, beautiful rooms filled with antique beds and gauzy white curtains framing a pastoral view. "About those rooms. In the actual hotel. How many of those are rentable?"

"You mean, right *now*? None of them. Unless you can convince Claudine to give up her rooms. Bing is living in the attic, so that's pretty well furnished, but getting him to move would require an act of God."

A steaming bowl of soup was placed in front of me with bits of potato and leek swimming in a pale, creamy broth. A basket of bread appeared, and as the waiter withdrew his hand, I grabbed it. "More wine, please?" I stared at the soup, trying to find something positive to latch on to. "Bing?"

"David Bingham. Rather a brash sort of fellow. He's a writer, kids' stuff. Been living here since the nineties. He and Claudine have a history. . . . Ah, Stavros, excellent soup, as always. This is Lucy Gianetti. She's the one who's going to turn the hotel around. Lucy, this is Stavros Collard. He owns this café and is also a partner in the hotel."

I stared at Colin. "A partner?"

"Well, of course. Claudine had to raise the money somehow. Stavros is a partner, as is Georges. They not only put up cash, they are part of the enterprise. Georges will provide all the transportation for guests to and from the train station. Stavros here will oversee the hotel kitchen."

I looked up.

Stavros Collard was tall, well over six feet, with broad shoulders and muscular arms practically bursting out of a pale blue T-shirt. His hair was thick and curled around his head like lamb's wool, gray and wiry. "We are all counting on you," he said in perfect English with barely an accent. "We have put our hopes in the hotel, and Andre assured us that you were the one to turn the old beauty around for us."

"It's a pleasure, Mr. Collard."

He took my hand and squeezed briefly. "Stavros. Please. After all, we will be seeing each other every day, no? Unless you want to share your meals with Claudine, and I can tell you, for a Frenchwoman she is a terrible cook. No, you will eat here, and we will become friends." His teeth were small and even as he smiled.

"Of course," I said faintly. He bobbed his head and backed away, and I looked down at my soup again. I took a spoonful, then another. It was delicious, and I found my strength growing with every swallow.

"By *Andre,* did he mean Andre Mollner?" I asked.

Colin nodded.

Andre Mollner had been a long-standing client of my lawyer's, and that's how he'd gotten my number. He'd called me out of nowhere and introduced himself by saying that he'd found the perfect job for me. The man insisted that no one in Rennes cared about what happened at The Fielding and that I would be welcomed with open arms.

Well, naturally they'd welcome me. I was probably the only one they could find who would take a job at a hotel without ever setting foot on the property, because if I had . . .

"Okay, Colin. I'm curious. Why did you hire *me*? Exactly?"

"Well, to be honest, we almost didn't. Here in Europe, to hire someone who is not a citizen of the EU for a job . . . well, you need a very good reason. But Claudine wanted someone who knew the American market, who would know what to say and do to attract American tourists. And someone who could design a website that catered to American tastes. She also wanted someone who did not have an accent, since she spoke no English at all. Hiring you was a lot of work. We were lucky that Andre recommended you. He knew of your, ah, situation, and, well . . ."

"And that I couldn't find a decent job anywhere in the US, so I had to take whatever crumbs got thrown my way?"

"Nonsense. Andre told us you had been completely innocent in the Fielding matter. He also insisted that you had been responsible for making The Fielding Hotel the talk of New York City. Why wouldn't we want that kind of expertise here?"

Man, he was good. "Claudine knew Andre how?"

"I have no idea. The woman has relations all over the world. Second cousin? On her ex-husband's side?"

"And all the investors you mentioned . . . Stavros and Georges?" I asked Colin.

"Yes. Also, Bing put up some money. So did I, for that matter. And Raoul, he is a carpenter. He didn't put up any cash, but he will be doing the renovations for us."

I ate more soup. "I see. You made it sound like there were a couple of billionaires who needed a bit of something to dabble in during their spare time." And I had envisioned having cocktails with those same French billionaires, sipping a martini on a terrace. Instead, I'd be eating soup and getting free rides in a Volvo.

"You also said—"

"Claudine said," Colin corrected. "I just translated, remember?"

I looked at him. "But what you translated wasn't the truth."

He drew back, looking hurt and surprised. "Of course it was the truth. I dare you to find one word I wrote that wasn't one hundred percent true. Go on."

I knew if I opened my laptop that very minute and went through every one of the twenty-seven emails that went back and forth between myself and Claudine Capuçon, he'd be right. He hadn't lied. He hadn't even shaded a single line. It was my own imagination, running wild at the idea of starting my career over as the manager of a small hotel a few hours away from Paris, that had colored every single word he had written.

Another plate was set before me. Beef and mushrooms in a gravy that smelled of herbs and red wine. I broke off a bit of bread and dipped it in, then put it in my mouth and chewed slowly.

Heaven.

Well, I was here. I had a place to live until the fall, and I had a salary. Not much of one, to be sure, but I didn't have to worry about rent. With my visa, I had health care paid for after three months, and if I could eat food like this every day, how bad would it be?

Besides, where else was I going to go?

Chapter Two

I hung up most of my clothes, and they just about fit into the
wardrobe on old-fashioned wire hangers. I had no clue what I
was going to do with the rest of my things. I carried my toiletries
into the bathroom. There was no place to put them but in the claw-
foot tub. I knew that back in the States, a claw-foot tub would have
drawn exclamations of jealousy and rapture, but all I could think
about was not being able to stand up under a shower of steaming-
hot water unless I held the nozzle over my head.

Who was I kidding? What were the chances of there even *being*
steaming-hot water?

With nothing else to do, I carefully made the bed, noting that
the pillows were made of real down, and the quilt was old but thick
and beautifully stitched.

"Lucy?" Colin called. "Claudine is back. Are you ready to meet
her?"

Was I? Who knew? Ordinarily, I'd have changed into my red
power suit, put on makeup, and slid my feet into killer heels to look
the part. But that red suit had fit like a glove twenty pounds ago,
and I imagined that I'd look like one of those balloon people that
clowns made at kids' parties if I put it on now.

Besides, I felt lied to (even though I knew I hadn't been), cheated (out of what? I hadn't done anything yet), and altogether scammed (even if it was probably all my fault). I had read every single email that I'd received from Claudine and reread the contract. The job had not been misrepresented in any way. I had just been an idiot. A miserable, exhausted, broke idiot who had been beaten down to a quivering mass of self-doubt and self-pity and had grabbed at the first straw that had drifted by.

The only straw.

I went back into the bathroom and looked in the small mirror that hung over the sink. I looked old. No. Not old. I looked my age, which I hadn't until this past year. I also looked tired, but that was easily explained. I'd just flown across the ocean, hadn't I? What I would not tolerate was looking like a complete loser. I crouched by the tub and hunted through the carry-on until I found what I needed. I carefully put on some lipstick and vigorously brushed my hair until it fluffed out from my head in bouncy curls. They may have been salt-and-pepper curls, but, by God, they were perky.

"Coming," I called. I grabbed my laptop off the kitchen table, pulled my very expensive pen and red leather notebook out of my purse, and followed Colin out of the room, across the twilit court-yard, and into Hotel Paradis.

The lobby was cool and dark, with a black-and-white marble-tiled floor and a massive chandelier that hung in darkness from the twelve-foot ceiling. This had once been the vestibule of a manor house, and the grandeur was still there. To the left was an alcove that housed a sweeping staircase to the second floor. Across from the front doors, I could see a huge salon, lost in darkness, its floor-to-ceiling windows shuttered tightly. To the right was a long counter made of dark wood that looked to be mahogany. Behind it, I could see the pigeonholes where room keys would have been kept. I stopped and stared. I had—literally—only seen those in the movies. There was a large library table in the center of the space with beautifully carved legs, and brass sconces along the walls provided a soft light.

It was a step back in time, and if I squinted to blur out the chipped wood and dull metal, the water-stained plaster and dingy windows, the place was magnificent.

"Wow," I whispered.

Colin must have heard me because he grinned over his shoulder. "She's something else, isn't she?"

Yes, she was.

And so was Claudine Capuçon. "*Bonjour,*" she sang out as she swept into the lobby.

What was I expecting? A chic and icy old woman in a severe suit and lots of diamonds? Or maybe a wild-haired, boho-chic, middle-aged hippie, dripping in gold necklaces and dangly earrings? A huddled crone, with a skinny black cigar between bright red lips and clawlike hands?

She looked to be older than me, probably by ten years, and I swear her hair was the same mix of gray curls and shaggy layers as mine. She was wearing bright, red-framed glasses and a simple sweater with slacks. She rushed over to me and hugged me, speaking so rapidly that even if she were speaking English, I doubt I could have understood it all.

"Claudine," Colin said, then rattled off some French, and Claudine stepped back.

"Welcome," she said carefully.

"*Merci,*" I answered, just as carefully.

We walked past the main staircase and down a narrow passage that opened to a room that was calm and simple, sleek lines of furniture completely out of sync with the plaster walls, tall windows, and ornate woodwork. We sat down at a small, round table covered in a vibrant, colorful cloth, and she poured wine. Colin sat with us, and the three of us clinked glasses.

"I know you speak French," Colin said, "but you did say you

weren't too sure of how proficient you were. If you don't mind, I'll just sit here and make sure there are no, ah, misinterpretations."

I was fine with that. While I could already feel my "ear" coming back, I didn't want to agree to anything that might be a disaster because of a misplaced vowel.

"Have you made any type of plan for your first few weeks here?" she asked.

I opened my laptop. "I've been thinking about a website." I made sure I spoke slowly and clearly. "What kind of budget were you thinking of? There are several options available, depending on what services we choose. Do we want people to be able to make reservations online? Because that requires rather expensive software, but we can probably find one of these companies to accommodate us."

She listened, then made a face. "There is no budget for a website. Can't you do it yourself? I've looked at a few, and it looks easy enough to do."

I continued to scroll through all my carefully researched website hosts, my mind racing. "I've never built a website on my own," I said.

"My godson has one. If a fifteen-year-old can do it, how hard can it be?"

My mind went over the emails I'd reread in the past hour. As a matter of fact, I *had* assured Claudine that I would be happy to help build a website that was easy to use and attractive to American travelers. Hmmm . . .

"Well, then I guess we can start by taking pictures of the rooms and getting all the rates online. Unless you already have pictures we can use?"

She shook her head. "No. You see, none of the rooms are ready to be photographed. They all need to be painted and decorated."

I sat back and stared at her, then at Colin. "What is she talking about?" I said to him in English. "Painted? These rooms aren't even *painted*?"

He shrugged and looked apologetic. "I told you the hotel had been essentially vacant since before the war."

"But . . ."

He leaned forward. "It says in your contract that you will be responsible for bringing all the existing accommodations up to a standard acceptable to American tourists."

"True. But I didn't think the baseline would be so . . . low. Is there someone already lined up to do all the painting and, I guess, decorating and cleaning?"

Colin listened and turned to Claudine. There was a lengthy and heated exchange, too fast for me to follow, before she turned back to me.

"That would be you," she said.

I closed my laptop and sat back, arms folded across my chest. "Now, wait just a minute . . ."

Claudine's smile never wavered, but her eyes were cold. "Lucy, do you know what your role *is* here? Did you have a lawyer look over your contract? What didn't you understand?"

"I understood it perfectly. I just assumed that my role would be more of a *supervisory* position. You know, telling people what to do."

Claudine stopped smiling. "I am the owner. I am the one telling *you* what to do."

I think my jaw dropped open. Oh, dear Lord, what had I gotten myself into?

In the section of the contract that was specifically about preparing the hotel for its opening, there was no mention of painting aged plaster walls or any other type of physical labor. As I geared myself up to argue, I realized there was nothing there that *exempted* any of that, and that *preparation* was a relative term. I had expected to be ordering around a bunch of worker bees who would be arranging priceless antiques and rehanging ancestral portraits, leaving me the less arduous duties of putting fresh flowers into crystal vases and plumping up linen pillows. That was not, apparently, Claudine's expectation.

"Well, I certainly can't do everything by myself," I stammered, trying to regroup. I hadn't painted a room since I'd moved into my first apartment in college.

Claudine was smiling again. "Of course not," she said. "Everyone living here will help you. We are all invested in making Hotel Paradis a success."

I felt every plan I had carefully formulated in my head fold up and scatter like a house of cards. I closed my eyes and took a few deep breaths.

"Lucy?" Claudine said, pronouncing slowly. "We have faith."

I opened my eyes and was surprised at the tears in them. "Why?"

She spoke gently. "Because no one works harder than a person with something to prove."

Back in my room, I reached for my phone. What time was it in the States, anyway? I didn't even try to do the math. I just dialed.

Julia Wilson answered on the third ring. "Oh my God! Are you there? Is it fabulous? Why aren't you on FaceTime so I can see your amazing new home?"

I sat on the edge of the wooden chair and looked around at my amazing new home. "Julia, it's a mess. This place is a relic. The rooms have been unused for decades, and my so-called apartment used to be a horse's stall. There's no staff; it's just me and the other people who live here, who I haven't even met, and there's no money for a website—how am *I* supposed to build a *website*?" I could feel the tears starting and my breath come up short. "It's all terrible, Julia. I'm such a fool to think *this* was going to solve all my problems."

"Okay, Lucy? Just take a few deep breaths." I pictured her, probably in her Upper West Side apartment, or maybe in her office at the small but prestigious Maxwell Gallery. She'd be wearing black—she always wore black until high summer—and she'd push back her short, perfectly dyed blond hair with one hand while holding her phone with the other. "Tell me from the beginning. You're there."

"Yes."

"In . . . Where are you again?"

"Rennes."

"Right. Is it a big city?"

"Yes. And beautiful. It's *old,* Julia, everything is so old and looks like something from the movies."

"So. You're *in* the city. Not some country estate?"

"No. I mean yes. Right in the city."

"And it's not what you'd pictured?"

"God, no."

"Well, honey, let's face it. You had built this place up in your head for weeks. To be honest, I couldn't imagine anything living up to your expectations. You kept talking like you were going to manage Downton Abbey."

I buried my face in one hand and with the other gripped the cell phone so tightly my fingers hurt. "I know, but . . . Julia, she thinks *I'm* going to paint all the rooms."

I think she was drinking because it sounded like she spit something out all over her phone.

"You? Paint all the rooms? Have you ever even held a paintbrush?"

"Of course I have," I shot back, feeling defensive.

"Oh, Lucy. My poor darling. I know you had so much riding on this. I'm so sorry it didn't work out. How terrible is this going to be for you, coming back after such a buildup about how wonderful this job was?"

I lifted my head slowly.

To say there had been a buildup to this job was putting it mildly. I had practically thrown it in the faces of my family, especially my little brother Frank, who had spent months making snarky comments about how the only hotel job I would ever get again would be as a dishwasher. My father had practically taken out an ad in the *Neighbor News* when I got the offer, he'd been so proud. And I'd spent weeks practicing French in the middle of the living room, at the top of my voice, whenever Mom had been around.

How terrible?

"I can't come back," I blurted.

"Wait . . . what? But, Lucy, you just told me it was awful."

"It is."

"And you're going to have to paint? Like, on a ladder and everything? Honey, we're looking at fifty. At our age, getting up on a ladder is dangerous."

"Julia, if I crawl back home now, without even trying, I'll die in my old bedroom, wearing really bad shoes and surrounded by cats."

"Oh, Lucy . . ." She was silent for a moment. "You know you can always move in here with me."

I felt a rush of gratitude. "I know. Of course, your husband wasn't thrilled the first time you offered, and I doubt he's changed his mind. And like I said, if I moved in with you, I'd never move out."

"So . . . what are you going to do?"

I had no idea. Until that moment, my mind had been in such a whirl I hadn't thought about anything beyond getting to the safety of this room. I swallowed. Hard. "I have to stay for at least six months."

"Six months?"

"That's how long my contract is. That's how long they have to give me a place to live and a paycheck, and that's more than I'd get if I went crawling back to New Jersey."

"True that." More silence. "What can I do? Do you need money?"

"I'm fine. I mean, I don't *have* any money. My lawyers took everything. But then, I have nothing to spend it on here. I have a place to live, and I guess they're going to feed me, and since I'll be spending the next few months painting walls and scrubbing floors, I won't be going anywhere . . ."

"Oh, honey. Just wait a minute. Aren't you, like, two hours from Paris?"

I finally smiled. "Yes. But I was saving that for you to show me."

"Well, don't. You grab that first day off, and you go and stand by the river Seine and send me a picture of your gorgeous face in front of the Eiffel Tower."

"Oh, Julia, I miss you already."

She sighed. "I miss you, too. And you know what? You can do anything you set your mind to, Lucy. I know you've had a few bad years, but remember before all this crap happened? Remember how great your life was? Remember how great *you* were?"

Yes, I did remember. I ran The Fielding Hotel like a well-oiled machine, and after a very rocky start, it began making money, making employees happy, making guests *very* happy. We'd been written up in everything from *New York* magazine to *The New York Times*. I had hobnobbed with the East Coast elite, or at least the Manhattan elite. And I had been in love with a marvelous, cultured, successful man who I'd thought loved me back until he ran off with millions of dollars and left me to deal with the unpaid staff, the angry guests, the FBI, the unions, and the investors—all of whom kept looking at me and saying, "But you *had* to have known. . . ."

I hadn't known. Not a bit. And I'd been just as shocked and devastated as everyone else.

But before that, boy, life had been grand.

I nodded to myself. "Yeah. You're right. I was hot stuff, wasn't I?"

"Baby, you still are."

"Yes. I am. And if anyone can take this wreck of a place and turn it into a showstopper, I can."

"There you go."

"Anyone can build a website these days."

"Absolutely."

I stood up and stared out of my window. "I can paint a room. How hard can that be? And you know how good I am about decorating."

"Your place was a stunner, Lucy."

"That's right. Why, I bet this place is loaded with great furniture and all sorts of beautiful things, just waiting for me."

"That's my girl."

"I'm good."

"Lucy, you're the best."

Outside, across the courtyard, I could see the attic rooms suddenly light up. "I can do this."

"Yes. You can."

"Thanks, Jules. I love you, and I'll talk to you soon."

I clicked off the phone and watched as the lights in the attic flickered. David Bingham, I presumed. I could see him pacing in front of one of the narrow windows. Otherwise, the courtyard was empty and quiet, pale light coming from a few windows along the stable row and a single window on the first floor of the hotel.

I stepped out into the middle of the courtyard. The air was cool, and I could hear the bare branches rustling in the breeze. The cat I'd seen earlier walked slowly out of the shadows, looked at me with slight regard, then vanished.

My kingdom. All I had to do was conquer it.

But first, I needed to find the plug adapter, recharge my phone and laptop, and start making new lists.

The mattress on the iron bed was surprisingly comfortable, and I woke up feeling slightly jet-lagged but mostly refreshed. I had opened the window just a crack before I'd gone to sleep the previous night, and I could hear a bit of noise outside. When I went to the window, I could see movement in the courtyard. I cautiously moved the curtain to peek.

Colin was standing toe-to-toe with a much younger, much larger man who was yelling and making wild gestures. I feared for Colin, thinking that one of those wildly flailing arms could easily knock him over. Their conversation was in French, and it was obvious the argument was about whether the young man was staying for the day or heading out to another job.

The third man, standing with his back to me, watched, shaking his head. Finally, he threw up his arms and yelled, "Colin, stop! You're being unreasonable. Let Raoul go. The poor man needs to make a living, and that woman probably packed her bags and ran off in the middle of the night as fast as her American legs could carry her."

Excuse me?

I was dressed in a striped sleep shirt that fell almost to my knees. Totally inappropriate attire for having a conversation first thing in the morning out of doors with three men I didn't know. But that was *me* he was talking about, and as my imaginary hackles rose, I left the bedroom, marched to the front door, and pulled it open. Colin stopped arguing and turned away from Raoul. As he did, he saw me.

He spoke English. "Well, look at that. She didn't run away at all. Lucy, this is Raoul Fournier. He is here to talk to you about what repairs need to be done to the rooms. And this one here? He's David Bingham. Bing, meet Lucia Gianetti."

I crossed my arms across my chest, partially as a defensive measure in a possibly hostile situation and partially to prevent my boobs from bouncing around too much. I lifted my chin. "Still here, Mr. Bingham. Sorry to disappoint you."

He turned, and can I tell you? My heart almost stopped.

He was not handsome. Well, okay. Maybe he was. His forehead was high, and his face angular. His hair was pewter gray and long, brushed back away from his face, Lord Byron–style. He had a beard, trimmed short, gray with flecks of white. His lips were very full, and he seemed to be gritting his teeth. He was slope-shouldered and dressed in jeans and an oxford shirt of crisp white cotton, sleeves rolled up, revealing hairy and muscular arms. He was not tall, barely taller than my five foot six. But there was something about him that hit me, hard, right in the gut.

"So, you're the one who's going to save us all? How are you going to do that?" His voice was deep and had a vague southern twang. All the cutting and succinct replies I had on the tip of my tongue slid back down my throat, leaving my brain and my mouth gasping like a dying fish.

I clenched my jaw. *Think, think, think.* "I have plans," I finally blurted.

"Like what, Miss Gianetti?" he countered. "Are you going to paint all the rooms soft green with billowing drapes and fluffy pillows, like every other small hotel in Rennes?"

I may have been knocked off-kilter by a sudden and inexplicable attraction to a man I didn't know and, from his obvious arrogance and swagger, would probably grow to despise, but I had done the work. "Most of the small hotels in Rennes are decorated in a very modern, almost minimalist style. If you do a bit of research online, you'll see that these places have completely stepped away from that shabby-chic Parisian look. So offering soft green and fluff would set us apart. But I'm going to go more classic. All the rooms will be white."

"Well, isn't that boring."

I mentally counted to three. "No, not boring at all. *Classic.* If you'd bother to look at any decorating magazine published in Europe in the last six months, you'd know that." I knew exactly how the rooms should look to draw top dollar from affluent tourists who wanted an authentic experience in a town known for its medieval buildings and centuries-long history. I wasn't going to let Mr. Sexy-Eyes mansplain my job to me. Now that I'd realized I'd be painting all those white walls myself, my enthusiasm had somewhat waned, but my vision hadn't changed.

I tore my eyes away from his and looked at Raoul. I spoke to him in French, thinking that I'd have to get faster at switching from one piece of my brain to another. "It's a pleasure to meet you, Raoul. I need to change and have some coffee. Why don't I meet you in the hotel lobby? I haven't seen any interiors yet, and we need a plan for getting these rooms in order. Give me fifteen minutes, okay?"

Raoul nodded and headed to the hotel.

David Bingham snorted out a laugh. "Fifteen minutes? I've never met a woman who could get herself ready in the morning in just fifteen minutes."

"Yes. Well, you've never met me before, have you, Mr. Bingham?"

Suddenly, he grinned, and the blast of charm almost knocked me back on the cobblestones. "It's Bing. Tell you what—if you can be out in fifteen minutes, I'll have coffee ready for you."

I needed a shower. I needed to do something with my hair to curb all those flyaway curls. I needed to find the perfect I'm-a-professional-but-can-still-be-sexy outfit. I needed to lose—or hide—fifteen pounds and all the wrinkles around my eyes.

"It's Lucy."

He shook his head slowly. "No. It's Lucia."

I held his eyes. "Fine. And it's a deal."

I managed it. Not the losing weight or wrinkle removal part of the wish list, but I was clean. My hair was up in a messy bun, but at least it was out of my face. I found my best-fitting jeans and a tunic in my favorite cobalt blue that hid the paunch around my middle. I pushed my way through the main doors of Hotel Paradis with two minutes to spare.

Last night, I had met with Claudine in rooms to the left of the lobby that made up her personal suite. I walked to the right now, behind the long counter, following the sound of voices to a narrow office, crowded with two massive wooden desks, a bookcase crammed with books and files, and a computer setup that looked to be at least ten years out of date.

Bing was leaning against an elaborate fireplace mantel, out of place among the twenty-first-century clutter.

He straightened when I came in. "Congratulations. You are the proud winner of one cup of coffee. I have American-style, if you'd like. Or café crème?"

I didn't know what café crème was, but if I was going to be living in this country, I should probably start acting like a bit of a native. "Café crème. Please."

He nodded and left. Raoul was perched on the edge of one of the desks, but he slid off and held out the chair for me. "Please, Miss Lucy. Sit."

"Thanks. And no 'miss,' please. After all, we'll be working together, yes?"

He smiled and practically lit up the entire room. He was a beautiful young man, probably in his early twenties, with broad shoulders and narrow hips in splotched painter's pants and a T-shirt, torn in a few places and showing smooth skin on what I imagined to be washboard abs. His eyes were bright blue, and they were smiling as well.

"Do you speak English?" I asked.

He shook his head, nodded, then shrugged. I decided to stay with English just to see where it all went. "So, have you been working on anything here yet? How does it look to you?"

"Well." He pulled up another chair, swung it around, and

straddled it, forearms dangling over the back. "In nineties, many improvements made. Lights, water . . . Much money spent. But since . . ." He shrugged. "More work needed."

Well, that didn't sound too promising. "Colin said you were going to do the repairs?"

He nodded. "Yes. Is my job. Plaster, wood, windows. All my job."

Well, that was a relief. "What about painting? And the floors?"

He shook his head. "That your job."

Bing came in, a steaming cup in each hand, and he put one cup in front of me. "I don't think he means that you are personally responsible for sanding and refinishing the wooden floors."

I took a sip. This was café crème? He couldn't have just called it a latte? Or was that a strictly Starbucks term?

"Thanks. But the painting is? My personal responsibility?"

Bing made a sort of snort that was almost a laugh as he and Raoul exchanged a look.

"Maybe. Probably," Bing said, a hint of a smile at his lips. "This was a perfectly functioning hotel at one time."

I sipped. Yep, this was latte, all right, but the coffee flavor was deep, and the milk tasted very different from what I was used to. "That was what, eighty years ago? Has everything been kept up to date?"

Bing made another one of those snort-laughs. "Barely."

I sipped again. "Is Claudine here? Maybe I should be talking to her as well."

"Claudine meant to be here, but there was an emergency of some kind at work. She did say she was going to try to come right back. She's, well . . . you would call her a CPA. She has her own firm," Bing explained. "Raoul and I can give you the grand tour and answer any questions you might have until she returns."

I found that looking at Bing was distracting. I watched his mouth move, and as I did, I wondered how the gray stubble on his upper lip would feel against my skin. I shifted my gaze to Raoul, who was much more pleasing to look at but did not elicit anywhere near the same response.

"Are you qualified to do this work? I hate to ask, but . . ." I certainly didn't need a well-meaning DIY-er doing repairs on two-hundred-year-old walls.

"Yes. I work with brother building houses. Many years. But Claudine says I can be partner if I work for her. Would be good to be business owner, yes?"

I drank more coffee, and as it hit my stomach, I was reminded that I hadn't eaten. "How many partners are there, exactly?"

Bing leaned back against the desk and cradled his coffee cup in both hands. "Colin put in a chunk. Stavros is going to be running the kitchen, providing free breakfast for the guests. No cash output, so he gets a smaller slice. Raoul has no cash, either, but he has a very real skill set, so he's in for a bigger cut."

"And you?" I asked, looking at him. His eyes were light. Gray? Hazel? Whatever color they were, they suddenly brightened.

"I put up the money for your salary. Claudine let me live here rent-free for a number of years, and I owed her, big-time."

"But that's a lot of money. Why would you do that?"

He frowned. "Because I don't want Claudine to be working in an office at eighty when all she wants to do is quit her job and be the charming, gracious hostess she was born to be. Raoul here should be making handcrafted furniture instead of hammering together two-by-fours. Colin needs to stop teaching music theory and start composing symphonies."

"Interesting. And what about Georges? Is he going to give up driving his car to design women's shoes?"

Bing stared a moment, then threw back his head and laughed. "That's very good. I was beginning to think you had no sense of humor at all. No, Georges will probably be buried in that Volvo. He's just one of Claudine's strays, looking for a place to belong."

He watched me as I finished the café crème. Best morning coffee I'd had in years.

"Did you eat?" he asked.

"What? No. But that's okay. I can get something later."

"No. Raoul, run across the street and grab whatever Stavros has handy. Come on, Lucia. Let me give you the grand tour."

Okay, then. Here we go.

Chapter Three

The grand stairs were just off the lobby, as was an elevator, obviously built in the twenties. It was small, barely big enough for two people and one suitcase, behind doors festooned with wrought iron in an art deco pattern. "Is this safe?" I asked.

"Absolutely. It was upgraded sometime in the sixties. Claudine remembers it as being a very big deal. And it really hasn't been used very much since then. I believe it was inspected recently."

We went up the stairs. "There are a few guest rooms on the ground floor," Bing explained, "but most of the work will be up here."

At the top of the stairs was a landing, with the obligatory chandelier and a spacious corridor with tall, carved doors leading to rooms on the front and back of the hotel.

"The rooms behind us overlook the side of the hotel. Basically, it's an alley. But the rest of the rooms have some sort of view." He led me forward and opened a tall wooden door, its creamy white paint peeling off in long curlicues.

"All the rooms on this side overlook the interior patio," Bing said.

I took a step in.

"On the other side, the rooms overlook the front courtyard. And at the other end there, those rooms look out on our garden."

"There's a garden?" I asked, taking another step. The first thing that caught my eye was a beautiful fireplace, its mantel made of carved marble.

"Yes, but it's a real garden. That is . . . well, we grow things there."

We? Who was "we"? And what kinds of things? "Oh?" I looked around. "Oh . . ."

The ceiling here was also twelve feet tall. Water stains darkened the plaster walls. The windows were almost to the ceiling and broad, a few panes cracked, with a simple diamond pattern across the very top of the glass. In the center of the filthy wooden floor was a cluster of furniture. Or at least I assumed furniture. There was a dusty tarp thrown over the top of the pile, but I could see the curved legs of a chair and possibly a bed underneath.

I walked past the fireplace. "Does this work?"

"Maybe."

I then went to the window and looked.

The entire back of the property was enclosed by another one of those high stone walls. Below me was an empty patio of gray slate, the silhouettes of barely leafed-out trees casting shadows in the pale sunlight.

"What a view!" I said, feeling a surge of excitement. "How about this balcony? Is it safe? Can guests have direct access to the courtyard from up here?"

Bing came up behind me to look over my shoulder. I could feel the heat of his body against my back, and I could smell something that reminded me of turpentine. Was he painting something? And did he really have to stand so close to me?

"The balconies are all safe. There's been some sort of inspection in the past year. And there's another stairway from this floor that leads directly down to the salon."

"It would be perfect," I said, my mind starting to spin. "Each balcony is big enough for a small table and a couple of chairs. And down on the patio, we can put iron tables and more chairs, lots of big clay pots with palms and ferns. Does it get much sun all day? Maybe geraniums."

That snort. "Claudine will kill you if you try to put a geranium back there. But ferns sound good. If you can talk her into it, that is."

I tried to open the window, but the hasp had been painted shut.

"They're called *portes-fenêtres,*" Bing explained. "They're windows, but open like doors. It's a French thing."

I looked at the floor. No water damage there, at least. The radiator was rusty. "Does *that* work?"

"Yes. All the basic mechanicals work. Things had just been neglected."

I opened a paneled door set into the wall. The bathroom. Very narrow, running probably half the length of the room. The floor was black-and-white hexagon tiles, mostly intact. A simple pedestal sink, toilet, and bidet, all lined up in a row. At the end sat a clawfoot tub with no shower attached. I looked into the tub. Stained rust and black. The stains in the sink and toilet were almost as bad.

"So, I guess there hasn't been any regular cleaning in the past eighty years?" I tried to keep my voice light, but my stomach was sinking fast.

"Actually," Bing said, "Claudine tends to the rooms on a regular basis. Just checking for mold and damp and airing things out. For the big stuff, she holds a party every Bastille Day, and we all drink wine and clean."

"We all?"

He shrugged. "We all who live here."

"So, once a year, six drunks get together to dust and vacuum?"

"Not just the six of us. Sometimes there are other invited guests." There was laughter in his voice, but he kept a straight face. "No vacuum. But we do have mops."

"I see," I breathed. I stepped out of the bathroom and looked at where the wall met the ceiling. "How old are those water stains? Please don't tell me the roof needs repair."

"It doesn't. The roof is slate and, to be honest, only started to give us trouble a few years ago. It's been fixed. This hotel was regularly maintained up until right before the war, and places like this were built to last. The damage looks bad, but it's mostly on the surface."

I pulled off the tarp, expecting a cloud of dust, but it slid off without much bother. Yes, there was a bed under there, an ornately carved headboard and footboard, with a mattress that looked like a body had bled out on it. There was also a small desk, obviously antique, and a dresser that looked like it had come out of a farmhouse, with simple lines and whitewashed wood.

"Very, ah, eclectic styles here," I said, leaning in to take a closer look.

"The furniture situation is very uneven. Some pieces are, seriously, original to the opening of the hotel back in the 1800s. Then you have bargain-basement pieces that were dragged in throughout the years."

"Well, that should make decorating a breeze," I muttered. "No closets?"

"Closets were never a thing in France. Especially not in the eighteenth or nineteenth century. We do have an extensive collection of armoires and wardrobes to choose from."

"Gotcha." There was a very ornate chandelier hanging in the middle of the room, half of its crystal pieces missing. "Is the electrical any good?"

"It's very good. Claudine never had a lot of money to keep the place up, but she always found, um, ways to get the important jobs done."

"Ways?"

His mouth twitched. "Well, she has an extensive list of clients, and she has a very unusual relationship with some of them. I believe the electrician slept here through the entire job."

"Ah." Well, then. At least *that* wasn't written into my contract. "So, is this pretty much what all the rooms look like?"

He nodded and crossed his arms against his chest. "Everything may look rough, but you have a lot to work with."

There was a challenge in his voice, and I immediately rose to meet it. "Yes, I think I do. There are a few similar properties in Rennes, so we have to make sure this one stands out. Le Magic Hall has kind of a similar vibe, but the interiors there are very modern. There's the Balthazar, but that's also very modern, and they have a spa, so that's a completely different kind of guest. We are going to be very niche, a very old-world vibe. You know"—I lifted an eyebrow—"billowing curtains and fluffy pillows."

He nodded slowly, as though to himself. "I see that you've done a little bit of work."

I closed my eyes and took a cleansing breath. If there was one thing I had been fighting my whole life, this was it. I opened my eyes and gave him what my brothers used to call "the look of death."

"Yes. I've done the work. I've been in hotels my entire adult life. I started busing tables at a Holiday Inn as a part-time job in high school, and I've hardly done anything else. I've worked in every department—housekeeping, reservations, I've prepped food in half a dozen kitchens. I even spent a summer following around the head of maintenance at the Marriott in Short Hills, New Jersey. This is my *job*, Bing. And I am very good at it. More than that, I love it. There have been plenty of screwups in my life that I deserve criticism for, but no one can fault my *work*. Especially not someone who obviously knows nothing about me *or* hotels."

I took a breath. Had I been shouting? I glanced over, and there stood Raoul, looking rather cowed and holding a large paper bag.

"I have food," he said.

Bing clapped his hands together. "Good. I think a little food is what we all need." He looked at me. "I apologize. I know what it means to love what you do. I will not make this mistake again." He followed Raoul out into the hallway.

I put my hand through my hair, tucking in a few curls that had escaped the bun.

Food would be good.

Back downstairs, the salon was dark, the floor-to-ceiling doors covered by interior shutters. Bing opened them up, and the room slowly filled with sunlight, revealing small wooden tables and an assortment of chairs pushed against the wall. He opened a few of the *portes-fenêtres,* and the cool, fresh air rushed in. The patio beyond was silent in the morning sun, without so much as a ripple in the branches of the trees. Raoul pulled one of the tables in front of the open window, then reached for a few of the chairs. I sat, and from the paper bag came the smell of warm baking.

Bing handed me a croissant, and my mouth began to water. He looked down at me. "Would you like some more coffee?"

I managed to not stuff a piece of the croissant into my mouth until after I said, "Yes, please."

He smiled, again with that blast of sudden charm, then walked through a set of double doors in the corner of the salon.

How could one person be so smug and patronizing one minute, then turn into something so yummy . . . Wait. That was the wrong word. That applied to the *croissant.* Not Bing. *Not* Bing.

"He is not such an asshole," Raoul said suddenly.

I looked at him, surprised. "What?"

"Bing is good man. He cares about us. But he can be real . . . what is it? *Douchebag?*" he looked at me hopefully. "Is that a good word?"

I burst out laughing. "Yes, that's a very good word." I found that breaking the croissant into small pieces kept me from wolfing it down like a maniac.

"So, tell me, Raoul. How long will it take to get all the rooms here in good working order?"

He was chewing on a piece of baguette, smeared with some sort of jam. "My part? Six weeks. We need to check lights and plumbing but is mostly good. I do mostly plasterwork. Some wood repair."

"That's pretty quick."

He nodded. "Yes, pretty quick. But not mean paint. Or clean. Or, what say . . . décor?"

Right. Because paint, clean, and décor . . . that was *my* part. "Tell me about the other people here. They're going to help me?"

He nodded. "Yes. Colin and Bing. They very much help. Marie Claude and Eliot are married. They both work but will help at night. Eliot very big."

"Eliot is huge," Bing said as he came back in and handed me a steaming cup. He smiled. "He needs direction."

"I'm good at that," I said. "Directing."

"I bet you are," Bing said, sitting down across from me. He was holding his own cup.

"And where is all this delicious coffee coming from?" I asked him.

He nodded to a set of double doors. "We have a complete kitchen here. And any French kitchen has an espresso machine. Is Raoul giving you the rundown of available personnel?"

"Yes. He said you and Colin are very much help." I raised both eyebrows. "Are you?"

He sipped coffee, but I saw that smile. "Very much."

"Marie Claude and Eliot are the night shift. Who else have I got?" Raoul made a face. "Vera."

"Now, Raoul, don't start, " Bing warned.

"Oh?" I reached for more croissant. "Vera?"

"Vera is alcoholic," Raoul said. "Very undependable. Claudine . . ."

"Claudine is Vera's very good friend," Bing explained. "And Vera has been sober for many years."

Raoul rolled his eyes. "Very undependable," he repeated. "Then there's Karl, who is so old is useless."

"He is not," Bing countered, but there was laughter in his voice. "He's very energetic for his age."

"Which is?" I asked.

"Eighty-three," Bing said, his mouth twitching.

I sipped more of that soothing, delicious coffee. "And does he have any particular skill? Like Raoul here?"

"You mean something useful? Like plumbing or masonry or tile work? He is a gardener." He was grinning now. "And a retired professor of history. What he is mostly good for is explaining things to you in much more detail than you ever realized you needed."

I felt desperate. "Can he hold a paint roller?" I asked.

"If you can give him a very good reason to do so," Bing answered.

"If this hotel fails, will he lose his home?" The croissant was finished, and I felt ready to take on the world.

Bing shrugged, and there was laughter again in his voice. "Not necessarily. After all, we've been limping along for years. But there's always a chance that Claudine may just give up, so . . . Yes. That might be just the reason he needs."

Raoul brushed his fingertips together, loosening crumbs. "Should we begin? I have all day today if you want work."

I sat, my mind going through the myriad of lists I'd put together last night before bed. "Go into each room. Start on the first floor, I guess. There are guest rooms here?"

Raoul nodded. "Yes. Three."

"Can you repair the plaster? All the walls need to be ready to paint, so any water damage needs to be fixed right away. Can you do that?"

He nodded as he stood. "Yes. I do that. Very good start."

"I want to look at this so-called garden. And figure out a plan for the patio here. I also need to inventory all the furnishings and see what can be used and where. Can Marie Claude and Eliot clean up the furniture? Polish light fixtures?"

Bing nodded slowly. "Yes. I'm sure they're capable of doing those things."

"How about Vera? Does she work during the day?"

"At university, in library there," Raoul said.

"So, she has lots of time to help or not?"

"Yes," Raoul said. "But she will not."

"We'll see," I said. "And Karl?"

"We can visit him right now, if you'd like," Bing said.

"No. This afternoon, after I find something suitable for him to do. Okay, then, Bing, how about the rest of the tour?"

He stood. "Of course. I'm very interested in what you have to say about the rest of our little hotel."

Why? What else could possibly be wrong with the *rest* of the hotel? And once again, there was laughter in his voice. Why did he find this all so funny? But I just smiled.

"Lead the way."

The rest of the rooms on the second floor were not all that much better than the first one we'd looked at. There were degrees, of course. Some plaster walls were smooth, just faded and ugly. Most of the floors were undamaged but filthy. In the center of each room was a pile of furnishings in varying degrees of repair and/or disrepair. All the bathrooms were either oh-my-God or almost oh-my-God.

I asked to see the garden, and we went down a back staircase, into the lobby, and out the front door. At the far corner of the hotel, through an archway in yet another wall, was the garden. It was a level patch, quite large, and enclosed on all sides. It was neatly planted, and there was a whole lot of growing going on. I recognized stakes for tomatoes, tepees for beans, and elaborate trellises. Pale green sprigs were everywhere, pushing up through dark, damp earth.

"This is practically a farm," I said.

Bing nodded. "This is all Karl's work. It's been years in the making."

"And it's beautiful, but we need this to be used as public space. How are we going to have guests sit out here among the vegetables?"

"On these benches. They're not very fashionable, but they're comfortable enough," Bing said easily. "This garden is a showplace. Look at it. It's as well laid out as any formal garden. And there are whole beds of flowers among all the vegetables. Does it matter that we can eat the things that grow here, instead of just looking at them?"

He was right. The broad flagstone paths divided heavily planted areas mulched with straw. Three simple benches were lined up in front of the tomato stakes. The air smelled fresh and earthy, birdsong was everywhere, and the bees hummed happily.

"Can we get here from the hotel lobby?" I asked.

He shook his head. "No. All the rooms on this side are guest rooms. There are three of them, and they open up directly on to the garden."

I looked around, then back at the hotel. "We can convert one of the guest rooms to public space. We're going to need more than just a dining room, anyway. We'll need somewhere for guests to work, plug in their laptops, copy things. Maybe we can create an office that can then open up to the garden."

"You'd lose a room. And the revenue of that room," Bing pointed out.

"Yes. But having a room with work space capability will be attractive to guests."

"Aren't these guests supposed to be on vacation?" There was laughter in his voice.

"Being on vacation won't stop them from checking emails and that sort of thing," I said. "Can you show me the first-floor rooms?"

He shrugged, and I followed him back. We went past the front desk down a window-lined corridor that turned to the back of the building. Raoul was in the first room, a tarp spread on the floor, tapping the walls gently with a hammer. I watched as chunks of plaster fell. The room was at the corner and overlooked the front courtyard and the garden.

"The next one?" I asked.

The second room was smaller but had a beautiful fireplace. There was no visible water damage, but it was bleak and charmless, with debris piled in the corners, cracked panes in the glass window, and wires dangling where a gleaming chandelier should have hung. "Maybe," I said.

At the end of the hallway was the other corner room. Tall windows opened on the garden side and to the interior patio. Here, the floor was scuffed but fairly clean, the windows intact, and the walls smooth. There was the expected pile in the center of the floor, chair legs peeking out from beneath a dusty tarp.

"This is it," I said. "Accessible to both the garden and the courtyard . . . Yes, this will work. And that doorway? Is the salon right there?"

He shook his head. "No. The bathroom." He opened the bathroom door. It was like the others, long and narrow, the toilet and sink at the far end, a claw-foot tub taking up most of the space.

"We can break through to the salon easily enough," I said, half to myself. "Make this a storage closet? Or powder room? Guests can go from breakfast to work, or outside to sit in the sun, or to the garden. Yes, this is perfect." I felt a mounting excitement, a familiar feeling that I hadn't felt in a long time. This was a plan coming together.

I walked to the floor-to-ceiling windows overlooking the garden and pushed one open, breathing in the sweet spring air. I turned back to the room and nodded. "We'll put in bookshelves and a few comfortable chairs, and in the corner, we'll have a desk."

"You think it's just that easy?"

"Yes, I do. Why? What would be so hard?"

That smile played around his lips again. "You just seem to think you can walk around and talk like you're actually going to accomplish something."

"Can I ask you something?" I said, stepping closer. There was no pitter-patter in my chest this time, just a slow, angry throb.

"Certainly."

"What about this do you find so damn amusing?"

His eyes flew open. "What?"

"You. This. Every time you open your mouth, you sound like you're going to burst out laughing. This is a monumental task, and you know it. There are completely unrealistic expectations here, and you know that, too. Or at least you *should* know it unless you're a complete idiot. At least I'm trying. I'm thinking and trying to figure out how to make this whole thing work. So tell me, what's so funny?"

He crossed his arms against his chest. "That you—or anyone else, for that matter—can think that this is even possible. Claudine is a brilliant woman, and I admire her very much, but her scheme to bring this hotel back to life is a pipe dream. She's convinced all of us—well, not me, but the rest of them—that it's possible. And then she got you to fly over here to sort everything out. Which, under the circumstances, I find absurd."

"And what circumstances are you talking about?"

He narrowed his eyes. "This charade of yours that you knew nothing about what Tony Fielding was doing and that you don't know where he is today. Aren't you just waiting for him to fly you to whatever island he's bought with all those millions, so you can go back to playing house?"

If this had been a movie from the 1940s, I would have slapped him in the face. If this had been Brooklyn in the 1980s, I would have taken out a gun and shot him. As it was, I just took three steps back and gulped for air.

I started to swear. In Italian, because I had found over the years that cursing in Italian was much more empowering, especially if the one you were swearing at didn't know Italian. Watching the facial expressions of a person who knew they were getting blasted, but not sure exactly *how,* added a whole other level of satisfaction.

Then, my hands started flying. I couldn't help it. First, they flipped around my face, then, as I took a step forward, they started inching toward his face and he began to back away. Good. Then the pointing began, and that's when I stopped even trying to control myself.

He blanched and kept moving back, and I kept moving forward, through the open window and out into the garden, and by then, I was shouting. Okay, maybe screaming. The birds and maybe the bees were silent as I raged on. I took a deep breath to possibly gather my thoughts, or maybe just get more oxygen in my lungs, when I heard someone applauding, quite loudly. And there was laughter.

It was Claudine, dressed in a simple black suit, a large tote bag over her shoulder. She was standing at the edge of the garden, grinning. "You are right," she called out. "He is a thoughtless pig with no manners. And although he usually does know what he's talking about, if this is about you and Tony Fielding, I'm on your side."

I glared at her, my chest heaving. "Your hotel is a total disaster!" I yelled at her in French.

"I know," she answered. "Can you save it?"

"Of course." I narrowed my eyes at Bing. "That's why you hired me, right?"

He took a step back, stuck his hands in his pockets, and went back through the open window.

Claudine waved a hand. "Come. Tell me all the wonderful things you are going to do to my hotel."

"He's really not an arrogant, no-nothing son of sea whore," Claudine said.

When Colin had said she could understand a bit of Italian, he'd been off the mark. She had understood everything I'd said.

I was feeling calmer, but not much. "He made a few assumptions that were completely false."

"So I gather. You speak Italian like a native."

"My parents were both from Rome. They went to the United States on their honeymoon and never left. It's what we spoke at home."

"That explains your grasp of the, ah, vernacular."

I grinned. "I have two younger brothers. The vernacular was pretty much all they spoke."

"That makes sense. But don't be too hard on Bing. He's quite a wonderful man. He is just a bit skeptical of my mission, and my choosing you to be part of it. He gave you the tour?" We walked back across the front courtyard into the hotel.

"Yes." I felt my anger easing. Talking business did that to me. "I was thinking that we have to turn a first-floor guest room into a public space. A kind of office work space and a way for guests to get to the garden without having to walk all the way around."

"The garden? Karl grows his beans and tomatoes. Marie Claude grows herbs. Why would anyone want to go to the garden?" she asked as we walked into the lobby.

"We need to utilize every inch of this place, Claudine. It's called maximizing the assets."

"And the garden is an asset? Interesting." Vague construction sounds were echoing. She looked at me. "You've put them to work already?"

"Just Raoul. He's repairing any damage to the walls so we can start to paint."

"Excellent."

We walked down that front corridor, past the open door where I could see Raoul up on a ladder, still tapping away at the softened plaster.

"We will hire someone to help him," she said. "He is very fast, but he can only work twelve hours a day."

Twelve? Were there no unions here? But then, he was a partner. I supposed I'd probably be working twelve-hour days as well. I watched Raoul as he worked. "How many rooms exactly?"

"There are sixteen rooms upstairs. And three on this floor. This is the ground floor, yes? I know in your country, this would be the first floor, but no. This is the ground floor. Upstairs is the first floor."

"And what about the attic? The second floor?"

She shrugged. "Bing lives there. There are empty rooms. But no elevator."

"That won't matter. We also need to accommodate housekeeping."

"We have an entire cellar for that, with washing machines and dryers. Commercial grade. And on each floor is a large closet for storing cleaning supplies and linens and towels. This was designed to the highest standard when the house was transformed into a hotel."

"Two hundred years ago," I muttered.

She smiled. "You'll see."

We continued walking.

"What about permits?" I asked.

"All plans have been approved, permits issued, and the proper palms have been oiled. The electrical work has already passed inspection, and the plumbing for the hotel is staying as is, so that's not an issue, either. There is no need for construction, just repair work and paint. Then we will do a bit of redecorating and open by the summer, yes?"

"Claudine, I think you need to realize that you're going to need more than a bit of redecorating."

"Not every room is bad," she said. "We will fix the best rooms first, so we have pictures to put on our new website."

Right. The website. That was a whole other list.

"Much has been done already," she said. "We have been working all winter." She opened the door to the last room, the corner room, the room I had chased Bing out of minutes before.

"This is what I want to use for the office," I told her. "We can just create a doorway here, through the bathroom, so guests can come right from the salon. So, maybe a little construction?"

She nodded. "Yes. We can have a bit of hallway here with no problem." She looked around. "We can make this your office space, if you'd like. I don't mind losing the revenue of this room. I would feel guilty renting it out to guests."

I was surprised. "Why? This goes right to the outside. Guests would love it."

She shook her head. "Maybe not. The courtyard is haunted," she said.

I mentally counted to five. Slowly. "The courtyard is haunted?"

"Yes. Not a bad ghost, you understand, but, well, some guests might be frightened." She looked very calm, just as though she hadn't just said something totally outrageous.

I reined in any urge to jump up and down, scream, and run like hell. "Do you know who it is? The ghost, I mean?"

She smiled and opened the tall window that led to the courtyard. I followed her slowly.

The air was sunlit and still. No traffic sounds came over the walls, although I knew that the street was right on the other side. No breeze ruffled the leaves gathered in the corners. No birds chirped from the eaves.

"I think she was a maid," Claudine said quietly. "Who knows? Many people have died here. You know that the original house burned to the ground in the great fire? Not in this exact location, of course. The estate was much larger then. They rebuilt here, where the fire had not reached." She motioned with her hand. "They used the local limestone for the new house. Simple but very beautiful. Then they renovated it to become a hotel. There was much money then. The Perrot family was on the right side of the revolution."

"Why do you want to bring it back?" I asked her. "It seems . . ."

"Impossible. I know," she said simply. "But what else can I do? Sell it? To whom? New owners might tear it down. I was born in this house, right in that upstairs room there." She pointed. "My brother and I played in this courtyard. We were not afraid of her, the ghost. My brother, Maris, named her Polly. Such an American name."

She sighed. "I have a new family here now. You can't throw out family. Where would they live? Bing has been here for thirty years. Karl just as long. Jacques, ah, I wish you could have met him. He died last Christmas, but he'd been here even longer." Her smile was wistful. "He was my brother-in-law. He moved in when Hubert and I first married, and after the divorce, well, he stayed. He was lovely." She looked around the courtyard. "Vera came here almost ten years ago. She was . . . Things were very bad. She had nowhere else to go. Now she is happy and has a good job and is making amends. This is her home, too."

I looked around and then up. I saw that the third-floor attic windows were much newer than the rest, wide expanses of glass.

"Bing put those in when he fixed the roof," she said. "He needed the light to work, he said."

"*He* fixed the roof?" I asked.

"Yes. It was a huge job. I am so grateful to him. For many things."

"He said you let him live here rent-free."

"And he has paid me back many times over." She ran her hands through her gray curls and shook herself. "I am getting very sentimental. Come, let's look upstairs. Bing spoke to me this morning and said you wanted white walls and fluffy pillows. I think that is very good. I trust you, Lucy. I know you will make good choices."

She turned and went back inside. I stood in the courtyard, and in the unnatural stillness, I could feel the weight of history, of family, of promises kept and promises broken. I took a deep breath. Yes, there was something here. Something that had nothing to do with rebranding a hotel or rebuilding my reputation.

She had talked about her new family. Was that even possible? My own family seemed very far away, with not just an ocean between us but years of resentment, anger, and disappointment. I sometimes felt that they lived in my head, rather than in my heart. How much of their coldness was I supposed to forgive?

"What am I doing here?" I whispered into the warmth and sunlight.

I waited for something: a touch, a whisper in the air, any kind of a sign.

"Are you coming?" Claudine called.

I walked back into Hotel Paradis.

Chapter Four

Claudine and I went to buy paint.

She had a short conversation with Bing before we left. As we walked across the courtyard, she explained the very simple security system. The gates locked automatically. They could be pushed open from inside the courtyard, but to open them from the street required a code.

"It is 230663," she explained. "Empress Joséphine's birthday. If you forget, just push the red button. The bell sounds inside the hotel, out in the garden, and up in Bing's rooms. Someone is always around to answer."

We then walked to a metro station, where she purchased a card for me and explained how it all worked, and we emerged a short ride later in a decidedly commercial area, crowded and noisy. The French version of a hardware store was narrow and badly lit, but she knew the proprietor, and after taking several paint sample cards out into the sunlight, we decided on three different shades of white. Yes, that's right, three. From almost thirty-four different choices. Perhaps a lesser woman would have crumbled, but I knew exactly what I wanted, and Claudine approved. Creamy white walls, a deeper cream for all the woodwork, and a bright white for the bathrooms.

"All the bathrooms are the same, black-and-white tile on the floor, and white fixtures everywhere. We have white towels. This is a good choice. Why complicate things?" she said approvingly.

"Agreed," I said. "That's the walls and trim. What about curtains, bedding, all of that?"

"What do you want?" she asked. I was trying hard to listen to her, but I was walking in France, and the streets were unlike anything I had seen before, the energy palpable, and the flow of a language I could not completely understand did nothing to dampen my excitement. This was *France*.

"Lucy, I feel I do not have your attention," she said.

I tried to look apologetic, but I was too busy gawking at the storefronts, into café windows, and at the crowds of people rushing by. "I've never been to France before," I told her. "I'm trying not to be a tourist."

She grabbed my elbow and steered me toward a tiny café table. "Then sit. We will have coffee. Or wine? It's lunchtime. Let's eat, and you can watch all the people. We will talk."

I sank gratefully into the wooden chair and felt my whole body relax. "I want the windows framed with curtains that are white and flowing. Linen, I think, would be best. Simple lines but lots of volume. That kind of thing says *luxury*. Where can we get something like that?"

"Vera will make them," she said, sinking into the chair beside me. "Do you trust me to order the fabric for you?"

"What? Oh yes. Absolutely. Who can make what?"

"Vera Sidibe. She lives at the hotel. She's a very talented seamstress, with an excellent sewing machine. We'll get her all the linen she needs, and she'll make whatever we want."

There was a rather lengthy exchange between Claudine and the waiter, so I took the time to watch a very elegant older woman, easily in her eighties but walking sprightly in beautifully made high heels. She was dressed in simple black, her cropped gray hair ruffling in the breeze.

"How do they do it?" I asked as the waiter left. "All these women look so effortless and put together. Women in New York always look like they're working at it."

Claudine laughed. "Women in France have, for decades, been applauded for their chic. They have nothing to prove."

"Raoul said that Vera was unreliable," I said.

Claudine made a face. "Raoul is a lovely boy, but he is also a racist. Vera has black skin, so he thinks she can do nothing right."

"Oh. But . . . he said she was an alcoholic."

"She is. She always will be. But she has been sober now for a longer time than she was not. That is his excuse. Young men can be very stupid. Ah, here's our cider. Cider is very Breton, and you must get used to local tradition. Let us drink to all our lovely paint, yes?"

We touched our glasses. The cider was cold and delicious.

"I have bed linens," she said. "Sheets and such that have been saved. And quilts. Handmade quilts that my aunt stitched herself."

"Like the one on my bed?" I asked. "That one is beautiful."

"Thank you. They are all beautiful. They are old but have been stored properly. I have paintings," she said, sitting back. "In a temperature-controlled unit. Some things must be carefully tended. And rugs. Do you know that there are hand-knotted rugs that are hundreds of years old? Some objects are more than objects. They are a testament to the dedication of artisans and craftsmen. They remind us that beauty has been around for centuries and will remain long after we are gone. When the original estate of the Perrot family burned, many things were pulled out and saved. That's what servants did five hundred years ago, saved the masters' valuables. Some of these things have not seen the light of day since before the war. It is time."

"You've been paying for storage for that long?"

She shrugged. "My father paid. Then my brother paid. And

when he died, it fell to me." She leaned forward. "Everything was hidden away when the Nazis came. When it was safe, basements were emptied and everything came back, but there was no money to reopen the hotel. My father made sure that nothing was sold off. They went hungry in the winters, my aunts and uncles. The years after the war were very hard. But nothing was sold. Everything was saved, and now, it is my job to bring it all back." She smiled. "That is why I am such a crazy woman. My time is running out. I am getting old, and I want to sit back and enjoy Hotel Paradis in its glory. And I want to see my son enjoy it as well. If I am very careful, there will be enough money. And I have you."

A plate was set before me.

"Another tradition," Claudine explained. "It's called a *galette saucisse*. It is a sausage surrounded by a crêpe made of buckwheat. You eat it like a—what is the American?—hot dog. Eat this like a hot dog."

I picked it up gingerly and took a bite. Flavors exploded in my mouth that I had never experienced before. *I am never going to lose weight,* I thought as I took another bite.

Claudine laughed. "It is very good. I try to make the galette, but I am a terrible cook. Luckily, Stavros will keep you fed. And we will buy you bread and cheese for your room. You may want to cook a few things for yourself."

I swallowed and took another swig of cider, and as I did, I wondered what the alcohol content was because I felt a bit of a buzz in the back of my brain. "There's no refrigerator."

"We'll find one."

"And there's no dresser for my clothes or a comfortable place to sit."

She tilted her head. "I suppose you are used to something very different?"

I nodded. "Very. I understand that this is a very unusual situation, but I need to feel comfortable. This is going to be my home for at least the next six months, and I don't want to dread it."

"Of course. You can have your pick of anything we have for your own rooms. We will get you a refrigerator. In fact, there's probably something in the cellar."

"We need electronics."

"What?"

"Televisions."

She frowned. "In every room?"

I nodded. "It will be expected. And Wi-Fi."

She shrugged. "That is not a problem. And we have—what do you call them—knickknacks?"

I shook my head. "No. Nothing that can fit in a suitcase and be carried out."

Her frown deepened. "Really?"

"Really. But we can use plants and flowers."

"That's easy."

"Not just for outside but in the rooms."

She nodded. "Of course. Karl planted many seeds this spring, so we will soon have cut flowers for every room. He complained. He insisted that the garden was his domain. I had to remind him that it is, in fact, *my* domain." She smiled, but there was steel behind those red lips.

Tony Fielding had also been made of steel. He ran his company with skill and ruthless decisiveness. He often said that The Fielding Hotel was more than just a name, it was his legacy. But greed and weakness had eroded whatever good intentions he had started with, and he had let his legacy collapse under debt and scandal.

I could tell that Claudine Capuçon would never let that happen. Hotel Paradis carried a family history dating back centuries, and she was the sole protector of that history. It was indeed her domain. She would not let anyone forget that.

Including me.

We were back in front of Hotel Paradis.

"We need to do something about all this rust," I said, looking up at the gate. "We can't have this be the first impression people have."

She nodded. "Yes. Colin will do this. He is good at the tiresome, fiddly things."

We pushed through the gate. The courtyard was still and peaceful in the sunlight. I could see the white cat curled up in his planter, asleep.

"Is that the hotel cat?" I asked as we walked to the front door.

She reached down to stroke the cat's fur. "Yes. This is Napoléon Bonaparte. Every cat we have is named Napoléon Bonaparte, and they are always white. He is friendly, for a cat."

Napoléon opened one eye, blinked slowly, then settled back to sleep.

We went into the lobby and back down the corridor. Raoul was still busy, now using a trowel to spread plaster over the various holes in the wall. He looked at us briefly, then went back to work.

"I think we need to get a bit of work done, you and me," Claudine said. "Let me change, and then we can look at the furniture. I told Bing to take the tarps off all those piles. We can see how useful he's been."

I went back to my *appart* and grabbed my pen and notebook. Making lists always soothed me, and I went back into the hotel feeling like an adventurer beginning a treasure hunt. Bing had mentioned antiques and armoires, and I imagined finding mahogany and rosewood, hand-carved and lovingly crafted.

Claudine called to me. "Have you been downstairs?"

No, I hadn't. We went through the kitchen, which was smaller than I had expected, gleaming stainless steel, and spotlessly clean. We turned down a narrow stone staircase and walked into another century.

There were fluorescent lights, but that did little to make me think I was in anything but a nineteenth-century wine cellar. The walls were rough, the floors flagstone, and the beamed ceiling low and dark. The air was surprisingly fresh and dry, and I could feel a faint breeze.

"That door there leads outside," Claudine said, pointing. "All the laundry was done down here. There used to be giant tubs where women churned the wash like butter; then it would be wrung out in a machine that looked like a medieval torture device. Then everything was brought up to dry along the side of the house. That is the south side, and there is sun all day."

Now there stood a row of stainless steel washers that were almost as tall as I was, and as many industrial dryers. A long table ran down the center of the space, with arched doorways along the walls.

"We still have wine here," she said, going through one of the archways. "Come."

Here, single bulbs dangled from swaying wires, and as she pulled the frayed string of one, a wall of wine appeared from the darkness, row upon row of dusty bottles like soldiers lying down for a rest.

"One day, before we open, I will have someone come down and look. There are bottles here that were laid down before the war." Claudine pulled out a bottle, wiped the dust, and squinted at the faded label. "Nineteen thirty-two. This might be valuable. It depends on the vintage, of course. Bad wine does not improve with age."

She went back into the vast laundry room and looked around. "We will have someone come three times a week to do the washing. We have an obscene amount of linen here, enough sheets to change the beds every day for a month." I must have looked skeptical because she laughed. "French linen lasts generations, Lucy. And my great-grandmother had a bit of a hoarding problem. Once a year, she would make a mysterious trip to an abbey in Nice and return with more and more sheets and pillowcases. My mother remembered the hotel before the war. She helped make the beds, and she used to say the closets overflowed. They still do."

We went up another set of stairs, the one leading outside. We stepped into brilliant sunlight, and I could see a few remaining clotheslines running between the side of the hotel and the wall. The flagstones were uneven, and many were broken.

"So, this is what those few second-floor rooms look down on?" I asked. "Bing said there was no view, and he's right. But we need to do something else here. We can't afford any useless space."

She shrugged. "The stable row is that way, and you can just walk around the corner there to get to the front courtyard." She looked in the other direction, where there was a solid wall. "The inside court-yard is there. This was for laundry. What else can we use it for?"

"We don't have to use it for anything," I said. *We just have to make it look good to guests looking out the window,* I thought. "How good a gardener is your Karl?"

"It is his passion."

"Okay, then, what about those fruit trees that get planted against the walls?"

"Espalier?"

"Yes. Can Karl do that?"

She began to smile. "I'm sure."

"We can plant roses here, with lavender and boxwood. We can make some sort of design. Pull up these broken flagstones and cre-ate a pattern that you'll be able to see from the windows."

She reached over and gave me a quick hug. "That is brilliant. Of course. And we can have roses to bring into the rooms all summer long. I never would have thought of that. I've been staring at this ugly yard for years, thinking it was useless. In two minutes, you have made it into a treasure."

I began to scribble in my notebook. "What should we grow? Apples and pears? Do apricots grow in France? We can offer guests fresh fruit in the morning from our own little orchard."

She laughed. "It will be a few years before we get any fruit."

"That's fine," I said, still writing. I had to research espalier. Roses—

they would have to be beautiful but also smell like heaven. And was there garden design software I could download for free?

I ignored the little voice in the back of my head, reminding me that I might not be here in a few years.

The furniture Claudine and I uncovered was exactly the treasure trove I'd imagined, with a vast and varied assortment to choose from. Most of the wooden pieces were obvious antiques, dusty but in good repair. Beds ranged from elaborate four-poster affairs to simple, classic sleigh beds. All the mattresses would have to be replaced, but she'd warned me about that. Every room had either a standing wardrobe with a combination of hanging space and built-in drawers or an armoire for hanging and a small dresser. There were desks and tables of varying sizes, some simple, some inlaid with marble or contrasting wood. I took pictures of each piece with my phone so I could mix and match more easily.

The upholstered pieces were the problem.

"This chair has been sitting here for decades, Claudine. There are probably bugs living in the cushions."

She shook her head. "Every three months, I come into each of these rooms. I take the cushions off and shake them out. I have a brush, and I beat the dust out of the furniture. This fabric is perfect. It hasn't seen sunlight in years, see? Not faded at all."

"But bugs . . ."

She glared at me. "There are no bugs in my hotel. There has been no damage from the damp, except when the roof leaked, but whatever was ruined was taken away. Everything here is good."

She may have been right. There was no sign or smell of mold or dampness, and as I sat on one of the chairs, no cloud of dust rose. And the pieces were beautiful. There were classic Louis XV chairs in rosewood and pale, striped silk. Wing chairs in floral tapestry. Slipper chairs trimmed with delicate fringe. Sloped channel-back chairs in lush green velvet. A graceful chaise longue in gold damask.

"Have you seen anything that you want?" she asked at last.

I was filthy and exhausted, and we had only made our way through half the rooms on the floor, but I felt as though I had accomplished quite a bit.

"I want? Oh, right. Ah, I'm not sure."

We were back in the hallway. "Send me the pictures of what you want, and I will have Eliot bring them over." Claudine looked at me. "I think you have done enough for today. You look very tired. And it is late! I am sorry." She took out her phone. "We did not get you bread. Or cheese. I will ask Marie Claude to pick them up for you. And wine, of course. You can eat at the café across the street. Stavros will feed you. He is a marvelous cook."

I was starting to feel my muscles ache just a bit, but I knew they'd be screaming before the night was through. This was more physical work than I'd done in the past two years. I was suddenly grateful for that claw-foot tub.

"Will you be around tomorrow?" I asked her as we went down into the lobby.

She shrugged. "I should be. I have not gotten any frantic messages, so maybe my office has not burned itself to the ground." She suddenly reached over and gave me a quick hug. "Thank you, Lucy. This was a good first day. Eat something. Take a long, hot bath. You will feel so much better."

"Yes. Well, good evening, Claudine. This is quite a lovely hotel you have here. I think we can make it a real success."

She put her hand on my shoulder. "I know we can."

I watched her go back into the hotel. Her home. I took a deep breath and started toward mine when a man darted out of the garden. He was tiny and stooped, with a black yarmulke pinned to a halo of white, bushy hair.

"Wait," he called. "Are you Lucia? Wait."

He hurried across the cobblestones and grabbed my hand in both of his. "Karl Levi. I am so glad to meet you. Bing said you were quite lovely, and he was right. And my garden? You like my garden?" His accent was German rather than French, and he spoke slowly. "I will help you all I can. I can still do much, even though I am an old man." He grinned, his watery eyes dancing. "I am young in my mind, even if my body does not always agree."

In his shabby clothes and rough boots, he looked like a garden gnome, and he radiated energy. I found myself smiling despite my growing fatigue, thinking it oddly appropriate that this little man would so easily fit the role of gardener.

"It's a real pleasure to meet you, Karl. Claudine and I have a few projects for you. We want a rose garden."

He continued to hold my hand. "Excellent. Most excellent. I have wanted a rose garden for many years. You were on your way back to your room? I will not hold you up. But you should come by. I am in number one, right there in front. After dinner? Have a drink with me?"

"I'm very tired, Karl, but if I have any energy left, I'll try."

He held my eyes for a few seconds, then shook himself and dropped my hand. "You remind me of someone I knew long ago. I will try not to stare. Welcome to Hotel Paradis. We have been waiting for someone like you for a long time."

"I'm glad to be here. Thank you. Excuse me, but I need a bath."

I slipped away from him and crossed the courtyard. Napoléon Bonaparte jumped out of his cast-iron pot and wrapped himself around my ankles before slipping off into the garden. I could hear noise coming from inside the hotel and the sound of a woman's laughter coming from flat number three. Wasn't that Colin's flat? Was he entertaining a guest? Did I even care?

I went through my own door and sat in the stiff wooden chair. I scrolled through the pictures of the furniture and sent a few of them to Claudine. An overstuffed chair, a small, round table, and a low dresser. That would make a good start.

I went into the bathroom, pulled all my toiletries out of the bottom of the tub, and began to fill it. I'd discovered that there was plenty of hot water to be had, but I wanted a deep soak, not a quick shower.

I dug through my pile of bath soaps, looking for something scented when it suddenly struck me.

Bing had told Karl I was lovely.

I was in the tub, possibly napping, when I heard a loud knocking on the door.

Now what? Who could want to see me or talk to me? Hadn't I already exhausted all the possibilities?

I pulled myself out of the tepid water and grabbed a towel. The towels, by the way, were fabulous—thick and soft and big enough to wrap around my body with plenty to spare.

At the door were Eliot and Marie Claude. At least that's who I assumed they were. They both looked to be in their twenties. He was roughly the size of a brown bear, and she was tiny, hair dyed bright blue. She was carrying a burlap bag, and I could see a baguette sticking out of the top. He was carrying the overstuffed chair I had claimed as my own.

I backed away from the door. "Come in, please. Can you give me a minute? I'll put on some clothes."

Eliot dropped the chair in the center of the room, said hello, and left.

Marie Claude smiled. "We'll be back," she said in English. "He is going to get your dresser. Here is some food. Take your time." She left the burlap sack on the chair and followed him out.

I went back into the bedroom. While I had hung most of my

clothes, anything that didn't belong in the armoire was still in a suitcase on the floor. I pulled on some underwear and a simple cotton dress, then darted into the bathroom for a quick look in the mirror. When I didn't burst into tears, I hurried out.

There was bread in the sack, butter wrapped in brown paper, a few chunks of unidentifiable cheese, three bottles of wine, and a basket of strawberries. There was nothing to store anything in, so I lined up my groceries on the table. I'd need some sort of cupboard. I'd also need dishes, glasses . . . Was I ever going to cook on that tiny stove? Then I'd need pots and bowls and all sorts of utensils that I hadn't had any use for in years. My mother, in the two years I'd lived back at home, had never let me in her kitchen to do anything more than take food out of the refrigerator or put away clean dishes. Her kitchen had been her kingdom, and even if I hadn't been completely inept, I was not welcome.

I reached for the wine and realized I didn't even have anything to open it with. I clutched the bottle in my hand, sank into the lovely, overstuffed chair that was the only comfortable thing to sit on, and felt tears building.

My body hurt; muscles that had never moved so much as a table lamp in two years moaned in protest. I stared at the palms of my hands. I had blisters coming up. I was so *tired*. I was hungry but couldn't slice the bread. I didn't have so much as a jam jar to drink my wine out of, even if I could open it.

I was going to have to start painting rooms soon, and what about that website? Was that Vera person really going to sew drapes for *all* those rooms? All that furniture—but what about the salon and furnishings for the office and then outside tables and chairs? Karl was a gardener. Could he also oversee planting all the pots and urns *besides* a rose garden and espalier? At least that would be one item I could take off the list, but . . .

A sob broke through, and I knew that if I let one out, a torrent would follow. I held my breath. That didn't help. Nothing was going to help. I let my head fall back, closed my eyes, and started to bawl.

"Lucia?" Someone was there, a man. Bing? "Lucia, are you hurt?" Then he began to yell.

I opened my eyes, and through a wash of tears, I saw Eliot pushing the dresser into the center of the room on a hand truck. Then he dropped on one knee in front of me, grabbed my hand, and began to pat it. Marie Claude rushed in, looked, pulled Eliot to his feet, and leaned down. "What is wrong? What do you need?"

I pushed the bottle of wine at her. "A corkscrew," I sobbed. "I don't have a corkscrew."

She said something over her shoulder, and Eliot practically ran out. "We will get you a corkscrew," Marie Claude soothed. "What else?"

"G-g-glasses. I don't have glasses or a dish or anything. I can't even c-c-cut this bread!" I was in full-out wailing mode now, but she remained unruffled.

"We will get your glasses, Lucy. And a knife. Claudine should have thought this out a bit more." She stood up, wiping her hands on the front of her flowered dress. She looked out the doorway and spoke sharply to someone to get Claudine. She was obviously reeling off a list as she pointed and then waved her hands. "Don't worry, Lucy. We will take care of you."

I felt a surge of emotion at her words. The last time I had heard anyone say that to me, it had been a junior law clerk as he took my check for the $100,000 that was used as my retainer. Taking care was something I had always done for myself, and the thought of someone else willing to take it on—for free—was overwhelming. I used both hands to wipe away tears and fought to keep my voice under control. "I'm sorry. I hate to cry."

"Nonsense. I love to cry. It gets out all the poison." She looked around. "You don't even have a tissue?" She went to the door, stuck out her head, and mumbled something to someone just outside.

There appeared to be a bit of an argument, but she just mumbled some more. She came back and went into the bathroom, returning with my damp towel.

"Here. Use this for now. You poor thing, did she even give you one day to settle in? I love that woman, but really . . ."

I covered my face with the towel and scrubbed hard. I took several deep breaths, and after what seemed to be a very long time, I let the towel drop and looked up.

I was surrounded. Marie Claude was still in front of me, her brown eyes wide. Eliot stood behind her holding a corkscrew and three wineglasses. Karl was there, his hands clasped and brow furrowed. Colin had a long-bladed knife in one hand and a box of tissues in the other. And there, just inside the doorway, stood Bing, holding a stack of plain white dishes.

"Better?" Marie Claude asked gently.

I nodded. "Thank you. Yes." I looked at the concerned faces around me. "I'm tired," I said, the lamest of all excuses, but no one seemed to notice.

Eliot went over to the table and began to open the bottle of wine. Colin set down his knife and handed me the tissues, which I took gratefully. Bing carried the dishes over to the sink, looked around, then went out again, taking Colin and the hand truck with him.

"We'll be right back," he said over his shoulder.

Karl began to slice the baguette. "Low blood sugar," he said solemnly. "Eat something and you will feel better." He handed me a slice of bread smeared with about an inch of butter, and I had never tasted anything more comforting in my life.

I finished the bread in silence, then took a glass of wine from Eliot. Marie Claude whispered something to him, and he left.

"You should probably go across the street," Marie Claude said. "Stavros will give you something hot and delicious, and then you can have a good night's sleep. I'm sure things will look so much better in the morning."

I drank all the wine in one gulp and nodded. "You're right. I should eat." I stood up. "Thank you again. Marie Claude?"

She nodded. "Yes. That is me. It is a pleasure to meet you, Lucy. Truly. Go and eat. We'll straighten up in here. Go. Please."

I left. If I passed anyone as I crossed the courtyard, it didn't even register. I don't think I would have noticed an elephant if it had been perched in Napoléon's cast-iron pot.

I sat alone by the window of the café. Stavros came over to greet me, ignoring my red eyes and tearstained face as he suggested roast chicken. I nodded and sipped the wine he had brought over.

Well. I finally met my neighbors. Perfect. These were the people who were supposed to be helping me in the impossible task of reviving Hotel Paradis, and I sat there, blubbering like a baby over the lack of a corkscrew. *That* was certainly a great start.

Two glasses of wine were probably my limit, but I had a third, and boy, did I feel so much better by the time my dinner was in front of me. I think it was delicious.

I sat long after my meal was done. The café was almost empty when I finally walked back to the hotel. I had waited until I thought everyone would be settled back into their respective *appartements*. I certainly didn't want to meet anyone in the courtyard after my earlier display of complete and utter lack of self-control. Had I really cried about not having a corkscrew?

No. I had cried for a stockpile of professional and personal injuries, real and imagined, that had all come together over fatigue, a sense of overwhelm, and a bottle of wine.

The courtyard was empty and quiet. I walked quickly to my door. There was a light burning in the window, but that was strange because I didn't have a light by the window. I pushed open the door thinking, *Are there locks? Should I ask for one?* I didn't want people to just open the door to my new home and do . . . whatever.

The overstuffed chair was in front of the window. Next to it was the small table I'd asked for. On top of the table was a small brass lamp, shining warmly.

The wooden table was covered by a cloth of deep blue, and in the center was a white bowl filled with oranges. There was a refrigerator next to the stove, roughly the same size as the one I'd had in my dorm room at college, humming quietly. A tall, narrow cabinet with glass doors sat next to the sink, and in it were stacked the white dishes and wineglasses. There were also blue-and-white mugs and a small clay flowerpot filled with mismatched cutlery. There were a few more white bowls, and in one of them, the strawberries peeked out from beneath a linen towel. The wine bottles were in a row along the bottom shelf.

One of the favorite books of my childhood had been *A Little Princess,* and at that moment I felt just like Sarah Crewe, opening the door to her attic room to find a fire burning and warm food waiting.

I turned at a quiet knock at the door. "Yes?"

Claudine opened the door, took a quick look around, and smiled. "This looks much better."

I smiled back. "Yes."

Claudine looked apologetic. "I'm sorry. They really gave it to me. I should have given you time to get used to this place. Do you even have a new phone?"

I shook my head.

"Tomorrow, you do what you have to do. Walk into town. Buy what you need. If you want help or company, take Bing away from whatever he may be doing." She glanced over her shoulder. "Marie Claude and Eliot are in the hotel. They have already started working on our furniture. They are a good team. Colin is helping them tonight. Even Karl asked me what he could do. Good night."

She closed the door behind her.

I went into the bathroom and peeled off my clothes. When I came out, I saw the dresser next to the bed, my suitcase on the floor beside it. On top of the dresser was a pretty porcelain tray, white with roses, just right for putting earrings or a watch in before going to bed.

Maybe everything wasn't going to be so horrible after all.

Chapter Five

I thought I could slip out early but was stopped halfway to the iron gates by a brisk, commanding voice.

"Are you Lucy? Claudine told me to talk to you. She also told me to be nice. One thing is harder than the other, but I'll try. I'm Vera Sidibe. We can have breakfast together." She walked past me and across the street to the café and, despite the slight chill in the air, sat at a table outside by the curb.

I followed her. I couldn't help it. Her voice, in clipped and heavily accented English, was not to be ignored or argued with. She was tall and broad-shouldered, white hair cut close to her beautifully shaped skull. She was dressed in a sleeveless blouse and blue cotton skirt, a long scarf around her neck and shoulders. She also had several stud earrings in one ear and a single hoop in the other.

I sat across from her. Her eyes were very round and dark, fringed in short, straight lashes. A young girl hurried out, and a quick exchange sent the girl scurrying back.

"She's bringing a menu. I assume you want to look at one? Breakfast here is very different from the US." Vera crossed her arms under her rather substantial breasts. "Claudine said you will want to buy things. A phone? What else do you need?"

Everything, I thought. "Your English is very good."

"My family migrated to the States from Mali when I was six. We lived there illegally for almost fifteen years. Then we had to leave. The government of France grants citizenship to anyone born in a former French colony. So, rather than return to Mali, I came here." She flashed a smile. "Your French is very good."

"I studied in high school, then all four years in college. It came in very handy when I worked in Quebec. *Merci.*" I took the laminated menu from the young girl when she returned. The menu was helpfully in both French and English but was noticeably lacking in the usual breakfast staples found on a menu in the US. Missing were items like pancakes, waffles, western omelets. And what, exactly, was *pain aux raisins*?

"Need help?" Bing asked. He pulled up a chair from the next table and sat between Vera and me. His hair was damp and brushed back, and I caught a whiff of something spicy. Or musky. Or both? "Are you looking for steak and eggs?" That laughter was in his voice. What was so funny *now*?

I snatched it back. "No," I snapped. I concentrated. "I just don't know what *pain aux raisins* is. I mean, I get the general idea, but . . ." I squinted. Did I really think that having the words *blurred* was going to help?

"I was telling her that French breakfasts are probably different from what she's used to," Vera said to Bing.

He made a kind of clucking noise. "I bet everything that has happened since she got here is different from what she's used to."

I glared at him over the top of the menu, then shifted my eyes as the young girl reappeared.

"Simone, this is Lucia. Lucy," Bing said in slow English. "She is at Hotel Paradis now. Lucia, Simone is one of Stavros's daughters."

"*Bonjour,* Simone," I said.

She smiled brightly. "We are putting American things on menu now," she said. Her English was hard to understand, but I got the gist. "Oatmeal. Froot Loops."

I handed back the menu. "Just tartine and café crème." The last was for Bing's benefit, and as I glanced at him, I caught his smile.

Vera and Bing both ordered, and we sat for a few minutes. Warm sunlight filtered through the trees, and the traffic sounds were very faint. This was nice. It was a new day. The sun was shining, breakfast was coming, and I was going shopping. Life, at that moment, felt very normal.

"I'm taking her shopping," Vera said to Bing. "For one thing, she needs a phone."

I pulled out my beloved iPhone. "Do I really?"

"Well, you need everything switched over to Orange. They're the biggest phone provider. But first, you need a bank account," Bing said.

"I don't have any money," I said. "Seriously. I have less than four hundred US dollars."

"That's enough. You don't get charged for having a low balance in French banks. It's not allowed. You can open a bank account with one dollar." He glanced at Simone as she set down our café crèmes. "*Merci,* Simone. What else do you need?"

"Clothes," I said.

Vera sat back. "Colin complained that your suitcases weighed a ton."

"Well, he's right," I said. "And they were all filled with clothes. But when I packed, I thought my job was going to involve sitting back in a nice, cushy office and pointing my finger at things to get them done. I have plenty of clothes for *that*. But for painting and scrubbing and repairing furniture . . . well, not so much."

Bing snorted, and Vera gave him a hard look as she spoke. "We'll find plenty at thrift stores. No reason to spend too much of your four hundred dollars on those kinds of clothes. So . . . bank, phone, thrift . . . what else?"

I looked at the perfectly toasted slices of heavenly smelling bread and the small portion of deep purple jam on the side of the plate. Could I eat every meal here, or did I want to at least try to cook on my own?

"Maybe I should get some food?" I said.

"No," said Vera. "Wait."

I spread a bit of jam and took a bite of my breakfast. Did everything taste that much better here? "For what?"

"Saturday market," Bing said. "I'll take you when I go. It's an experience unlike any other."

I swallowed a few more bites of toast. "It's a market?"

"You will see," Vera promised. "You will have to bring a very big bag. We'll get one of those today, too."

"A bag?" This simple shopping expedition was getting complicated. "Why do I need a bag?"

Bing was eating his way through a bowl of fruit and toast spread thinly with butter. "Stores here don't have bags. Everyone has to bring their own."

I stared at him. "What?"

He chuckled. "Living in France is going to take a bit of an adjustment. There are hundreds of small things you'll have to get used to. Like bringing your own bag when you shop."

"And very good, very cheap wine," Vera said.

"Eggs that don't have to be refrigerated," Bing said.

"Vegetables that look ugly and taste wonderful."

"Only paying thirty bucks a month for your phone."

That got my attention away from my food. "Really? Thirty bucks?" I asked Bing.

He grinned. "Or whatever twenty-six euros comes out to. And believe it or not, the communications companies still manage to make a profit. Living here is a joy. Sure, there are problems, but . . ." He shrugged. "I came here thirty-two years ago from a small town outside of Atlanta, and I've never even thought about moving back."

I looked back down at my half-eaten breakfast. Would *I* be moving back? If I managed to pull this whole thing off, would I be living in France for the rest of my life? I'd been so eager to take the job and get away from everything that was dragging me down at home, I never thought past the end of the six-month contract.

"Why did you come here?" I asked Bing, trying to distract myself from thinking too hard about . . . anything.

"I was just out of art school. Where else should I have gone?"

"Colin said you were a writer. Kids' books?"

He nodded. "I wrote them to pay the bills until I made money off my paintings. And I am in the middle of something right now, so I must go. Vera, I know you work this afternoon, so if there is anything else that needs doing, I'm on Lucia duty." He turned to me. "I'll be happy to help you organize the furniture if you want to finish that up. I took the tarps off everything and tried to put all the pieces in some sort of order."

"Thanks. And you did a great job, by the way," I said, keeping my face straight. "Of folding all those tarps, I mean. If this art thing falls through, this may be a new career path."

Vera laughed out loud.

"I'll keep that in mind," he said, his eyes dancing. "Go on, ladies. You have lots of things to do, and the morning is slipping away."

Vera and I got up and left him, sipping what remained of his café crème, sitting alone in the dappled sunlight.

Vera had left me at the metro station, having to go to work. I made it the rest of the way myself, proud that I recognized some of the street signs and landmarks. Coming into the courtyard, my two mesh bags loaded with thrift store jeans and T-shirts, I saw the doors to the right-hand stable row standing open with several cans of paint stacked in front of the wooden doorway. Karl was moving them, one at a time, onto shelves.

"Lucy," he called when he saw me. "Your paint has been delivered."

I put on a bright smile. "I'll be right there," I answered. I went into my *appartement* and dumped my purchases in the middle of the floor, then went out to look.

Yes, the paint was there, all right. There seemed to be thirty or forty cans, as well as brushes, rollers, painting trays, everything needed to paint two-hundred-plus-year-old plaster walls.

Oh boy.

Karl moved deliberately, lining up each can on a tall metal shelf, one at a time. I helped him, significantly speeding up the process, then looked around.

This was obviously the workroom for the hotel. In addition to the shelves reaching up to the beamed ceiling, there was a long wooden table crowded with tools, ladders propped against the walls, and cardboard boxes with descriptions of the contents scrawled in black marker, and all along the back, various pots and gardening implements.

"I guess this is where Raoul keeps all his tools?" I asked.

"Raoul, yes. And all of mine as well. And many years' worth of other guests and workmen. There's old furniture in some of the other bays, and more tools, and lots of kitchen necessities. Things tend to find their way in and never leave." He smiled. His teeth were stained and uneven, and his whole face shone.

I examined the paint cans and pulled one off the shelves. "This one is for Colin," I told him. "All the rust and peeling paint has to be scraped off the front gate, and it all has to be repainted. It's the first thing people will see when they come up to Hotel Paradis, so it needs to be perfect. Claudine said Colin would be the one for the job."

He bobbed his head. "Yes. Colin is very patient. I know there's a metal brush here somewhere. I'll put this aside for him. But what about the rose garden?"

"And espalier. Along the side yard, where the laundry was hung?

Claudine said it got sun all day long. That would be good for roses, yes?"

He nodded, but disappointment changed his smile. "But no one will be able to see them back there."

"I want them seen from the second-story rooms. There needs to be a view there just as beautiful as the rooms that overlook the garden. What do you think?"

His face changed again, and I could see the sparkle in his eyes. "We will have to design from, what is the phrase . . . bird's-eye? That is a challenge, but I am up to the task."

I believed him. I had faith in his spirit. "That's good to know, Karl. Thank you. I'm going to change. I need to finish looking at all the rooms and figuring out the furniture."

He nodded, and I went back into my *appart,* quickly changed, and was almost out the door when my cell phone rang. I took a quick look. Mom and Dad.

I took a breath and swiped, girding myself for an ordeal.

Talking to my parents was not in itself particularly trying, but my father's grasp of technology was dependent on the day of the week, the time of day, and the position of the moon in relation to the stars. He insisted on FaceTime, and he sat at his computer for the call. His computer was so old that he had a separate camera attached to it, as well as a separate microphone. That provided multiple opportunities for the camera to be pointing to the ceiling or the floor, or not turned on at all. Mom was usually in another room, yelling her portion of the conversation, so the mic had to be picked up and moved from where he was sitting at his desk and stretched as far as the cord would go in the general direction of whatever room my mom was in. You'd think after years of such phone calls, they would have gotten some sort of system down. But . . . no.

"Hi, Dad. What time is it there?"

"It's late, but since you never told us you got there safely, your mother made me call."

"Dad, I texted you the day I arrived."

"What text?" I could hear my mother yell.

I watched as Dad picked up the mic and held it off to the left. She must be in the kitchen. "Dad texted me and I answered back that I landed. Didn't you get the text?" I raised my voice, hoping she would hear me. Some conversations with Mom were held at concert pitch.

"No. Bruno, she texted? Why don't you ever check your phone? This call is costing money."

"Dad, listen, I got a phone plan here, and I can call you for free."

"FaceTime?"

I sighed. "No. Does it have to be?"

"Maybe we can do that Skype thing. Do I have to download a Skype thing?"

"Yes, Dad. Do we *really* need to see each other? When I lived in Ohio, we talked all the time without FaceTime."

"That was Ohio," my mother called. "Now you're in France."

"Yes, but you can still hear me just the same."

"But your face," she argued.

"Mom, you're always in another room. You never *see* my face."

"I know, but your father."

"Dad. Really?"

He put the mic back down on his desk. "Just a regular phone call?"

"Yes."

"Like, on the landline?"

"Or your cell, Dad. Whichever you prefer."

"The landline. That way, I can sit in the kitchen with your mother. Maybe tomorrow. I'm glad you're safe."

"Good. Quick, before I go, how are the boys?" My brothers were forty-one and forty-three, but they would forever be boys in my mind.

"Frankie got a promotion," Dad said.

"Great. Good for him."

"And Joey is the same." *The same* meant he was not drinking. Joey not drinking was a big deal. He had always had a drinking problem, and it had intensified when his wife, Sara, died of cancer three years before. He had not pulled himself out of the deep depression that followed. He had not rallied to care for his two confused and grieving daughters. But he had finally put himself into rehab and been sober for almost eight months now, and the whole family breathed a daily sigh of relief at "the same." His twin daughters spent most of their time with Nana and PopPop, which was not ideal. My parents had never been warm and demonstrative, and the girls tended to just sit in their room all day unless someone, who had usually been me, took them out for a walk, shopping, anything. Still, it was better than them being alone in a rented apartment, waiting for their father to come home.

"Billy called!" I heard my mother yell.

"Nice, Mom!" I yelled back. Billy was William Forrester, my first and only husband. We married the weekend after we both graduated college, and he followed me from job to job for almost twelve years before finally finding someplace he didn't want to leave. Our parting had been sad but amicable, and my mother never stopped thinking of him as her son-in-law. Probably because I never gave her another option.

My dad rolled his eyes. "He's a good man."

"Yes, Dad. Very good."

"Your mother, well, you know your mother. Listen, I gotta go. I love you."

I nodded. "I love you, too, Daddy."

He ended the call, and I stood, staring at my phone.

I had worked in hotels across North America during my career, slowly gaining experience and something of a reputation. Before The Fielding, the weekly phone calls with my parents had always been short and sweet. After moving back east, FaceTime kicked in, even though I lived only forty miles away and saw my parents once a month instead of only three or four times a year. Now that I was a whole ocean away . . .

I stuck the phone into the pocket of my thrift store jeans. They were men's jeans and fit me pretty well except for the length, but after rolling up the cuffs, they were just fine. My T-shirt was also a man's size XL, a little too large, but I couldn't resist the AC/DC logo, faded but readable, across the chest.

Time to work.

I went back upstairs and into a room overlooking the back courtyard. I still had six rooms full of furniture to look at and access, with pictures to take. I had not seen or heard from Claudine, which was a shame, because the two of us would be much faster than I was alone.

But there was Bing.

I knew where the stairs to the attic were, tucked into a corner right next to the elevator. I opened a door to a steep stairway, and I could hear footsteps above.

"Bing?" I called. "Is that you up there? Or do we have another ghost?"

I heard his laughter. "Come on up."

The stairway was steep and dark, but as I turned on the landing, there was a sudden flood of light, and I found myself in a wide, open space, a wall of windows letting in the afternoon sunlight, the smell of oil paint and turpentine in the air.

It was a studio. Color was everywhere, on the walls in a sea of paintings, and a floor covered in vibrant oriental rugs. There was a long, narrow table down the center of the room, and three separate easels stood before the wall of glass. There was a cluster of comfortable chairs around a low, round table, and at the far end of the room, I could see a four-poster bed behind a thin curtain of lace.

"I've just finished," Bing said. "Seriously. I just cleaned up ten minutes ago, and I was on my way down to find you. What's your plan for the afternoon? I know you were trying to organize all our beds and chairs. I'm happy to help."

I gazed around me in wonder. There were oil portraits and watercolor landscapes of such delicacy and purity of line that I could not find words to speak. I just motioned with one hand, my mouth hanging open.

"Your work?" I asked, then felt like kicking myself in the teeth. Of course it was his work. "This is . . . I mean . . . Bing, you're *good*."

His mouth twitched. "Thanks. I happen to think so, too, but it's nice to get a second opinion. I was thinking that—"

"It's Boodily!" I squealed. "Boodily and Flap!"

Hanging above a bookcase that ran along the back wall were beautiful watercolors of two of the most famous and beloved characters in children's books. I knew them both because they had been a favorite of all my nieces, and I had bought all the books, all the stuffed toys, all the DVDs of the adventures of Boodily the pig and his best friend, Flap the duck. I walked over to take a closer look, then saw the bookcase held copies of the books, including several foreign-language versions. I pulled out a copy from Russia, or maybe Turkey, and ran my hand over the cover. The title was unreadable to me, but the author's name was clear enough: Bing Davis.

I turned and stared at him. "Is this *you*? You're Bing Davis?"

He shrugged modestly. "Yes."

"But . . ." I slipped the book back into its place. There were at least twelve picture books in the Boodily and Flap series, and three other series by Bing Davis that I recognized, all beautifully illustrated and written in a charming, whimsical style. "This isn't just kids' books. I mean, you practically have an *empire*."

He threw his head back and laughed. "I never thought of it that way, but I suppose you're right. I do control something of a media syndicate right now."

I stared. Was he *kidding*? Boodily and Flap had been around for at least fifteen years and were still going strong. One of his other series, Marnie and Pug, had released a full-length animated movie that winter. I knew because I had seen it, twice, with my nieces Mimi and Cara. Books, movies, a CGI television series that was still in reruns, toys, a video game . . .

"But you must be—" Doing well? Loaded? Filthy rich?

He waved a hand. "I get by."

"Then why are you living here?" Boy, did that come out wrong. "I mean, don't you rich writers live on oceanfront estates, surrounded by minions?"

He laughed again, harder this time. "Possibly bestselling *adult fiction* writers," he said at last. "But I have no interest in oceanfront estates. Or minions. I love living here. In Rennes, in France. In Hotel Paradis. I'm surrounded by friends in a vibrant city that I know and enjoy, I can go anywhere in Europe by just hopping on a train, and when I do go back home, I can indulge in the best." He stuck his hands in the front pockets of his jeans. "When I went to New York to see my editors, I always stayed at The Fielding."

I met his look. "Really?"

"Yes. It was my favorite hotel in the city. I was really upset when it shut down."

Yeah, Bing. Me, too. "I didn't realize the foreign press picked it up."

"Just in the beginning. I spent a lot of time following what happened online. I loved The Millhouse."

I found myself suddenly choked up. I had loved The Millhouse, too. That had been the bar in The Fielding, right on the ground floor off the lobby, a snug, comfortable place with leather banquettes and framed black-and-white photos of New York City on the walls. It had been my favorite bar in all of Manhattan, and I had been in many of them in eight years.

I nodded. "Jackie did a great gimlet," I said. Jack Fortuna had been the bartender there. I had hired him, and I thought we were friends until the scandal broke and he had sought me out, screaming in my face, "You were sleeping with him! How did you not know?"

He nodded. "Yes, he did. And I loved the concierge there, the woman . . . Phyl?"

I cleared my throat. "Yes. Phyllis Wentworth. It sounds like you were a regular. Why didn't we ever meet? I always tried to have a word with the VIPs."

He shook his head. "I wasn't a VIP. I was David Bingham, artist, from Rennes."

"Flew in under the radar? Very crafty of you."

"It wouldn't have made all that much of a difference. Your staff was superb. They treated everyone the same."

"Yes. They were. I was very proud of them." I swallowed hard. I had to ask. "Did you ever meet Tony?"

His eyes never left my face. "A few times. My editor, Joe Whatley, introduced us. Joe liked to rub elbows with the local celebs, and Tony was a catch. I never liked him, though. Tony, I mean."

What could I say to that? Other people had said the same thing about Tony, and I saw their point. Tony was charming, but he was also too glib, too quick with the cutting remark. It hadn't mattered to me, though. I loved him just as fiercely the day he left as when I'd first fallen, years before, in Quebec, when we had met at a conference and spent four days across from each other at meetings and four nights together in his hotel room.

"Well." I cleared my throat. "Yes, I was going to try to finish the furniture today. Can you help? It will go much faster with the two of us."

He ran his hand through his hair as he nodded. "Right. Let's go."

I turned, out of the sunlight and color, back down the narrow stairs.

"I love this style of chair," I said, getting a bit closer and taking its picture.

"It's a bergère. Very comfortable," Bing explained. He had been separating tables and chairs from the huddled piles they had been in all afternoon, offering explanations and even design tips. "This one here? It would go well in number twelve. The carving is like the carving on the desk there."

"How can you remember something like that?" I asked.

He shrugged. "I'm very visual."

Of course. He had also reeled in the skepticism a bit, although I could still hear the laughter in his voice if I waxed too rhapsodic over a carved headboard or drape of silk.

We shut the door to the last room we needed to look at. Done for the day.

"So, how many children do you have?" he asked as we headed for the stairs.

"None. Why do you think I had children?"

He tilted his head at me. "Well, most childless people do not instantly recognize characters from children's books."

"Ah. Yes, well, I have four nieces. The oldest, Heather, just turned eighteen. She was the perfect age when Boodily and Flap first came out. I bought her all the books, then the stuffed animals . . . Wasn't there a farmyard set? And then her sister, Brianne, fell in love, just like she had. The babies are Mimi and Cara, nine-year-old twins. They are, I must admit, the loves of my life. We saw *The Adventures of Marnie and Pug*. In January. Twice."

"Why, thank you for your support," he said, bowing graciously.

My back ached and one of the blisters on my hand had broken open, but I felt surer of myself than when I had first arrived, so when I smiled at him, it wasn't forced. "It's been a pleasure exploring your books through the eyes of those girls. You hide your cynical streak very well."

"It comes out quite strongly in my more serious work," he said. "My last show was the object of much discussion. I believe the consensus was that I was not aging gracefully but was rather fighting the process tooth and nail."

"That's how I'm fighting it," I told him. "If gray hair wasn't suddenly so fashionable, I'd be chestnut brown number twenty-four right now."

He laughed. "Your gray hair is quite attractive. Please, forget all about chestnut brown number twenty-four."

I felt myself blushing, and as I did, I wanted to kick myself. Really? Sliding down slowly into fifty and a sideways compliment like that could make me blush? If Bing noticed, he didn't show it but instead bent to pick up Napoléon Bonaparte, who sat at the top of the stairs.

"Are you a cat person?" Bing asked.

I shook my head. "I don't know. I've never had a cat. Or a dog."

He raised an eyebrow. "You've never had a pet?"

I shrugged. "My mother was allergic, and after college, I moved around too much to feel comfortable getting a pet. And then, I lived mostly in hotels. One of the perks, you know. The general manager usually got free room and board."

He stroked Napoléon's head, and the cat closed its eyes. I could hear it start to purr. "I like cats. I love dogs, but a dog is not suited to this kind of life. A dog needs grass to run around in and squirrels to chase. But Napoléon—that is, *this* Napoléon—I like very much. Are you done for the day? I'm going to make myself an espresso. Would you like to join me?"

I wanted a bath. I needed to sit down and go over all my lists. I was itching to make some sort of flow chart, or maybe an Excel spreadsheet, with all the furniture. I smiled. "That would be great."

He nodded. "Wait for me in the garden. It's still warm out there in the afternoons. We can sit there."

Napoléon jumped from his arms, trotted across the lobby, and jumped out through a half-open window.

"Is everything unlocked around here?" I asked.

"Sometimes. I'll explain."

I went out to the front courtyard. It was later than I'd thought, and the shadows were growing long. I walked into the garden and sat on one of the benches. Bing was right that it was not uncomfortable at all, but I would bring in more conventional chairs and small tables with bright green umbrellas to guard guests against the summer sun.

I closed my eyes and felt my body relax. There was the faint sound of traffic, and somewhere, a woman laughed. Was Claudine back? I shifted my shoulders against the wooden back of the bench, mentally checking off items on my furniture list. All the rooms had been looked at. I needed a chart of all the rooms, their numbers, and what was needed in each. Then, I'd have to play musical chairs and move all the pieces where they would fit the best. The rugs and artwork Claudine mentioned? That should wait until the last week, after all the rooms were painted and polished, furniture gleaming, linen drapes billowing . . .

"Here."

I opened my eyes, and Bing set a small tray on the bench between us. Two small cups and a silver coffeepot with a long, wooden handle. He poured.

"There are no air conditioners?" I asked.

He stretched his legs out in front of him and took a quick sip. "No. It is not a thing here. There are also no screens."

I frowned. "But . . ."

He shook his head. "No screens. And about the locks, well, no one can get in the front gate without the code, so until now, everyone has felt quite safe. Of course, once guests arrive, things will change. We will put locks on the doors to our *appartements* and figure out a way to secure the hotel. We may need some expert advice about that."

"Yes. We might. I don't have any hands-on experience with security." Of course, I had no hands-on experience with painting rooms or creating a website, but security was not mentioned in my contract, so I felt on safer ground.

"How about you?" I asked. "Any kids?"

He nodded, shifted on the bench, and crossed his ankles. "A son. He is living in Quebec now, working a crap job and painting. I'm pretty sure he's also studying nubile young Canadians."

I laughed. "I lived in Montreal for a few years. Canadian girls are quite lovely."

He nodded. "So are Canadian boys. Philippe is what you would call an equal opportunity admirer. While the Southern Baptist born-and-raised American in me is shocked and appalled, the Francophile bohemian artist in me is quite pleased. Things are very different here in France."

"So, you're divorced, then?"

He shook his head. "His mother and I were not married."

"But you are in his life?"

He looked sideways at me. "Very much so. Claudine is his mother."

"What . . . oh." I took another mouthful of strong coffee and felt a jolt all the way to my toes. "Are you and Claudine still together?"

"Oh, no. Our affair fizzled out after five or six years. She finally ended it because her husband insisted. And I was even getting ready to pack up my canvas and paints and find another place to live, but he decided to divorce, anyway, so I stayed. It worked out well because she and I raised him together."

"So, he grew up here? When did he leave?"

He glanced at me. "Five years ago. He ran away from a broken heart."

"Oh, poor Philippe."

"Yes. He was in love with Marie Claude."

I sat up straighter. "Our Marie Claude?"

"The very same. Her mother was an old friend of Claudine's, and she came here to live when she turned eighteen. Problems at home, I believe. She fell in love with Philippe, but she wanted to live here in Rennes. He wanted to travel the world and paint. She said, 'But if you loved me, you'd stay.' He said, 'But if you loved me, you'd go.'" He shrugged. "So, she stayed, and he left. Two years ago, she married Eliot, who is a perfectly nice young man but, if I may say so, dreadfully dull."

"Does he come home to visit? Philippe?"

"Yes. Every summer, when Marie Claude goes back to visit Eliot's family in Lyon for three weeks."

I watched his face. "You must miss him."

He nodded. "I do. We talk all the time. We're very close. But it's not the same." His mouth twisted. "Claudine misses him much more. She is lonely, you see, without her only son."

"She never remarried?"

"No."

"And you never married?"

"I did, very briefly, but she realized that the life of an artist that she imagined was not the life that I had any interest in leading."

A thought hit me. "So, your son will inherit Hotel Paradis?"

He set his empty cup on the tray. "Yes. He's not terribly enthusiastic about it, which is why he felt the need to run all over the world to paint while he was still young and not tied down. But he understands how important it is. And he will have my studio to use for his work. He is so much more talented than I, with a real gift. He will be important someday."

"I don't know, Bing. Boodily and Flap are pretty important."

He threw back his head and laughed, the sound echoing off the stone walls and up to the darkening sky. "Yes, I suppose you're right. At least important enough that he will never have to worry about finding the money the next time the roof needs repair. Are you done? I'll bring this inside. I have a call to make in a few minutes."

I set the cup down. "That was good. Thank you. I'll see you tomorrow?"

"Of course. And Colin will be around all day. We can work out a plan."

I watched as he disappeared behind the garden wall.

No screens.

No air-conditioning.

No locks on the doors.

I stood and stretched.

He and Claudine had a son.

They still lived under—literally—the same roof, yet he had married another woman.

That son would someday own the Hotel Paradis.

Bing scoffed at the idea that Claudine could bring the hotel back to its glory.

Bing was right. Things were very different in France.

Chapter Six

I made the grave error of googling "painting plaster walls" and went down a rabbit hole that even Alice in Wonderland would have found overwhelming. Two hours and nine YouTube videos later, I thought I was ready. But standing in an empty room with twelve-foot ceilings, windows almost as tall, with crown molding and a picture rail, not to mention base molding almost a foot high *and* two doors, I could feel my confidence slipping away slowly like water down a clogged drain.

"You have no idea what you're doing, do you?" Bing asked, straight-faced but with laughter bubbling just under the surface of his voice.

"Shut up," I muttered between clenched teeth. "We start with the ceiling. Then walls. Moldings and trim last. All perfectly logical."

"Perfectly." He cleared his throat. "But shouldn't we prime first? You've got new plaster and some water staining."

Right. Primer. I knew that. I looked at the cans lined up on the floor. I had primer. Good start. "Of *course,* we'll prime first. What do you want? Ceiling or walls?"

He looked carefully at the tall but somewhat disreputable-looking ladder in the middle of the room. "How are you with heights?"

Did I want to get up on that ladder and try to balance myself while maneuvering a paint roller at the end of a six-foot pole? Did I want to have to climb up and down that ladder several times to put new paint on the roller, as well as moving the ladder from one place to the other? Did I want to crane my neck while squinting up at an almost-white ceiling to make sure I was covering every inch with primer that was almost the exact same color?

No. Of course not. "I have no problem with heights at all."

His mouth twitched. "Why don't I take the ceiling first?"

I did not throw myself at his feet, weeping with relief. "Sounds like a plan."

We spread tarps, which the hotel seemed to have in abundance, opened paint cans, and poured.

"Maybe we should have gotten one of those sprayer things?" I asked, half to myself.

"Have you ever used one before?" Bing asked.

"No. But how hard can it be? Point and spray, right?"

He made a noise that may or may not have been a snort. "It's a bit more complicated than that," he said in a tone that suggested I should have known.

I was willing to take his word for it. Besides, I had rollers, brushes, and poles, not to mention trays and tarps. I had everything I needed.

I loaded up my roller and began to paint the wall. *Apply the paint in a W pattern,* I kept thinking. W. And another W. And another. Then reload the roller and do it all over again. And again. And again. And . . .

"Ah, Lucia?"

I glanced up at Bing. He had managed to prime half the ceiling in the time it had taken me to cover the wall between two of the windows. He did not have primer splashed halfway up his arms. His fingers were not blotchy. His T-shirt was not spattered.

"Yes?"

He backed down the ladder and put down his roller. "May I make a suggestion?"

Oh, please, God, yes. "Sure."

"You need longer strokes. Load up your roller."

I dipped the roller into the paint tray and moved it back and forth.

"Just once or twice is sufficient," Bing told me. "The roller can only hold so much. Physics, you know?"

Really? It's *physics*?

"May I?" he asked.

May he what? I nodded.

He turned me to face the wall and stood directly behind me, his chest against my back, and I swear I could feel his heartbeat. He reached around and covered my hand with his.

"Longer strokes," he said again, moving my arm up and then down in a sweeping motion. "See?"

"Yep." I did see. I was also having trouble breathing, and the heat of him against me was more distracting than it had a right to be.

He let go of my hand and stepped back. "Go on."

I reloaded the brush and tried again. Why did I think those silly little W shapes were going to get the job done?

"Better?"

I nodded. "Thank you."

He went back up the ladder, and we continued to work in silence.

Once I got into a different rhythm, things moved more quickly, but Bing was done with the ceiling long before I was done with the walls. He switched from roller to brush and began to work around the windows and molding.

I could feel a whole new set of aches starting in both of my arms and my back. Was I really this out of shape? I mentally shook my head. No, I wasn't. I had to stop beating myself up for things that were out of my control. If I had sore and achy muscles tomorrow, it would be because I hadn't used them for anything as strenuous as painting walls in years.

"How about a break?" Bing suggested. "I'll make some espresso."

I tried not to look too relieved. "That would be great, thanks. I could use a pick-me-up."

I started to wipe my hands on my thrift store jeans, then stopped and looked around for the rags I knew I had brought in for the sole purpose of wiping my hands. They were in a small pile on the other side of the room. As I stepped off the tarp to get them, I looked back to see a trail of faint footprints on the scuffed wooden floor.

How had I managed to get primer on the *bottom* of my shoes? I picked up a rag, wiped my hands, then knelt and tried to wipe the faint footprint. Instead of magically disappearing into the rag, it became a larger, slightly fainter footprint, more a milky sort of blotch that seemed to grow larger with each swipe. I stood to get another rag. I also had primer on the knees of my jeans, because there were new spots in the exact area where I had tried to clean. I took a step back. Another footprint.

I closed my eyes and took several long, deep breaths. This was not terrible. This was easily fixable. All I had to do was strip off all my clothes and hope that I hadn't gotten any primer on my actual *skin*.

"Lucia?"

I opened my eyes.

Bing was standing in the doorway, holding a small tray and looking at me in an odd sort of way. "What did you do now?"

I managed a big smile instead of hurling the entire bucket of paint at him. "I didn't do anything. I just tried to walk from one part of the room to the other."

He shook his head and put on a "Not again" kind of expression. "And yet you somehow managed to create a disaster."

"This," I said, trying to keep my voice level, "is not a disaster. It's just a bit of a mess. I'm tracking footprints everywhere, but all I have to do is strip naked to clean them up."

"Well, I doubt that's true, but I'll be happy to watch and take notes if you really want to try it out." His mouth twitched. "You can't clean up with dry rags, Lucia."

"Why not? Is that another physics thing?"

He shook his head impatiently. "No. It's just a common-sense thing."

"You're suggesting that I lack common sense." Just three minutes ago, he was the sweet, thoughtful man suggesting a break and making espresso. Now, he was back to being an insufferable know-it-all.

"Well, you're the one tracking primer all over the floor and then trying to clean it with *dry* rags," he said.

"And perhaps it's because I have never primed or painted rooms on this scale and am ignorant of the process, rather than lacking common sense."

He shifted his weight from one foot to the other. "That's another possibility," he said. "Why don't you take off your shoes, follow me, have a little espresso, and we'll figure this all out."

He turned and was gone. I slipped off my shoes, balanced carefully as I checked to make sure there wasn't anything on my socks, and padded after him.

He wasn't in the salon. He was sitting outside on the patio, pouring espresso from a small copper pot into tiny china cups. The air was still. I sat and took a sip, closed my eyes, and felt the bitter coffee against my throat. The jolt came a few seconds later, and I opened my eyes. He was looking at me with that half smile on his lips.

I wanted to ask him if he was always such an insufferable jackass. I wanted to wipe that slightly smug smile off his face. I also wanted to kiss that smile off his face, a thought that came out of left field and threw me off. So . . .

"Do you believe there's a ghost?" I asked him.

He raised both eyebrows. "Where on earth did that come from?"

I shrugged. "I like it out here. No bad juju. In fact, I'm more relaxed out here than anywhere else in the hotel."

"Maybe because this is one of the few places in the hotel that doesn't need a massive overhaul?"

"I hadn't thought about it quite like that. You're probably right."

He leaned back. "Some people are more intuitive than others. Claudine is convinced. She says she feels her, the ghost. Karl and Vera also have said they can tell when she's here. And Marie Claude, why, she feels like this spirit is a long-lost friend. But then, she is a very fanciful young woman. I have never felt anything at all, in all the years I've been here. But that doesn't mean I don't believe. I've lived long enough to know that you should never discount another person's beliefs just because they aren't in line with your own."

"Wise words."

He chuckled. "I'm old."

"How old?"

"Fifty-five."

I sniffed. "That's not old. Sixty is the new forty, haven't you heard?"

He smiled. "They have been fifty-five very *long* years." He shrugged. "But they mostly have been good years." He stretched out his legs. "How about you?"

I drank more espresso. "I'll be fifty in three months. I had planned on retiring at fifty. I had a bunch of money in a private pension fund, managed by Fielding Enterprises. I had a separate IRA. I had my eye on a little condo in Cape Cod, right on the bay, where I was going to spend the next thirty or so years sitting on a beach and writing bad poetry. Then Tony Fielding cleaned out all the money—mine and everyone else's who worked for him—and dropped off the face of the earth. I spent every penny of my IRA to keep out of jail. The little condo is still there, though. I check on it occasionally. It's a rental now."

He reached over and put his hand on my arm, giving it a gentle squeeze. "I'm sorry," he said quietly.

I took a breath. I had talked this out so many times—with myself, my lawyers, Julia, my parents—but I heard words coming out of my mouth I had never said before. "He asked me to go away with him. I didn't know at the time what he was planning. But he asked me, just a few weeks before it happened, if I would run away with him, leave everything behind and spend the rest of our days together in a cabin in the woods somewhere. I said no." I moved away from him, just enough that he dropped his hand. "I didn't think he was serious. Who says something like that and *means* it?" I put my empty cup on the tray and closed my eyes again.

"Knowing what you know now, would you have said yes?"

I felt tears begin, tears I thought had long ago been cried out and brushed away. "I loved him. With all my heart and soul. I would have followed him anywhere."

I felt the wetness on my cheeks, and then the cool air dried them, and finally, I opened my eyes and Bing was still just sitting, his arms folded against his chest. He looked over at me and spoke quietly. "We need to clean up the floor and finish priming our room."

I nodded. "Yes. And tomorrow we paint, and by the end of the week, we can move in furniture and maybe have one room complete."

"Hopefully, things will speed up as we figure out what works and what doesn't," he said.

"Hopefully."

"And on the weekends, Claudine and Colin will help."

"Yes."

"And once Raoul is done with all his work, I'm sure he'll pitch in."

"Yes."

"So, you have a plan."

I managed a smile. "I always have a plan."

He was still, then nodded. "Yes. I'm sure you do."

Bing met me as I crossed the courtyard, walking into the hotel. He stood in front of me and shook his head.

"Change," he said briefly.

"Why?" I was dressed in my painting uniform: rolled-up men's jeans and a now paint-spattered T-shirt.

"Because it's Saturday, and we're going to the market."

Right, Saturday market. I was about to argue. After all, we'd just started getting into a rhythm with the painting of the rooms. But I felt the ache in my shoulders, felt the new blister on my thumb, and nodded. "Change into what?"

He shrugged. "I'm not familiar with your wardrobe. All I can tell you is that Frenchwomen dress well to walk the dog. And make sure you have comfortable shoes."

Fifteen minutes later, in a pair of black linen pants and a colorful tunic, with my feet in comfy oxfords and my newly acquired mesh shopping bag over my shoulder, we set out.

It was a fairly short walk. Bing pointed out a few landmarks, gave a brief history lesson of the rebellious Bretons, and as we suddenly turned a corner, I stopped and stared.

Sloping gently down an incline, the morning sun was bright on the various stalls and vendors that lined the cobblestone street before me. All was color and noise, stretching out for what seemed to be forever. Was there an end to this? And if there was, how could I possibly run this gauntlet with just one single mesh bag?

Everything I saw I wanted to buy: fresh flowers, live plants, vegetables of every description. Separate stalls for herbs, mushrooms, leafy greens I'd never seen before in my life, tomatoes in shapes and

colors that defied logic, fruit in woven baskets that seemed to mock
the grocery stores of what I thought was the greatest food city in
the world, New York.

Bing knew some of the vendors and greeted them by name.
I just followed him, mouth hanging open, occasionally stopping
because I simply could not take another step without six of those
small, blush-red apples, a bunch of fragrant lilies, or a basket of
pearl onions. Just when I thought I had seen it all, we turned into
a row of prepared foods, men and women cooking on giant grills
and propane-fueled cooktops. My mouth began to water, and we
stopped to buy a few pastries, delicate buttery rolls wrapped around
berries and honey.

"We'll come back and get something for lunch," Bing said in
my ear. "Come on."

Inside a large, lofty building were the butchers. Meat and poul-
try and fish lay on beds of ice. Here were the cheese sellers and
smiling women selling pots of homemade jam and jars of honey.

Bing had his favorites, and he bargained loudly and with a smile.
Some sort of fish I'd never seen before, not even in an aquarium. A
piece of beef as red as blood, a chicken small and pink.

"Why doesn't meat look like this in the States?" I asked.

"Here, the small farmer is encouraged. All these people sell their
own goods, not something raised or bred for some megacorpora-
tion." We watched as two thick pork chops were wrapped in brown
paper. "This is how meat is supposed to look." He grinned at me.
"Something else you'll have to get used to."

Finally, we found an empty bench and opened cardboard containers filled with something Bing had purchased from a smiling woman
wearing a hijab. I didn't know what I was eating, but it was delicious:
rice and chopped vegetables and spicy, tender chicken in strips.

"You come here every week?" I asked, taking a swig of cold cider
from a bottle.

He nodded. "I don't cook much. I only have two burners and

not much skill, but with this food, it's hard to make a bad meal." He grinned. "Unless you're Claudine."

"Really?"

He brushed the crumbs from the flatbread off his fingers. "Never accept an invitation for anything other than wine and cheese. Marie Claude is an excellent cook. So is Vera. Colin still prepares food in the English style he grew up with, so unless you like overcooked lamb and mushy peas, find an excuse."

"Don't you all have communal meals? Big potluck feasts? Aren't you all one big happy family?"

He stretched out his legs. "Yes and no. Most of us have been living at the hotel for a very long time. We used to share meals more often. But we all value each other's privacy very much. We have to, or we'd become *too* much like family and start quarreling with each other over the littlest things. As it is, we all try to live our separate lives. And when we do get together, we tend to enjoy each other's company very much."

I was full. Actually, I'd been full three-quarters of the way through the container, but it was so good I'd finished every bite. "Has there ever been someone living at the hotel who didn't fit in?"

He pursed his lips and thought. "Well, we've had a few other so-called general managers try their hand at what you're supposed to be doing. They didn't last long. They were all overrated and underqualified. And they were, to a man, arrogant know-it-alls who tried to tell Claudine the job was impossible."

I looked at him and raised an eyebrow. "And yet," I said, "here *you* are."

He stared for a moment, then threw back his head and laughed. "Two points to you. Yes, I think this is impossible. But . . ." He turned slightly on the bench, his body leaning toward mine. "I think you're different. I haven't figured out how or why. It's an interesting puzzle for me, and I like interesting things." His eyes held mine, and I felt the color start to rise in my cheeks.

"Maybe," I said, looking away from him to gather my napkins from where they had drifted to the ground, "I'll get the job done because I'm good at this. I used to be highly respected. I once had an entire magazine article written about how I had turned The Fielding from midtown's version of Motel 6 into a five-star showplace."

He nodded slowly. "I found that article. *The New Yorker*."

I looked at him in surprise. I still had the framed article that had once been on the wall in the lobby of The Fielding. It was in one of my suitcases, under my bed.

I stood and walked to the trash can, dropped in my used napkins and the empty container, and rubbed my palms against the rough linen of my pants. As I turned, Bing handed me my mesh bag, laden with my treasures.

"Can I come with you again?" I asked.

"Of course," he said. "I'm here every Saturday. You can come with me anytime."

"Thanks," I said, and we walked back to Hotel Paradis.

Chapter Seven

The chandelier in the lobby of the hotel was brass and crystal, with small light bulbs shaped like candle flames. Half the bulbs were missing. The brass had turned black. And most of the crystals were in a box on the floor.

I looked over at Claudine. "This," I said emphatically, "was *not* in my contract."

She smiled. "No. Marie Claude and Colin are going to take the rest of the crystals down, scrub them clean, polish the brass, replace the bulbs, and put all the crystals back."

"I thought Eliot was her partner in crime."

She made a face. "I think Eliot is not as enthusiastic about helping out as he once was. Besides, Colin is perfect for something as tedious as this."

I sighed. "When do you think they'll be finished? July?"

She laughed. "You have so little faith, Lucy. It will only take a few days."

I looked back up toward the chandelier. "Who's going to stand on the ladder for all that time?"

She shook her head. "Ah, no. Nothing so difficult. There is a mechanism that lowers the whole thing down for cleaning. In the office. I'll show you."

I followed her down the corridor and into the office. I hadn't been in there more than once or twice since I'd arrived, because it was just another outdated mess that I was going to have to clean, update, and improve without any money.

The office was long and narrow, with frosted windows on two opposite walls to let in the light from the corridor on one side, and the salon on the other. Two large wooden desks were pushed against the back wall. On one of them, there was a desktop computer, so old I knew that if I powered it up, I'd get a flashing C: prompt. There was not a printer in sight, nor a fax machine, not even a phone. There was a large safe, looking about a hundred years old, open and empty. And there were boxes everywhere, stacks of papers, and yellowed manila folders crammed in the bookcase.

I'd been having nightmares about this office intermittently since the last time I'd peeked in, about two weeks ago.

Claudine moved a few boxes from in front of a narrow door in the corner and opened it. There was a handle sticking out of the wall, and she cranked it slowly. I could hear the creak of metal against metal, and I went back out to the lobby to watch as the entire chandelier lowered itself slowly until it stopped three feet from the marble-tiled floor.

I couldn't help myself. I felt a grin. "That is so cool," I called to Claudine.

She walked up beside me and sighed. "I know. It was my job, as a child, to dust the crystals. My father lowered this once a month, and I used a feather duster to clean it. Now, we will need a good soak with ammonia, and it will be back to its glorious self."

I nodded, still smiling. The lobby looked perfect. We had primed and painted the walls and trim, scrubbed and polished the marble floor, waxed the long mahogany counter, and dusted every pigeonhole behind it. We had moved the library table into what had become—quite successfully—the guest office space. It now served as a desk, pushed against a freshly painted wall, across from a small and quite lovely bookcase where, I envisioned, we would have guidebooks and brochures available for our guests.

"Urns with palm trees," I said, waving at the double front doors in their creamy new paint. "And art on the walls. A cluster of chairs with a few tables, and maybe a few more chairs on either side of the salon doors. And ferns in pretty pots. I love ferns. I think that's all we'll need."

"All doable," she said. "Easily."

I stepped back and looked into the office. "Listen, Claudine . . ."

She followed my gaze. "I know. It is a disaster."

"We're going to need all sorts of stuff. At least two desktops, a printer—"

She waved a hand, cutting me off. "We already have all of that. In my office in town. I've sold it, you know. The practice. Well, the client list, anyway. But all the office equipment, including desks and chairs that were manufactured in this century, are mine. We will be officially closing the office the first of June, and then we will bring everything here."

The relief was so intense I could have kissed her. I'd kept my mouth shut about so many things over the past few weeks, mainly because it was painfully clear that money was a real issue. Other than making sure I knew there were very limited funds, she never talked about money. She had shown me a budget, a simple spreadsheet with a list of items and amounts in euros. But I did not have a copy, and I was sure it was not accurate, which made me uncomfortable.

One of the reasons Tony so efficiently cleaned out all the accounts at The Fielding was because he had, in the nine months before his abrupt departure, slowly steered me away from the financial side of the business. He had claimed that I had too many other responsibilities, especially since he had allegedly been planning a second hotel in Miami, and I had been meeting with architects and schmoozing investors. I still saw the daily sheets, of course, but had stopped receiving monthly reports from the accountant. When Tony left, I had no idea how much money had been slowly building in accounts that had been earmarked for the new hotel. When I found how much had been involved, I was stunned. Millions of dollars for the development of the Miami project had vanished, along with everything in the operating accounts, the pension fund, and the reserve.

I was sure Claudine was not sitting on anything even close to that kind of money. And I was also sure that she would start selling body parts to realize her dream of reopening Hotel Paradis if that's what it took. But I was still uneasy when she made it quite clear that the money side of the business was hers and hers alone.

I walked back into the office and pulled a manila folder from the bookcase and opened it up. The paper inside was so old it crumbled. I was holding a sheaf for registration sheets, with the fleur-de-lis logo of Hotel Paradis on the top and the ornately printed sheets filled in by hand. The date was September 23, 1938.

I glanced up at her. "All of these go back this far?" I asked, incredulous.

She took the folder from my hands and read the top sheet, then turned it over carefully. "They never opened the hotel back up after the war. We just lived here, surrounded by empty rooms and echoes. I suppose we can get rid of all this now."

I shook my head. "No. We can frame these. We'll put an old registration in each of the rooms. This is history. We can't just throw it away."

She raised an eyebrow. "Are you going through all these? Because we still have serious work to do."

She was right. In the seven weeks I'd been there, we had completely redone the ground-floor guests' rooms, the salon, the office space, and, once the chandelier was cleaned, the lobby.

After going through the rooms of Hotel Paradis, we were like a well-oiled machine. Bing, Colin, and I had done most of that work; Bing did the ceilings, I did the walls, and Colin came in last to do all the trim. Karl helped by coming in after we were done and cleaning all the drips and smudges and polishing the tall windows until they sparkled. Marie Claude and Eliot had finished with the furniture. Eliot seemed to have dropped away from work around the hotel, but Marie Claude happily stepped in wherever she was needed.

We had moved up to the first floor. Raoul was three rooms ahead of us, working his way through the building, patching plaster and replacing broken molding, and all I could think about was his finishing all the repair work so we could give him a brush and roller. Vera had produced yards of drapery, styled like opera house curtains, which could hang straight to the floor, puddling softly, or could be drawn up with a single tug of the cord to open, revealing cleaned and sparkling *portes-fenêtres*. She had insisted on organza, rather than linen, and the final effect was perfectly sheer and luxurious.

But more than half the rooms were uninhabitable.

Claudine cleared her throat. "I'm thinking about calling in a few favors with a journalist or two. Get some local press about the renovation and the reopening."

I brushed the dust of the crumbling paper from my hands. "Do you have an opening date in mind?"

"July 1."

I mentally went over the most recent timeline I'd created. It was the fifth timeline I'd sweated over in as many weeks. July 1 was a few weeks ahead of my projections but was not unreasonable. "That's less than two months," I said slowly.

She nodded. "I know, but look how far we've come. Can the website be up and running next week?"

Ah, the website. It was a real thing now, with a registered domain name, an email address, and a URL that opened to a landing page, complete with a full-color photo of a stately mansion that I'd lifted from Google images.

"No. We don't have anything in the way of pictures, Claudine. Just a few rooms are finished, and we don't have them completely styled. The salon looks fine, and the lobby will be ready as soon as Marie Claude and Colin finish, but the courtyard is still a mess. I don't even have a good picture of the front of the hotel."

She pursed her lips. "Colin has finished with the front gate," she said.

"Yes, and that looks terrific, but we can't photograph the front gate without also photographing the courtyard and the front facade of the hotel. It's a problem."

"What do we need in the courtyard?" she asked.

I leaned against the doorjamb. "I wanted to pressure wash the whole courtyard. Just to blast away some of the grime and moss."

She nodded. "That's not grime. That's patina. And moss conveys graceful aging."

I grinned at her. "If you say so."

"I do. What else?"

"All the urns in front need to be filled. Palms with trailing vines, maybe? Or ferns? The front windows need to be repaired and cleaned and drapes put up in all the windows. The outside of the door needs to be repainted, and all the exterior trim."

She made a face. "That's a lot."

"Yep. I think it's too soon for photos."

"But we need to start getting the word out. You know that, as of July 1, the whole of Europe goes on vacation. We need to grab some of that trade. And when do people in the US go on vacation? Summers, right?"

"Yes. But we need somewhere to download the software we're going to use. I can't use my laptop, and—"

"I'll get something from work this week and see what we can get going."

I had found free, open-source hotel management software. Who knew? The Fielding had the best software money could buy, sophisticated and complex, with customer support for the smallest of glitches available to us around the clock. I was surprised to find free options out there for smaller hotels and decided which one would work best for us, but without any workstations, it was a moot point.

"We need to finish off the rooms that *are* done. What about artwork? And your rugs?" I asked.

She nodded. "Yes. I'll get them here. We can dress the rooms we have."

We spoke in French, and I was surprised how naturally the language came to me now. I spoke English to Colin and Bing, but the rest of my day, surrounded by French-speaking natives, had tuned my ear and quickened my tongue. No one would mistake me for a natural-born French speaker, but no one cringed at my accent, either.

Claudine narrowed her eyes, and I recognized that as a sign she was thinking hard. "I know someone who can get us greenery," she said slowly. "Very cheaply."

"Cheap is good," I said, wondering if I should question her further, but decided against it. Claudine had a way of producing things we needed without receipts or even packaging. She had miraculously produced keyless locks for all the doors, the kind that opened with the swipe of a card, but had presented them, a whole two dozen, jumbled together in a cardboard box. Raoul had installed them, and I had had to scan the internet for instructions on how to program them.

I nodded. "And art. And rugs. And anything else you may have stored away."

"I'll make the calls," she said. "Maybe two weeks? If I can get you plants? And everything else? Then we can take pictures for the website?"

I looked at her. "We shouldn't be taking these pictures on an iPhone," I told her.

She nodded. "I have a client. No worries." I wondered what kind of deal she would make as I remembered the accommodating electrician.

There was a clatter in the lobby, and I looked to see Marie Claude, in faded overalls, and Colin, in his uniform khaki pants and denim shirt, standing next to the chandelier. Claudine hurried over to them.

"Perfect," she crowed. "Just in time. Let's get a few buckets, and I'll show you what to do."

Marie Claude nodded and, seeing me, gave me a broad smile. She was a delightful young woman, sweet and very smart, and I liked her. Her husband, Eliot, not so much. As Bing had said, he was very dull, slow to join in conversation, and never sat with the rest of us when we gathered in the garden in the evenings. I didn't know what she saw in him, but I had long ago lost any right to pass judgment on romantic relationships, being such a dismal failure at my own.

I looked back into the office. I'd need garbage bins, plastic bags, a broom. . . .

I sighed and started to work.

There was a knock on my door, just loud enough to wake me out of a sound sleep. I glanced at my phone. Just after five in the morning. The knock came again, and I hurried out of bed and looked out the window.

There was a flatbed truck in the courtyard, and Claudine was standing at my door.

I opened the door. "What's the matter? Is something wrong?"

She jerked her head toward the truck. "We need to unload. Can you help?"

I nodded, shut the door, and hastily threw on jeans and a sweat-shirt. *Unload what?*

The truck had moved up closer to the hotel, and the back panel was down, and I saw that it was filled with greens: palm trees, pot-ted ferns, cardboard boxes with all sorts of vines spilling over the top. I ran up to the back of the truck.

There were two men pulling items from the truck bed and handing them to Karl, Claudine, and now me. No one said a word, and in the semidarkness, I really couldn't see what we were off-loading, except that there was a lot of it and there was spilled dirt everywhere. It took us several minutes to empty the back of the truck. Then, the two men jumped down, turned the truck around, and drove out of the courtyard. Claudine followed, closing the gate behind them.

There were all the plants I'd mentioned to Claudine earlier in the week, as well as additions that Karl had brought me later. Obviously, Claudine had made an extensive list of plantings and had placed an order with a local nursery or landscaping company.

But as I looked closer, I realized that none of the items looked like they had come from a nursery. The palm trees were in very attractive and expensive ceramic pots, but none of them matched. The same with the ferns. I poked into one of the cardboard boxes, filled with traditional ivy, and saw that there were leaves, roots, and dirt, but no pots. As though they had been just dug out of the ground and . . .

"Claudine?" I called. "Where did all of this come from? Were those men from a nursery?"

Claudine and Karl exchanged a glance. "Not exactly," she said.

"These pots? I mean, they're very nice, but why aren't these palm trees in plain black plastic pots? These all look like they came off somebody's front porch."

Karl began to whistle tunelessly between his teeth.

I stared at Claudine. "Where's the invoice?"

She picked up a large potted palm tree and hoisted it onto her hip. "There is no invoice," she said shortly. "Can you get the door for me?"

I hurried ahead and opened the front door and watched as she placed the palm tree next to the door to the salon.

"Are you going to help me or not?" she asked somewhat crossly as she went back outside.

"Where did all this come from?" I asked again, even as I lifted another palm with both hands and followed her back to the foyer.

"Over by the stairs, I think," she said.

I set the palm down carefully. It was thick and healthy, with delicate leaves as tall as I was, in a lovely emerald-green pot.

Back outside, Karl had taken the ferns from their variety of pots and had replanted the first of them in one of the cast-iron urns. He lifted a green-and-white vine from another box, shaking the dirt from the roots, and, with a small trowel, dug in the vine into the dirt at the base of the fern.

"Isn't this beautiful?" he asked. "It's variegated plectranthus. Good in sun or shade. These should do well, don't you think?"

Claudine handed me another palm tree. "In the salon," she said, giving me a small push.

I trotted through to the salon and set it down near the door to the outside patio. The sun was stronger now, and I could see where we had scattered iron tables and chairs around. We could put a few palms out there as well, along with flowering annuals, since we suddenly seemed to be enjoying a wealth of green plants. In fact, we practically had an entire greenhouse's worth.

Claudine carried in another palm, set it on the other side of the salon door, and made a face. "I wish those pots matched," she groused. "We may have to buy something . . ."

She hurried out, and I was right behind her.

"Claudine, stop. What do you mean, 'buy something'? Didn't you buy all of *this*?"

She shrugged. "Well, I paid money, that's for sure. I had to give Stefan fifty euros."

"For what?" I asked.

She gave me another potted palm tree. "Acquisition fee. Put this in the salon, too? Maybe by the new hallway to the office?"

"You're not going to give me a straight answer, are you?"

She rolled her eyes. "Stefan is a client of mine, and he provided a service, and now we have lots of beautiful green plants, just like you wanted. Can't you just say, 'Thank you'?" She went through the front doors.

Karl was working on the second urn, and I had to admit it looked lovely. The fern was thick and dark green, and he'd planted a tall, pale grass behind it; the green-and-white vine spilled over the edge of the pot and trailed almost to the ground. There were several more of the large cast-iron urns, and I saw that he had more than enough to fill them. They were going to look perfect for pictures, adding just the right air of elegance. And the additional ferns could be put out in the patio, along with some very nice topiaries, also in very expensive planters.

I stood, holding a palm tree, watching Karl as he carefully separated a vine and snuggled it in at the base of the fern.

"Do you have everything you need?" I asked him.

He straightened, rubbed his back, and smiled at me. "Oh yes. It took me almost a week to find everything, but it was worth the effort."

"And where, exactly, did you find everything?" I shifted the palm from one hip to the other.

His smile never faltered. "We started in Cesson-Sévigné, just east of Rennes."

"Oh?" I asked innocently. "Is there a garden center there?"

"No, but many beautiful homes with gardens."

"So . . . these all came out of people's *yards*? Did you just drive through neighborhoods, taking stuff?"

He looked indignant and shook his head. "Of course not. Most neighborhoods are gated. You can't just drive through them, especially at night."

"Oh."

"And we never took more than one thing from someone's garden. I am not heartless, you know. I wouldn't take so much that it would be a burden to replace. A palm here, a fern there . . . that's why it took us so long. Stefan grew rather impatient with me."

"I can imagine. And those vines and—" I motioned to the cardboard boxes, overfilled with plantings.

"Ah. Well, we had to be careful there. I didn't want there to be gaps, you know. I took a little bit from here and there, so no one would even notice."

Claudine came back out and glared. "Are you going to just stand here all morning? Or are you going to help?"

"Claudine, all of this was stolen."

"Which is why we are going to do some transplanting. This pottery is very nice, but some of it is distinctive and very expensive. I'd hate for someone to read about our opening and recognize something of theirs in the photographs. That would not be so good."

"And you don't care about them being *stolen*? I thought there was an item in your budget for plants and flowers."

"There was. And then you decided that we needed a rose garden. Do you have any idea how much roses cost? Not to mention the espalier you wanted. And those silly little boxwood plants?"

"Wait. This is *my* fault?"

"Not at all. I manage the expenses, not you, so the responsibility is of course mine." She looked at Karl, who had gone back to his digging. "But we're not talking grand larceny here. No one is going to miss one potted plant, Lucy. Now, see that one there? Out to the patio, I think." She picked up two of the ferns, one and each hand, and went inside.

I looked at the topiary. It was some sort of evergreen and looked like a green lollipop. She was right. Perfect for the patio.

Chapter Eight

"The mattresses are here," Colin called.

We were painting one of the rooms overlooking the garden. Colin had gone downstairs at the sound of the bell, and I heard a truck out in the courtyard. I put down my roller. "What did she do?" I muttered to myself. "Send someone to raid people's bedrooms?"

Bing heard me and burst out laughing. "Are you talking about our ill-begotten foliage?"

I brushed back my hair. "I suppose you had no problem with that whole thing?"

He came down from the ladder and put down his roller. "Yes, of course I did. I even felt a twinge of guilt as I was driving around with Karl."

I stared. "What do you mean, driving around with Karl?"

He made a face. "Karl and I drove around—well, Georges drove, Karl and I just looked—and we noted all the places that looked like they would be worth, ah, revisiting."

"You were in on that?"

"Karl is certainly spry for his age, but, well . . . he needed help."

I folded my arms across my chest. "And what, exactly, did you do?"

He looked thoughtful. "I just wrote down addresses. We went out after dinner, before it got dark, and drove around. It took us four trips to target everything he wanted." Bing chuckled. "He had some very specific items on his wish list."

I closed my eyes and shook my head. "Unbelievable. You have no faith in Claudine, her vision, my ability to carry out that vision, but you drive around making a literal hit list." I threw up my hands. "You're ridiculous."

He reached and caught my wrists in his hands. "No, I'm not. Yes, I may have doubts about, well, everything, but this hotel is my son's legacy, and no matter how absurd I may think this endeavor is, I will do anything and everything Claudine asks of me." He moved closer, and his grip loosened as my hands fell to my sides. I could feel his smooth palms against my skin, and as his hands opened, they lingered, a cool caress.

I took a step away from him. "So how long did it take you to scout out eighteen mattresses?"

He threw his head back and laughed again. "The mattresses are from IKEA." He nodded toward the hallway. "Hear that? They're delivering them now."

We went out to the landing, and two men were coming up the staircase, carrying between them what looked to be a rug, long and tightly rolled, wrapped in white plastic.

"That's a mattress?" I asked, skeptical.

"Is there an elevator?" one of the men asked.

"Yes," I said. "But I don't think it's big enough for two men and a mattress."

He scowled at me. "Where do you want them?" he asked in French.

"Put one in each of the rooms up here," I told him. "All the doors are open. And the last two are downstairs."

The two men nodded, and I watched them disappear through a doorway.

"Seriously?" I asked Bing.

He shrugged. "You unroll them, and they expand to a regular mattress."

I frowned. "Where's the box spring?"

"There is no box spring."

"What? That must be like sleeping on the floor," I said.

He snorted. "Is *your* bed comfortable? Without a box spring? I would have thought you'd pay attention to something like that."

"Something like what?"

"You climb into bed every night. How clueless do you have to be not to notice what you're sleeping on?"

"There you go again," I said hotly.

"What?" he growled.

"Making assumptions. And being a jerk," I said. Maybe yelled.

"I'm not a jerk!" he yelled back.

"But you're making assumptions. Remember that first day? When you said you jumped to conclusions, and it was a major flaw? And you were going to *work on it*?"

He glared. "So?"

"When are you going to start?"

Colin came up the stairs. "Uh," he said nervously. "I can hear you. Actually, everyone can hear you."

"Good," I muttered and went back to work.

Claudine had scheduled the press event for a Monday morning. Local journalists, travel agents, and a few regional bloggers were invited, as well as someone from the Ministry of Tourism.

A photographer was arriving early on Saturday to take pictures for the brochure and website. I planned to download a few of the best images and plug them into our self-designed trifold, which we would distribute to all our invited guests at the press event. I figured I could paste and plug what I needed and print them off faster and much cheaper than sending the job out to a professional. Eliot helped me there—grudgingly. When he wasn't hiding away from the rest of us in the tiny *appartement* he shared with Marie Claude, he worked for a graphic design firm. He put together a professional-looking brochure in the time it had taken me to finish three glasses of wine.

The previous week had been spent in a whirlwind of activity. Everyone had finished all the items on their punch lists, including Vera, who had somehow finished the drapery for all the rooms, even those that weren't quite ready for them. The public rooms were immaculate. We had eight individual rooms styled for photographs. All the exterior spaces, including the side rose garden, were complete. The front of the hotel was postcard-perfect, the exterior trim and front doors once again a peacock blue. The illicitly planted cast-iron urns were thriving. The back patio looked so lovely and inviting that no one would ever guess there was a former domestic in residence.

Claudine had made good on her promise of office equipment that didn't cause me to hyperventilate every time I looked at it. She had the equipment delivered much earlier than I'd expected, but since her office was still technically open, I wondered what her staff was using to work on. The software had been installed. The website was ready to go live as soon as the images were uploaded.

Claudine had arranged for all her treasure—the artwork, rugs, and miscellany that had been in storage for decades—to be delivered. The truck was late, but I'd gotten used to deliveries being late. Karl wandered off to his garden, and I followed him. It was one of my favorite spaces, and not just because it was one of the few places that I didn't have to fix. It was quiet until you really listened, and then you could hear the hum of bees and the soft chirping of birds. The abundance of growth was heartwarming, and it seemed as though if I sat there long enough, I would be able to see the tomato plants stretching toward the sun.

I settled on a bench. We had put cast-iron café chairs and tables around on the flagstone paths, but I preferred the benches. I watched as Karl fussed in the beds, pulling stray weeds and nipping back unwanted growth. He hummed as he worked. That was something else I'd grown used to, just as I'd grown used to many things in the ten weeks I'd been at Hotel Paradis.

I could make my own café crème now. The hulking machine back in the kitchen no longer caused me panic, and I made the espresso and steamed milk with the confidence of a Starbucks barista.

I took my mesh bag everywhere. If you bought anything from anywhere in Rennes, you had to figure out a way to carry it out of the store on your own. It only took me two solo trips to the bakery for me to put my mesh carry-all on a hook right by the door, right there in my face, so that I remembered to take it whenever I left the flat.

I called my parents every Sunday, on their landline. No, I couldn't see my dad's face, but now, when I talked to him, it was just to him, unless he passed the phone to Mom. No longer were our conversations interrupted by the disembodied voice of my mother from wherever in the house she wanted to be, instead of near enough to hear her daughter's voice.

Mimi, Cara, and I had a weekly Facebook video date on Monday nights. Joe and I worked it out so that I could call them just as they came home from school, and he had his laptop set up for them. When I was their age, the idea of talking to someone face-to-face across an ocean would have seemed magical. They took it in stride from the very first conversation, slipping in front of the screen, snacks in hand, bursting with questions.

"Is your new hotel pretty?" Cara asked.

"Beautiful," I lied. Not a lie, exactly. Soon, it would be.

"What are you doing now?" Mimi asked.

"Painting," I answered promptly.

They both giggled. "Painting? Like a picture?" Mimi asked.

"No. Painting, like the walls."

Cara frowned. "Did you do that at your other hotel?"

"No. But this hotel is different. And special."

"Do you talk French all the time there?" Mimi asked.

I nodded. "Yes. And the more I speak it, the easier it gets."

"Like riding a bike," Cara offered.

"Exactly."

"When can we learn French?" Cara asked.

I thought. "Probably in middle school. Definitely in high school. Do you want to learn French?"

They both nodded. "So when we come to visit," Cara explained, "we can talk to all your friends."

I didn't know what the bigger pipe dream was—that they would be visiting me or that I had friends. Was I warming up to the people around me? Yes, I was. But did I consider any of them friends? Not really.

And the idea that Joe could afford to send them to France in the first place was absurd. My parents helped pay his rent.

"Well, that's something to work for," I said, keeping the conversation away from delicate subjects.

"We miss you." Cara sighed. "Sunday, Nana was in a bad mood, and PopPop said his back hurt, and nobody would take us to the park."

They had dinner every Sunday afternoon at my parents' house, a tradition that began even before Sara had become ill. I had not joined them very often back then. It seemed I never had the time. Truth was, I never made the time. Of the few positive things that had resulted from the whole Fielding debacle, the greatest was my connecting with these two girls in a way that would have never otherwise been possible.

I felt my eyes suddenly burn. "I miss you guys, too. Like crazy. Which is why we're going to talk like this every week, okay?"

Cara, always the more cautious, narrowed her eyes. "Promise? What if you have something else to do?"

I shook my head. "It's practically my bedtime all the way over here. I don't do anything so close to bedtime."

Cara stuck out her lower lip, thinking. "What if you get sick?"

I made a face. "I can do this in my bed."

She persisted. "What if you're still painting?"

I shook my head. "I can't paint in the dark."

She wasn't giving up yet. "What if you have a date?"

"Then I guess you both will get to meet him."

They burst into giggles, and we said goodbye a few minutes later.

Julia and I texted each other, often at night, just an odd line or two, but I could hear her laughter as I tried to explain what my life was like now: thrift store jeans and broken fingernails, hardening muscles and long soaks in tepid water, wine at every meal with crusty bread slathered with butter that tasted like fresh-mown grass, going to the market every Saturday morning with Bing and finding even more foods and flowers I had never imagined existed.

You sound happy, she texted me.

Maybe I am, I texted back. Or maybe I'm too tired to be sad.

What's with Bing?

Nothing.

No. Really.

He's attractive and too complicated.

And he was. Attractive. He was charming and funny and smart, and whenever we got physically close, I expected actual sparks to jump between our bodies. But he was still a high-minded, arrogant know-it-all who managed to irritate the hell out of me by the end of most of our conversations. And any invitation to further intimacy, emotional or physical, real or imagined, I quickly threw off. I didn't know how long it would take before I trusted myself to make sound and reasonable decisions about my personal life again, but I was pretty sure that Bing was a risk, and I wasn't willing to take any risks just yet.

I had also become something of a cat person. Napoléon Bonaparte now slept at the foot of my bed every night. I don't know where he had slept before I arrived, but he settled into my little *appart* very nicely. I always had a small bowl of water for him. He ate in Claudine's rooms and wandered the grounds quite happily, but he always managed to find me as I opened my door in the evening, slipping in and curling up for the night.

Today, as I sat waiting, I watched him skulk around the garden. He was hunting. Voles, Karl had said, and he froze, the tip of his tail twitching, as he tracked some unseen creature through the rows of pole beans.

"Lucia?"

It was Bing, interrupting the hunt. He walked across the gravel and sat beside me. Napoléon sat, glared at Bing, and began washing his front paw.

"Why is Napoléon giving me the side-eye?" Bing asked.

"He was hunting. Still no truck?"

Bing shook his head. "It could take until midnight. The French have an odd concept of time."

"Are we sure all these things belong to Claudine? I mean, she's not above a bit of petty larceny to further her cause."

Bing smiled. "No, these are all her family heirlooms. She has a photograph of every item in a large notebook. She used to take it out and talk about the rugs like they were close, personal friends." He stretched his arm out along the back of the bench. I was aware that the nape of my neck was inches from his arm, and all I had to do was slouch down a little bit . . .

"I think you're doing well," he said, quite unexpectedly. "Things are moving along much faster than I'd thought possible."

"If I remember correctly, when I first got here, your expectations were rather dim. Nonexistent."

He nodded. "Yes. That's an accurate assessment. Aren't you impressed that I can freely admit when I'm wrong?"

I made a noise. "Why should that impress me? Isn't that something everyone should be able to do?"

"Yes, but if you knew me back in the day, you'd not only be impressed, you'd also be gobsmacked."

I smiled. "That's a great word. Gobsmacked."

"Yes, it is. I love words."

We sat together in silence. It was not one of those awkward, what-do-I-say-next kinds of silences. Rather, the silence between two people comfortable enough with each other to not have to fill in the empty. Tony Fielding had hated the emptiness and had filled it with talk, snapping fingers, or tapping toes. It had been exhausting at times.

"What?" asked Bing.

I realized I had made a kind of snort. "I was just thinking about what we're willing to put up with for love."

"Ah. Yes. Love."

"Deep subject."

"Very deep. I much prefer lust."

I sat up. "Excuse me?"

He grinned. "Lust. It's very direct. Straightforward. Just as powerful as love, but without all that thinking."

I laughed out loud. "That's an excellent way to put it. I'll have to remember that."

He turned his head. "The truck is here. Let's look."

Karl joined us as we walked. He was talking about Aubusson rugs, how they had been named for the town of Aubusson, on the banks of the Creuse River.

Bing shot me a look, and I giggled as Karl continued, out of the garden, onto the cobblestones, where the history of the Perrot family waited to be unloaded.

Claudine had her notebook on the check-in counter in the lobby, and three men were standing there, two holding a rolled-up rug wrapped in brown paper, and the third carrying a rectangular crate, antique-picture-size. A fourth man, in a stylish gray suit, was arguing with Claudine.

"We spent two days wrapping all these items to protect them from any damage. I will not spend any more time unwrapping them all just so you can check them," he said.

She tapped the open page of her notebook. "What if there is something wrong? What if a frame is broken? Or a rug is stained?"

"Madam, your family has paid my company thousands over the past eighty years. You are one of our oldest and most valued customers. Do you think that if something had happened to even one corner of one rug, we would not have immediately told you?"

She looked at him, frowned, looked at me, then shrugged. "You have a point. All the rugs upstairs." She gestured. "And the paintings can all be lined up against the wall here in the salon."

He looked at the sweeping staircase. "Upstairs?"

"Yes. Most of the guest rooms are upstairs. There is an elevator. Small, but you can use it for the rugs. Take them up and line them all up in the hallway."

He did not look happy, but he shrugged. "There are very many paintings," the man said.

"I know," said Claudine. "There's more than enough room in there." She turned to Bing, Colin, Karl, and me. "You can start to unwrap the rugs. Roll them out a foot or two and take a picture so I can match them against my list. We'll do the art last."

We went upstairs and followed the first rug from the elevator to the wide hallway. Colin carefully cut open the brown wrapping, revealing the rolled-up rug. We helped him unroll a foot or two.

"Oh," I whispered.

Colin whistled through his teeth. "Wow."

Karl squatted down next to Colin. "There are over one hundred of these rugs at Versailles," he said. He pushed a little harder, and the rug unrolled a bit more.

I had seen pictures of these rugs, of course, but the depth of color and close texture took me by surprise, especially since the rug was so old. And it was large, at least ten feet long.

"I pictured smaller area rugs," I said.

Karl stood. "Oh, no. These rugs were a sign of wealth. They were all made on a very grand scale. Each will cover most of the floor in every room."

"If I had known that," I muttered, "I wouldn't have spent so much time and money fixing the floors."

Bing laughed, pulled out his phone, and took a picture. "Where do you want this?" he asked.

We had finished the rooms overlooking the back patio. I opened the door to one of the rooms. The walls were painted, the furniture was clean and gleamed softly after Marie Claude and Eliot's ministrations, and soft drapery covered both windows.

"In here," I called. "I want to see how it looks."

Bing and Colin carried it in. We moved the furniture to allow for the rug to be fully unrolled. It was a pale blue with cream, soft green, and blush pink. We put the furniture back in place.

"We need to dress the bed," I muttered.

"First," Bing pointed out, "we need a mattress." The mattress was still rolled up and leaning in a corner of the room. He and Karl eased it onto the bed as I hurried out.

I headed for the housekeeping closet tucked into a windowless corner at the end of the hallway. Inside, by the light of a single, dangling light bulb, I pulled out a set of linen, three pillows, and one of the many quilts hanging from the wooden rack.

I hurried back to the room. We needed art. There was a picture rail in every room, dropped down about two feet from the ceiling. Trying to hang a picture on the wall was impractical, as it would have required a small spike and a sledgehammer to puncture the plaster. Pictures were hung on wire and attached to small hooks that slipped onto the rail.

I dumped my linens on the graceful bergère and headed downstairs.

Claudine had uncrated two paintings and was standing, arms crossed, and smiling. As I came up to her, she grinned broadly. "Look. Isn't she lovely?"

I stared. It was a portrait of a young woman, her dark hair swept up, her face calm and lovely, smiling from an elaborate gilt frame. "Wow. Oh, Claudine . . ." I reached out a hand, then snatched it back. This was going to hang on a wall? Where anyone could touch it? It belonged in a museum.

"Odette Perrot," Claudine said. "Painted in 1843."

The second painting was a landscape, a river flowing through a wheat field, horses in the background pulling a cart. It was so beautiful that my breath caught in my throat.

Claudine sidled up beside me and poked me in the ribs. "You didn't believe me, did you?"

I shook my head slowly. "It's not that I didn't believe you. It's just . . ." I put my arm around her shoulder and gave her a quick hug. "I just never imagined anything like this."

There were tears in her eyes. "I've never seen them," she whispered. "Not in real life. Just the pictures."

"Well, wait until you see your rugs. Can I take these upstairs?"

"Of course. I'll come with you."

I shook my head as I took Odette in both hands. "No. Not yet." I gestured at the young workman who came in carrying another crate. "Could you grab that for me? Please?"

He nodded and picked up the landscape, and upstairs we went.

Bing had the mattress on the bed. The headboard and footboard were carved mahogany. The mattress was unrolled, a pile of plastic wrapping heaped on the floor, but only looked four inches high. I carefully leaned Odette against the footboard and stared.

"What's wrong with it?" I asked.

Karl looked confused. "What do you mean?"

"It's flat."

"Of course," Karl said. "You have to give it time to expand."

"How much time?" I asked.

"Two, three days," he answered.

I shook my head. "We don't have three days. The photographer is coming the day after tomorrow. Bring in three or four more." I looked at Bing and Colin. "Please?"

I turned to Karl. "Do we have any flowers yet?"

He shook his head. "No. Not yet. But . . ." He frowned. "I have something." He hurried out.

Colin and Bing returned, and after unwrapping three more mattresses, we had something that looked like a regular mattress on the bed.

"Colin, can you hang these?" I asked, motioning toward the paintings. "Do you know where the hooks are?"

Colin nodded and left, dragging the mountain of plastic behind him, while Bing helped me make the bed. The quilt was made of cream-colored cotton, the intricate stitching outlining patterns of birds and roses.

Colin came back in, the small brass hooks in hand, and Odette was hung next to the door. The landscape filled the wall next to the armoire.

Karl came trotting back in, breathless, carrying a slender glass vase under one arm and graceful fronds that I recognized as coming from the tall grasses growing in the urns. He set the vase on the small table next to the bed and arranged the grasses.

He smiled at me. "Yes?"

I nodded. "Oh yes." I pulled open the drapes and pushed the tall windows open, revealing a bit of the balcony. Then I ran over to the doorway and surveyed the entire room.

"It needs more," I muttered.

Bing stood beside me. "Yes."

"Karl," I called. "Any ferns left?"

He nodded. "Yes."

I ran my eyes around the room. "Good. Can you bring one in here? Over by the bathroom door, just to fill up that bit of space." I turned to Bing. "Let's look at a few more of Claudine's treasures."

Downstairs, they had brought in two large wooden crates that were pushed up against the mahogany counter. Both had been opened, and the once nailed-on lids were askew.

I pointed. "What's in there?"

Bing went over, knelt, and dug his hands into the packing material. He pulled out a large, round object wrapped in brown paper. He peeled the paper off and revealed a large porcelain bowl, creamy white, sprayed with pink roses and faded gold.

"Perfect," I breathed. "What else?"

He rooted around some more, then turned with a grin. "Candelabra?"

"Bring it up." I grabbed the bowl, blew off the dust, and hurried back upstairs. "Colin," I called from the landing. "Any chance of candles?"

"Certainly," he called back and came out of the room and headed down the back staircase.

It took us longer than I'd thought it would, but finally, we looked at each other, grinning with satisfaction.

"Karl," I said. "You get her."

We could hear her grousing all the way up the stairs.

"What is so important?" Claudine asked. "I have rather a few things to do."

And then, right in the doorway, she stopped, and we could hear her gasp.

The room was beautiful. It was a step back into a more gracious time. The open windows let in a breeze that ruffled the pale curtains. The bedclothes were turned down, the pillows plump against the cream of the linen bedsheets. The furniture shone, and the candles flickered on the delicate writing table next to the bed.

She took a step in. Odette smiled, and Claudine smiled back. "I think you've done it, Lucy," she said softly.

"We've done it," I said.

She walked farther into the room, her steps muffled by the thick rug, taking in the soft pillow across the back of the flowered slipper chair by the window. She touched the grass in its vase and trailed her fingers across the fronds of the fern. "Yes. This is what I had always imagined." There were tears in her eyes as she smiled. Then she shook herself. "But where will we put the television you insist we need?"

"It's not like we're getting sixty-four-inch HDTVs in here," I said. "We can probably hide a small screen in the armoire."

She nodded. "Perhaps. We need more lighting."

"I know."

"And we certainly can't have open flames in the candelabras."

I kept my voice even. "We'll get the flameless candles. Anything else?"

She shook her head. "No. The fern here is a nice touch."

Karl beamed. "Yes. And I know where we can get many more, if you'd like."

I closed my eyes briefly, and when I opened them, everyone was looking at me.

I felt Bing's warm breath in my ear. "Well done," he whispered.

And as I smiled, Claudine clapped her hands. "Yes. Well done."

The rooms were set. Pictures had been hung, rugs rolled out, and Karl had been assigned the job of going to the Saturday market first thing in the morning to buy fresh flowers. Claudine couldn't afford to put large bouquets in each of the rooms, and I had a brief vision of her sending us out into predawn Rennes to steal flowers from people's gardens. Instead, Karl insisted he could rearrange the flowers in every room, giving a different look in every photograph. I allowed myself to relax. When Gaspard, the photographer, arrived the next morning, we would be ready.

Except . . .

Now that the weather was warm, we had taken to sitting out in the garden after dinner, usually with a bottle or two of wine. One of the most endearing traits of the French, I decided, was their belief that you didn't need an event to drink good wine. In fact, drinking *was* the event.

Claudine made her pitch as though she were offering each of them a chance of a lifetime. "We need people in the pictures," Claudine began. "You know. Guests."

"You don't have guests," Colin pointed out.

"Ah yes," Claudine agreed. "But I have all of you. You can pretend to be guests. You know, checking in, sitting in the garden, opening a suitcase . . . you all can be on the website!"

No one jumped up in excitement. No one raised their glass to toast such a splendid idea.

Vera spoke first. "You may not take my picture," she said. "I don't photograph well."

Bing was laughing very quietly, his shoulders shaking as he shook his head.

"I don't think so," Marie Claude mumbled. Eliot had not joined us. Again. "I have nothing to wear."

Claudine and I had offered Marie Claude a job as a desk clerk once the hotel opened. Her living on-site was certainly one reason, but she was a smart, capable young woman who was working in a bank, and I reasoned that she had the customer service experience needed for the job.

Claudine looked at Marie Claude. "You'll wear what you will wear once we open. A white shirt and a black skirt or pants. Do you mean to tell me you don't own a white shirt? I was going to have you photographed behind the front desk with Lucy. Checking in Vera and Bing."

Bing raised an eyebrow. "What?"

Vera cleared her throat and said again, a bit louder, "You may not take my picture."

Claudine rolled her eyes. "You are beautiful, Vera. Don't be silly. I'm sure you will look amazing. As will Bing. You will make a striking couple. And it will send the right message, no?"

"What message is that?" Bing asked. "That old people are welcome here?"

Claudine scowled. "Don't be difficult. That *everyone* is welcome here."

"I don't feel comfortable," Vera said stiffly, "being the token person of color."

Claudine made a face. "That has nothing to do with anything, Vera. You should know that by now. The color of your skin is a very nice, politically correct plus, but even if you were a bland, blond Swede, I'd ask you. I need a couple to check in to my hotel. Lucy and Marie Claude will be doing the checking in. I can't have them pretending to be guests. They are legitimate employees. Bing needs to be with someone, so it's either you or Colin. And the two of you make such an attractive couple "

Vera's face softened. "Very well."

Karl leaned back and said, "Then perhaps we can ask Stavros's oldest daughter? You know, the one with four children? To show that we welcome families as well?"

She narrowed her eyes as Vera and Bing both burst out laughing.

Karl's eyes were dancing. "I know how happy you will be to see small children running around, making all that noise and bumping into things."

"Stop it," she snapped. "Of course families are welcome, but we do not have the appropriate space. You know that. We can only accommodate two persons in each room."

Colin leaned over and said in my ear in a mock whisper, "Her love of children is practically urban myth."

"I *do* like children," Claudine said loudly. "I love them. Ask Philippe. He will tell you that he had a wonderful childhood. Didn't he, Bing?"

Bing swirled the wine in his glass. "I'm sure he did. What child wouldn't, growing up here? He had the run of the local haunted house. But I seem to remember that when he brought his friends over to play, well, sometimes that didn't go over so well."

"That," Claudine declared, "is because his friends were hooligans, running around here like a pack of wolves."

Bing threw his head back and laughed. "They were boys, Claudine. How did you expect them to act?"

Karl had a broad smile on his face. "This is an ongoing conversation," he said to me. "Claudine's patience with boisterous children has long been the subject of much debate."

I smiled back at him and relaxed in my chair, watching their faces. Even Marie Claude, who I know hadn't lived here nearly as long as Bing or Karl, was in on the joke. But then, she had known Philippe, and he may have told her the stories of his childhood, spent in an empty and echoing hotel, his mother scolding as he and his friends slid down the long banister of the grand staircase.

There was a familiar ease among them all, a feeling of belonging, and I ached to be a part of that. I had never felt embraced and accepted by my own family, and years of moving from one place to another had never given me the deep roots of long friendships.

At The Fielding, I knew every employee and had felt closer to some than others. There were a few who would call me for a drink after work or just to sit and chat in the lobby after an event. But after Tony left, not one of those people reached out in comfort or support. Instead, they looked at me as a coconspirator, and nothing I could say or do changed anyone's mind. Even those I'd imagined as friends turned their backs. I couldn't blame them, I suppose.

Tony and I had moved in tandem in the years we were together. His betrayal was seen as mine as well. It did no good to try to explain to anyone that Tony had been one of my greatest mistakes.

I considered myself lucky to have Julia, someone I had known in college, and we had somehow remained connected through all my many moves.

As much as I wanted to relax enough to let these people in, I had held back, still so distrustful of my own instincts that I sometimes worried that I would never again put any kind of faith in another person.

Claudine looked at me and explained. "They are all being overly critical. True, Philippe and I had a few issues as he was growing up, but that is true of all parents and their children. And to be honest"—she smiled wistfully—"I had wanted a daughter so badly. Oh, to have had a little girl to dress and teach to cook and play with."

Bing nodded. "Although, I must admit, she tried. Poor Philippe, he was the only boy in kindergarten who had a pink winter coat."

"That was not pink," Claudine shot back and then looked chagrined. "Okay, maybe it was." She pointed at Marie Claude. "When you finally get down to having *your* children, I want nothing but little girls. Understood?"

Marie Claude smiled. "I'm not quite ready for that, Claudine, but I will certainly keep your request in mind when the time comes." She looked at me. "She always gets what she wants."

I nodded. "Yes, I've noticed that. So, I guess we'll all pose for the camera tomorrow morning?"

Vera sniffed. "What about Colin and Karl? Will they be another couple?"

Colin sat up, grinning at Karl. "What do you say?"

Karl looked thoughtful and finally said, "Sorry, Colin. You're much too old for me."

We all burst out laughing.

Claudine waved a hand. "Colin, you will be a guest in the salon, having breakfast. Stavros will be here, of course, and has already agreed to be photographed. Karl, you can lounge out in the garden, sipping a glass of wine."

Karl grinned wickedly. "Certainly. And tell us, Claudine, how will *you* be photographed?"

She narrowed her eyes, opened her mouth to say something, decided against it, then grinned broadly. "I will sit out with you in the garden. We can hold hands, if you'd like. Or perhaps share a kiss for the camera?"

Karl blushed as he burst into laughter, and we all joined in. I felt a surge of something.

Maybe a wave of confidence that the first hurdle was almost over.

Maybe a growing sense that the hotel would open on time and be as successful as I wanted it to be.

Maybe a feeling that yes, I did belong here after all.

Chapter Nine

Karl and Georges entered the lobby, arms full of colorful flowers. Karl hurried into the back office, where a large selection of vases and containers were lined up on both desks.

Claudine had unpacked a vast collection of decorative objects from the wooden crates that had been delivered earlier in the week, including sterling silver vases that stood three feet tall, porcelain jars of exquisite color and delicacy (Limoges, Karl explained, giving a brief history as they were unpacked), and crystal bowls (Lalique, if you're interested). They were all antiques and probably extremely valuable, but Claudine wanted them all used.

"They've been packed away for too long," she said, somewhat wistfully, as though speaking of old, forgotten friends. "They need to be looked at and admired again."

The plan was simple. Karl and Marie Claude would arrange the various bouquets and deliver them as needed ahead of the photographer, Gaspard, who immediately understood the situation.

He began outside in the bright morning sun, avoiding the shabby stable block that served as storage, instead shooting the now-imposing facade: through the black iron gates, close up to the freshly painted double doors, looking around the corner from the just-blooming rose garden. Even Napoléon got his own headshot and another of him curled up among the ferns in his favorite urn.

Bing and Vera, as well-heeled guests, looked amazing: Bing in his usual jeans and T-shirt, but also wearing a crisp linen sports jacket and a long silk scarf wrapped around his neck, Vera imposing and sophisticated in a pale pantsuit. Marie Claude and I, in white shirts and black skirts, smiled and went through the motions as Gaspard clicked away.

"Vera," he instructed, "turn toward me and smile."

"Marie Claude, your hair keeps falling in your face. Please brush it back."

"Bing, put your hand on Vera's back."

"Vera, stop frowning. He's supposed to be your partner."

"Lucy, don't hide behind the flowers."

The tall silver vase filled with colorful blooms was strategically placed to block the credit card machine and the other, less attractive electronics, all necessary but not photogenic. I hadn't been hiding, exactly. "I'm scanning their credit card," I explained.

"You're hiding," Gaspard scolded. "Vera, please, smile. This is not that hard."

Vera shot him a look that could have stopped a charging rhino, and Gaspard blanched.

"We're done here," he said.

There was a flurry of activity as ferns and flowers were whisked into the salon, where Stavros, a red apron covering his white shirt and black pants, stood stiffly, waiting. Colin sat at a table covered in starched white linen, a bowl of spring-green ivy in the center, as though a three-star Michelin meal were waiting in the wings.

"Closer to the windows," Gaspard instructed. "The light is better, and we can get the patio flowers in the background."

Another flurry as everything and everyone moved, and Gaspard was satisfied.

"Stavros, stand on the other side. Now, pour the coffee."

Stavros bent over awkwardly and tilted the copper coffeepot. Nothing came out.

"Where's the coffee?" Gaspard asked.

Stavros looked confused. "I didn't make any. It would just get cold."

Gaspard shook his head. "Who cares if it's cold? You can't have him sitting there in front of an empty coffee cup. And where's the food?"

Stavros looked blank. "Food?"

I ran out of the hotel, through the iron gate, and into the café across the street. "Simone?" I called.

The young girl hurried from the kitchen, wiping her hands on her apron. She was slightly flushed, her hair up in a ponytail, her black apron powdered with floured handprints.

"Are you alone?" I asked her.

She shook her head. "No. Josiane is here." Josiane was the oldest of Stavros's daughters, the mother of the four children.

"Can you come over? And help?" I asked. "Your father is camera shy."

She rolled her eyes. "Of course."

"And we need food."

"I'll be right over," she promised, and I ran out and back to the hotel.

"Simone is coming," I called as I went into the dining room.

"Thank God," Claudine muttered.

Gaspard was standing out in the patio. I went out and touched him on the shoulder, and he jumped.

"What?"

"Simone is coming," I told him. "Stavros's daughter. She's bringing food."

He nodded, and as we walked back inside, he glanced over his shoulder. "Did you hear her?" he whispered.

I felt a chill. I did not want any reminders of our longest-staying guest.

Simone arrived a few minutes later. Stavros had filled his coffeepot with espresso. Simone exchanged her apron for her father's more photogenic one, arranged a few croissants and a peeled and sectioned orange on a lovely blue plate, and set it in front of Colin.

"Ready?" she asked Gaspard.

He nodded, and she went to work, pouring, smiling, listening with apparent fascination to whatever Colin was saying. Then she poured the espresso back in the pot and did it all over again, from the other side.

And again. And again. And behind the salon, in the bright sunlight, pots of fern and delphinium peeked through the tall windows.

Next came the office, its tall, glass doors open to the garden, pots of ferns clustered at the base of the elegant bookcase.

Upstairs, we had stacked mattresses high enough to be a stage set for *Once Upon a Mattress* with pillows plumped on pale quilts. Curtains billowed in a soft breeze. Thick white towels hung over the edge of a glistening claw-foot tub. In one room, Vera posed by the window, gazing out, so that Gaspard didn't have to coach her into smiling. In another, Bing lounged on the outside balcony, sitting in a small chair, a wineglass on the marble-topped table. Both declined to sit in the tub, in chest-high bubbles, reading and sipping champagne. It had been Claudine's idea, and I think she suggested the whole thing just to annoy Bing and Vera.

As we moved from room to room, Karl and Marie Claude rearranged flowers, positioned ferns, and strategically placed vases and bowls just inside the camera frame.

Back downstairs for a set of photos in the garden, with Bing on one of the benches, his arm stretched out along its back.

When he was done, Gaspard sighed. "He should be smoking

a Gauloises," he said, mentioning the famous French cigarettes. "American advertising is still very anti-smoking."

"Don't tempt me," Bing said, following us inside. "I gave them up many years ago but would go back in a heartbeat. In fact," he said, his eyes dancing, "once I hit seventy-five, I'm going back to all my old habits. Smoking, red meat every day, sex with younger women."

Claudine laughed at that, her head shaking. "You never liked sex with younger women," she said. "You always liked us more experienced types."

Bing put his arm around her shoulder and nuzzled her hair. "Yes. And thank you very much."

Vera shook her head. "You two are impossible," she muttered.

We ended back in the lobby, its chandelier gleaming, elegant tables placed between comfortable chairs, more ferns and potted palm trees strategically placed. Hotel Paradis looked magnificent.

The so-called guests all acted accordingly, and, with the exception of Stavros, all photographed beautifully.

Gaspard, clicking away, muttered, "Your real guests are going to be disappointed that there aren't really as many ferns and flowers around."

Claudine shot me a look, then smiled. "No worries. I can always get more."

And did I mention that Bing looked . . . Never mind.

Gaspard sat down next to me at my desk in the back office, leaves and fallen petals littering the floor, the strong sent of carnations in the air.

"Are you really going to get the rest of these rooms ready by July?" he asked as we waited for his digital files to load onto my desktop.

I looked up at him. "Great question. The stock answer is *yes,* of course. That's what we'll tell them on Monday. Between you and me, there will be a lot of long nights ahead. But we know how long it took us to get this far, and it's not an impossible task."

Gaspard chuckled. "Claudine has an iron will. That alone might get it done."

I nodded in agreement. "Yes. There is that. I've learned to never underestimate what that woman can accomplish once she puts her mind to something." I glanced up at him. "Have you known her long?"

"Almost twenty years. The studio I worked for was a client of hers, so when I went out on my own, I stayed with her. She has a way about her. She inspires loyalty. I am heartbroken that she is retiring, but I know what this place means to her. I am happy she will finally get her dream realized."

We went through his photos one at a time. It was tedious work, and he discarded half of them with just a glance, and then went back, studying each shot critically.

"The light here is good."

"That one is perfect."

"Why doesn't Vera smile? She's a very attractive woman."

"Marie Claude looks good in this one, but I have to crop. May I?"

I left him at my computer and walked outside. It was late afternoon. Gaspard had spent the better part of the day at the hotel, and seeing how long it was taking him to review his work, along with all the editing I realized he wanted to do, it would be a while before I got the eight or ten pictures I needed.

Napoléon came around the corner, meowed at me, then darted off to the rose garden. I followed him. There hadn't been any pictures taken of it, despite Karl's insistence that his creation was going to become a major draw for guests. I liked the narrow side alley. The roses were just beginning to bloom, and there was a faint, sweet scent in the air. The intention had never been for guests to linger here. This had always been just a view from the upper floor with the possibility of pears and apricots at some future date. But Karl had insisted on a small bench, and it was there I sat, smelling the light scent coming from the flowering roses. Each was a different variety. Karl had explained in great detail each rosebush, its history, how long it would bloom, and when. He carefully planned for them to bloom at different times during the summer, giving a continuous show.

Napoléon wrapped himself around my ankles, purring, then jumped up on the bench and settled beside me, almost but not quite touching my thigh.

"Are you done?" Vera asked. She poked her head around the corner.

I shook my head. "No. Gaspard is going through all his pictures. He's kept the ones he's deemed worthy, and now he's cropping or something."

She came around and leaned her back against the stone side of the hotel. She closed her eyes and took a deep breath. "I like it back here, too." She sighed. "Those roses are going to be glorious in a few years. Karl will tend to them like beloved children." She opened her eyes. "Things went well today."

I smiled tiredly. "It wasn't that bad, was it?"

She made a face. "Claudine is too much sometimes. In the bathtub?"

I laughed. "You know she only suggested that to get your hackles up."

"I should have taken her up in it. Both Bing and I. Together. That would have shut her down fast enough."

I thought about that, confused. "What do you mean?"

Vera narrowed her eyes, and I could practically see her deciding about what to say next. "I'm not sure she ever got over him," she said at last.

I sat up straighter. "Bing?"

Vera nodded. "I've known her a long time. I wasn't living here when it was happening, their affair, but I know her well. Bing moved on. She never did. It may be because of Philippe, and she feels the connection more strongly through him. But I had just moved here when he was married, and she was not good. At all. She hid it well from him. From everyone. But she would talk to me."

I felt something deep in my chest, a heavy, dull ache. "Really?"

Her eyes were shrewd and watchful. "You like him." It was not a question.

I waited a beat. "Yes. Even though he makes me crazy sometimes."

She smiled. "I imagine he makes you crazy most of the time. He can be a very annoying man."

I had to smile. "Yes, he can be."

"Don't take it personally," she said. "Like many intelligent and successful men, he automatically assumes he's the smartest person in the room. You just have to remind him that he's not, and eventually, he takes a step back." She shot me a look. "I think he likes you, because he wants you to succeed. You're not the first person given this job, you know. Since I've lived here, Claudine has hired three other so-called general managers. Not one of them lasted this long. Not one of them came close to doing all you've done."

I nodded. "So I've heard."

"In the end, it was Bing who chased them off. If they had any gumption at all, he wouldn't have been able to, but you are different."

I had no idea what to say about that, so I said nothing.

"Well." She straightened. "You did good work today. And no, it wasn't that bad. Gaspard showed me some of the pictures, and I looked much better than I'd thought I would. I'm pleased. And I know Claudine is, too." She waved a hand and turned rather abruptly and disappeared around the corner, leaving Napoléon and me sitting in the gathering dusk.

Claudine had never gotten over Bing?

I sighed. I could certainly understand that. I imagined that once you'd given your heart to him, it would be almost impossible to have it handed back to you in one piece.

Gaspard did not finish until quite late, and I crawled into bed without getting any of my own work done. Tomorrow would be busy, I thought. I had to cut and paste the selected photos into my brochure, print off a hundred or so copies, and fold them. Then I would upload to the website, recheck every line of information and every link, and get us live.

No big deal at all, launching a website. I closed my eyes.

Right.

I was up and out of bed before Napoléon the next morning. The cat opened one eye, closed it again, and burrowed deeper into the bedclothes as I hurriedly dressed and grabbed my usual baguette and butter to take with me for breakfast.

The kitchen had been slowly filling with cutlery, dishware, and copper pots. I made my café crème, examining the hodgepodge of plates, cups, and saucers. Claudine had managed to unearth dinner plates from the clown car of a storage shed, which seemed to give up box after box of preciously saved items dating back to prewar Hotel Paradis glory. There were deep bowls, tiny demitasse cups and saucers, and large platters, all white with scalloped edges.

The Fielding had specially made dinnerware, with the logo tastefully scrolling along the edges of the plates. Here, there was just a simple fleur-de-lis, a symbol found all over France, in the center of each plate, in a faded peacock blue. Simple, elegant, and lovely. Just what I wanted for Hotel Paradis.

The office had been painted by Colin and Marie Claude, and with Claudine's state-of-the art equipment, it was now a pleasure to walk into every day. The old safe was still there, its heavy door removed, filled now with reams of paper, printer cartridges, and boxes of number 2 pencils. My desk was adorned only with the pictures of my nieces, the desktop, and a neatly organized stack of folders. The chipped bud vase held a single blossom of whatever Karl brought in every few days. My new happy place.

Gaspard had winnowed down his over one hundred images to twenty he deemed good enough for public consumption, and they were all stunning. They weren't just beautiful photographs, they also captured the spirit of the hotel: the old-world charm, the slow and graceful pace, the quiet, unobtrusive service. We looked great.

I plugged the images into the website and slowly pointed and clicked every link to make sure there would be no surprises. Then, I clicked on the most important button on the screen, the one that made our website live and out there for all the world to see. I waited. I heard no fanfare of trumpets. There was no thunderous applause. Not one piece of confetti fluttered down from the ceiling.

"Ta-da!" I said softly to myself.

"What are we celebrating?" Bing asked, right behind me.

I jumped. The man was like a ninja. I turned and would have scowled at him, but . . . we were *live*. "The website is up and running."

He was sipping his morning espresso. "I see. And you're . . . What? Waiting to see all those hundreds of reservations to come flowing in?"

"Of course not," I snapped. "I still have to put us on Vrbo. And Airbnb. And the Rennes tourism website." I reached over to grab a folder, riffled through the pages inside, and thrust a sheet at him. "And we need to be on all *these* places. Want to help?"

He read down the list, his eyebrows raised. "All these places? Are you sure?"

"Yes. I'm sure. It's my job, remember?"

He sat down at the desk across from me. "Okay. What do I do?"

"Go to each site," I explained. "They ask for the same information, and it's all on that first sheet there. Just input everything and download the . . . Wait. One of the three pictures in the file that reads *exterior*."

"What about interiors?"

"They won't ask for interior photos."

"How do you know?" he had that tone in his voice again, the "Are you serious about this?" tone. "Did you already look at all of these?"

I took a breath. "Of course I looked at them. I looked at almost one hundred different sites, and those are the ones with the most traffic. They're highly ranked in other places, too. I spent hours scrolling through garbage to find the diamonds." I glared at him. "How do you think I chose them? Coin toss?"

He shrugged. "That seems, well . . ."

"Boring as hell? Yes, it was. That's how I've spent every night for the last three weeks."

His eyes narrowed. "Every night?"

I shook my head. "What else was there for me to do?" I muttered, then instantly regretted it. Talk about sounding like a total loser with nothing to do except troll travel websites. But it *was* my job.

"You need to get out," he said.

I sighed. "And go where?"

"To the Place Sainte-Anne. You and I will go."

"What's that?"

"A surprise. We'll eat and walk, and you can see something of this city besides hardware stores and thrift shops. Sundays are usually quiet, with most things closed, but not there."

Suddenly, walking and eating and seeing Place Sainte-Anne sounded like the best idea in the world, even though I had no idea what it was. After staring at the same series of walls and doors for weeks, I would have welcomed a trip to the city dump.

"I have to finish all this," I said.

"Finish what?"

I gestured at the computer. "I need to finish the brochure, make copies, and fold them in time for the dog and pony show Claudine has planned for tomorrow."

He thought. "Then let's change places. I can probably do that much faster than all this."

We switched, and once I found my rhythm, it became easier to copy and paste, click, and save. I finished just in time to see Bing standing by the giant printer, waiting.

A single slick sheet slid out. He looked at it briefly, then carefully folded it in thirds. "Here," he said. "I think it's very good."

I looked at it carefully. Yes, it was good. It was great. The pictures were clear and crisp: the front courtyard, the open front doors, giving a glimpse into the elegant lobby, a smiling couple being checked in, the sun-drenched garden, the calm and classic bedroom. I would have booked myself a room in a heartbeat.

The text was in French, but Claudine and Colin had both said it was fine. I had an English version as well, but that could wait.

"Okay. This is good. We need at least one hundred copies made, then they need to be folded, then—"

He held up his hand. "Tell Claudine she can do this. Tell her we're taking a walk."

"A walk? That sounds so . . . simple."

He smiled. "There is nothing wrong with simple. Put on good shoes. I'll meet you in the courtyard in ten minutes."

I put my hands to my head, felt the wild curls, and made a lame attempt to pat them down. "Should I change? I mean, I probably look like a crazy person."

He shook his head. "You look perfect," he said, and left me sitting behind my desk, holding the brochure, grinning like an idiot.

Place Sainte-Anne looked like a picture postcard. The buildings were tall, half-timbered, with flower boxes spilling color from three and four stories up, open windows aflutter with lace curtains and the occasional cat, sitting in the fading sunlight. Everywhere there were people sitting and talking and eating. That, I had discovered, is what the French did. They found a good place with wine and food and sat for hours. No one was staring at a phone. Instead, they all looked at each other and talked. And talked. And talked some more.

French is a musical language, and to hear an entire street of people, all talking, was like listening to a symphony of words.

We sat and ordered wine. It was too early for dinner, especially in France, where people ate the main meal of the day after the sun had set. We sat and drank, munching on a small dish of nuts, not talking so much as watching the crowds and making quiet commentary.

"I would never wear that color."

"No, that is not a very good choice."

"That couple is having quite the argument."

"I can see that. She's trying very hard not to beat him over the head with her wineglass."

"But *that* couple—"

"—should get a room. And soon."

"Are all dogs in France so well behaved?"

"Yes. They're specially bred for crowds."

"No, they're not. Are they?"

He laughed. "You are very gullible sometimes."

"Actually, I'm pretty cynical and skeptical about most things. It's just that you insist on baiting me."

"I can't help it if you're an easy target," he said. "We aren't going to eat here. Let's walk some more."

We did. Walking could be tricky in the older parts of the city, where the cobblestones were old and uneven, but that's where the good walking shoes came in. We moved slowly, looking into shop windows and reading the menus posted outside various cafés.

Finally, Bing found whatever he was looking for, because we sat and ordered more wine.

"Can I order?" he asked. "They have a few specialties here that I know you'll love."

How did he know what I'd love? My hackles started to go up, but I realized my reaction was a little over the top. He probably *did* know about local specialties. Why shouldn't he order? If I was going to get defensive every time the man offered *anything*...

"Sure," I said. "I have to make a call. It's my weekly call to my parents. Do you mind?"

He shook his head, and I dialed.

Dad answered. Dad always answered. I know that they didn't have caller ID on their phone, yet my mother somehow always knew when I called and did not answer. It had been that way for years. And I also knew, having lived with them both for two years, that she answered the phone on a regular basis. Sometimes, the universe had a way of telling you things you wouldn't ordinarily know.

"Dad, hi. How was your week?"

Usually, I got a litany of small complaints and sly observations about the local political climate. But not today.

"Joey's drinking."

I felt my stomach lurch. "Since when?"

He sighed. "Wednesday was three years."

Three years since his wife, Sara, had died after a brief but brutal bout of cancer. Three years since he had to quit his job in IT to care for his twin daughters. Three years in a less demanding and lower-paying job at a big-box store that allowed for flexible hours to work around the girls' school schedule. Three years since he started drinking vodka every night to numb the pain.

"How bad?"

"He didn't pick up the girls from school on Wednesday. We had to get them. He didn't show up until after dinner, and he was wrecked."

I closed my eyes and tried to breathe slowly. "What did he say?"

"That it wouldn't happen again. He went to a meeting."

"What do you think?"

"He's drinking again."

At the height of his drinking, eighteen months before, in the weeks before and during rehab, the twins had moved in with my parents. It was then that I really began to know them, and they became more than just my little brother's kids. It wasn't just that they had become a distraction from my own seemingly endless troubles. They burrowed deep into my heart and stayed there. I had been the one to take them to and from school and ferry them to all their activities while my parents scrambled to try to piece their younger son back together. I had been the one they talked to. Dreamed with. Cried to. And now, I was in France.

"What about Frank?" I asked, but I knew the answer. My brother Frank had successfully removed himself from Joey's life—and mine—as soon as he married his raging bitch of a wife who had no use for any of the Gianetti family. Elena's contempt trickled down past the immediate family all the way to second cousins. In the years he'd been married to her, he'd evolved from the usual troubled but tolerable middle child to a man with no concern or empathy for his parents or his siblings. In fact, our problems became something he could revel in. My disgrace had probably been the highlight of his life, bringing him greater joy than even Joey's fall.

"Frank says we shouldn't be surprised."

Of course.

"What are you going to do?" I asked. I reached for the glass of wine that had been set down before me and drank it down in one gulp. Bing raised an eyebrow.

"The girls are here. We're going to ask Vivian to help out."

Vivian was the twins' other grandmother, Sara's ultraconservative mother, who had embraced her recent widowhood with religious fervor, telling anyone who would listen that her recently deceased husband had in fact been murdered by the deep state. It would have been laughable if it didn't directly spill into the lives of the two little girls.

"Oh, Daddy . . ."

"Honey, what else can we do? You know what it took to get him help last time."

Yes, I did know, and for the first time since I'd set foot in France, I wished I were home.

The golden glow of the early evening disappeared abruptly. It didn't matter that I was away from work, in a beautiful old city, drinking wine with the promise of a fabulous meal before me. It didn't matter that tomorrow, Hotel Paradis would be officially introduced to the world after weeks and weeks of backbreaking work. It didn't matter that Bing and I had managed to spend the entire afternoon together without my feeling like I needed to smack him upside the head because of his mansplaining.

My brother was in trouble again, and I was on the other side of the ocean, unable to help. And my two precious nieces were once again in the line of fire.

"I don't know what I can do," I whispered into the phone, trying to keep my voice from cracking.

"Honey, just think good thoughts," my father said, his voice weary. "I'm beginning to think that's all any of us can do."

"Okay." I felt my fingers tighten on the phone. "Tell the girls I love them."

"I will."

"I talk to them on Facebook. Can I do it on your laptop?"

"Of course."

"Monday. Around four your time."

"We'll be ready for you."

"And tell Joey I love him, too. Will you do that?"

He sighed. "Sure. Bye." He hung up.

I clicked off the phone and stared at the screen. Two beautiful, smiling little faces beamed up at me. Those dear little girls . . .

"Everything okay?" Bing asked, his voice gentle.

I cleared my throat. "My brother is an alcoholic. He slipped again."

"I'm sorry."

I lifted my eyes to his, and the kindness reflected back almost broke me. "It's just that he has two daughters, and he's had to raise them by himself the past few years, and we all thought he'd kind of turned a corner." I shrugged. "But he turned back."

"Do you want to talk?"

I thought. "Not about that. Instead, tell me about Philippe. Will he be back this summer?" Was I really interested? Not really, but it was the safest thing I could think of. And it was as far away from my own problem as I could get.

Bing signaled for more wine. "Yes. He'll be here in a few weeks, I think. When Marie Claude and Eliot are gone."

"Yes, but . . ." I thought. "Marie Claude is going to be working the desk. She won't be able to take time off. Not in the beginning, anyway. I have no idea how many people will be working and what the schedules will be like. She can't leave the hotel in the middle of the summer."

Something in his face changed. "I hadn't thought of that."

"But it's been what, five years since their involvement? Surely he's over her by now."

Bing sighed. "I don't think he will ever get over her. Watching them together was like nothing I'd ever seen before. They were like two souls in a single body. Remarkable."

Our food was set down, what looked to be a white fish, grilled beautifully, with slender stalks of asparagus and tiny roasted potatoes. My wineglass was refilled.

"This looks amazing," I said. I looked up and caught his expression. "What?"

"Have you ever loved like that?" he asked.

I thought about the times I had told myself I'd been in love.

High school didn't count. Besides, that had been 99 percent lust. My first husband had been a sweet man who was my best friend, and yes, I had loved him. But leaving him had been more of an inconvenience than a heartbreak. But Tony? Two souls . . . yes, that had been us. Two souls in a single body. But were we really? Had we ever been that, when one could have so carelessly turned away from the other?

"I used to think so," I said, picking up my fork. "But maybe it's still something I can look forward to."

He nodded. "Maybe."

Chapter Ten

The lobby of Hotel Paradis was quiet. The flowers still looked fresh, the wooden surfaces shone, the air was scented a faint lavender. Marie Claude stood behind the desk, her hands pressed primly at her side. I was right at the front door, watching as the small crowd gathered in the courtyard. Claudine was chatting happily at her guests, her arms waving expressively as she pointed and smiled.

I glanced back into the salon. Through the closed glass doors, I could see the long table, bedecked with more flowers and simple white platters heaped with fruit and cheese, fragrant baguettes, and thinly sliced meats, with another table of empty glasses and decanted open bottles from Claudine's cellar.

I was in the uniform: simple black skirt, a white blouse, black ballet flats. I had a red rose pinned to my lapel, as did Marie Claude. She cleared her throat. She was officially working for us now, having turned in her notice at the bank where she'd worked. Her contract was sitting on my desk in the back office. Reading and signing it had been a very eye-opening experience.

It seemed that every working person in France had a contract for employment, a contract that was very specific not only about the wage, which was considerably higher than what new employees at The Fielding had started out at, but also about hours worked per day, per week, vacation time off, and a long list of other days off. Claudine had been very particular about the contract, as we were going to need the most employees when most everyone else in France was on vacation.

Eliot had not been happy with his wife working through the weeks they had always taken off to go to Lyon. Maybe it had occurred to him about Philippe. I don't know if Marie Claude had made the realization, but something in the way she and Claudine had managed the conversation made me think they were both very aware that he would be visiting and, for the first time in years, she would be right there.

She gave me a nervous smile, patted her bright blue hair, and ran her fingers lightly over the stack of brochures at the end of the desk.

"These are very good," she said.

"Yes. They are. Eliot was a great help," I told her, even though his help had been given quite grudgingly.

The door suddenly opened, and Claudine held it as a stream of men and women, dressed from casual linen to sharp black suits, came in, all chattering happily. Claudine clapped her hands.

"I would like you all to meet Lucia Gianetti, our general manager, and the woman responsible for all that you will be seeing this morning," she sang out and began to applaud.

I felt myself starting to blush as everyone joined her. I smiled and tried not to look slightly panicked as I realized I didn't know anyone's name. I had suggested Claudine create name tags, but she'd scoffed at the idea.

"That would be an insult," she said. "These people are all well known in their field, and everyone knows who they are."

"I don't," I countered.

"I'll introduce you, of course."

"To what, thirty people? And I'll remember their names how?"

She sighed. "Well, the press will have passes around their necks. They probably wear those things everywhere; they think it gives them importance. You won't have to remember too many people."

I had not been reassured, and since I knew all about schmoozing, I hoped I wouldn't call anyone by the wrong names.

A man in the back of the pack raised his hand. "Ah, I'd like to ask Miss Gianetti—"

"Marc," Claudine interrupted smoothly, "why don't we take the tour first? There's so much to see. I have a lovely luncheon prepared, and then we can all sit and chat." She looked upward. "So, as you can see, the original chandelier is still here. As a child, my job was to dust all those crystals. Luckily, I can order someone else to do that now."

There was an appreciative murmur of laughter.

"Let's start with the ground-floor rooms and the garden," she said. "Lucia will be with us, of course. She oversaw all the renovations, and I'm sure she can fill in any gaps in my knowledge."

Who was she kidding? She knew everything there was to know about every square inch of this hotel, renovations or no.

The tour began, and Claudine was absolutely *on*. She laughed and charmed and answered the most mundane questions as though they were sent directly from the gods. As they stepped out into the gardens, the oohs and aahs competed with the clicking of digital cameras.

And the garden looked beautiful. Karl had worked all weekend, and there wasn't a weed to be found. A much-older gentleman stepped away from the crowd and sat on one of the benches, his folded hands across the top of his cane.

I stood beside him. "It's lovely out here, isn't it?" I asked.

He nodded. "Yes. I knew Claudine's father and often visited here. I was much younger then, of course, and the two of us would sit out here, together, just talking. It was a smaller garden, just a few vegetables that he grew for the family." He looked up at me and smiled. "Claudine has done a good job. This will be a very successful place, I think. And she has you to thank."

"She could have done this without me," I said.

He shook his head. "No. If she could have done this without you, it would have been done years ago. Claudine has vision, she can inspire, but she's not able to create."

Claudine was calling and waving her arms for everyone to follow her back inside. The gentleman sighed, leaned on his cane, and stood. "I probably won't make it up to the second floor," he muttered.

"Then you can wait in the salon," I told him. "I'll be happy to sneak you in. And although I would never dream of attempting to influence a review, I'll even pour you a glass of wine."

He chuckled. "I'm not with the press. I'm the minister of, among other things, tourism for France."

Oh my. "Well, then," I said, "I'll make sure you get a very *large* glass of wine."

He laughed then and offered me his arm. I took it, and we walked back in through the doors that led to the office and the salon beyond.

He glanced out the tall windows to the patio, tranquil and lovely with large urns of pale blossoms and trailing ivy. "Do you still have the ghost?"

I pulled out a chair for him to sit. "Yes, but please don't tell anyone."

"I always wanted to meet her," he said, dropping his voice. "But now that I'm closer to her reality, I'm not as eager."

I smiled and poured some wine. "I have to go upstairs."

"Of course." He regarded me steadily. "This must be a very different experience for you. The Fielding was much larger, was it not?"

I was still. "Yes."

"And when you first went there, it was not a very good hotel. You made it a success."

"Yes."

"So, turning Hotel Paradis into a success must be easy for you?"

I burst out laughing. I couldn't help it. "When I got to The Fielding, I had to deal with a few hundred disgruntled employees, unions, the New York City Department of Health, dozens of websites and advertisers, the Hotel Association of New York City . . ." I sighed. "But I never had to pick up a paintbrush or print my own brochures. So, *easy* is a relative term."

He smiled, sipped the wine, and nodded approvingly. "I see. So, there is a different level of satisfaction?"

I thought. "Yes. Very different."

"And was it worth leaving your friends and family?"

That one really got to me. What friends? The friends I'd made in New York had been Tony's friends first, and while it was true they welcomed me with open arms, none of them had reached out to me after they realized Tony had stolen millions, and some of it had been their own money. And as for my family, well, those relationships had been difficult for so long I considered France a welcome respite.

"Yes," I answered simply.

He waved his wineglass. "Go. Do your duty. I can assure you, everyone is enchanted, and soon you'll have more guests than you can handle."

I left him then, and by the end of the day, I thought he might be right. Everyone seemed pleased and enthusiastic. Much food was eaten and wine drunk, and after everyone had left and the salon was cleaned and empty, and I felt like I was going to drop from exhaustion. I sat at my desk to see if, in fact, we had any reservations.

We had six reservations for our opening week. I was so pleased and surprised I had to look twice. I scrolled through the short list, stopped, and almost burst into tears.

Our very first reservation was for one Julia Wilson of New York City.

My Julia. Here for our opening day.

I sent her a text that was just a series of emojis across the screen.

She texted back immediately. But of course.

Once Marie Claude and Claudine became permanent members of the painting and cleaning crew, things moved more quickly than I could have hoped.

"Maybe we can move up the opening date?" Claudine asked.

I shook my head. "We're still on a very tight schedule. We don't want guests here while we're still painting rooms. It's not such a good look to be in the middle of renovations while our guests are trying to relax and enjoy the pleasures of an authentic Rennes experience."

She made a face. "To be honest, being in the middle of a construction site basically *is* an authentic Rennes experience."

"Okay, then. Let's go for the fantasy Rennes experience."

We were scrubbing one of the bathrooms.

"I had no idea that owning a boutique hotel was going to be so glamorous," she muttered.

I sat back and plunged my brush into a pail of hot, soapy water. "We could hire a housekeeping crew now," I suggested.

She shook her head. "No. Housekeeping and kitchen will wait until the last minute. I can't afford to pay people to do what I can do myself for free. But soon."

Claudine and I were still not in agreement on how many staff we were going to hire. Claudine was very much in the "bare bones" camp, insisting that since three paid staff members lived on-site, one of us could easily jump in at any time if needed to fill in a gap in staffing.

"That may work for now, but once we're up and running, things will be very different," I said. "And Marie Claude has a contract that is very specific about her hours. I don't see her bringing up clean towels in the middle of the night."

She made a face. "Marie Claude is a lovely girl, but she is a bit of a princess. But you're right. She won't be at anyone's beck and call."

I sat back, curious. "What's going to happen when Philippe is here?"

She sighed. "I've been thinking about that. She will be working, of course. I don't know if Eliot will be here or not. He may very well go to Lyon without her. She and Philippe have not seen each other in five years. Can a person carry a torch for that long? I don't know. First love is very strong, and I know that there has never been anyone else for Philippe who has lasted more than a few months. And Eliot, well, he is a very nice young man, but he's no Philippe." She carefully wiped the tile clean of sudsy water. "My son is an extraordinary person. This is not just love talking. You will understand when you meet him. He is very much like Bing in many ways." She smiled. "And he is very handsome. He was quite spoiled as a child, but most of his brattiness has disappeared. He's quite a nice man now. And a very good artist."

"How does he feel about the hotel?"

She sighed. "I am hoping he will see a successful, well-run business that he can step into and take over while still pursuing his art. Then, maybe, he will stay."

I stood and stretched, then tossed my scrub brush back into the pail. I walked back into the bedroom.

All the rooms were painted the same creamy shades, but the bedspread in this one was pale lilac. The quilting technique, as Karl had patiently explained to me, in detail, several times, was a variation on the Marseilles corded quilting, or *piqué marseillais*. The bed was a mahogany four-poster, and the small writing desk beside the bed was delicate walnut, carved and softly gleaming. There was a tall armoire, a small chair by the desk, and two overstuffed chairs by the windows, upholstered in pale-green-striped silk. Green and violet pillows were strewn across the bed, and in addition to the small chandelier, there were two floor lamps for light. We hadn't hung the artwork yet, but three small still life watercolors leaned against the wall. Like all the rooms we had finished this far, this had its own personality: calm and decidedly feminine, with a bit of whimsey in the embroidered pillows. I found myself having very strong feelings about some of our rooms, and this was one of my favorites.

"How are we doing?" Claudine asked, coming up behind me.

In the three weeks since the website had gone live, we'd received enough reservations that we were currently at a 50 percent occupancy for June and July, slightly higher in August. She knew that; she saw the numbers every morning, standing behind me as I went through the reservations on my computer.

I knew what she was really asking.

"For a literally unknown entity, we aren't doing badly. We have more European bookings than anything, but that's because your little press junket was such a success. The only real exposure in North or South America we're getting is through Vrbo and a few small, free booking sites. We're going to have to depend on word of mouth unless we spend big bucks on an advertising campaign, and we don't have big bucks."

"There is a huge Canadian market," she said.

"Yes. I know."

"How do we reach it? Didn't you work in Quebec?"

"Many years ago."

She raised her eyebrows. "Did you have any contacts?"

"Several. And I guess I could try to track them down, but like I said, that was over ten years ago." Somewhere I had a battered notebook with thirty years' worth of names and phone numbers. I had thought about burning it at a particularly low point, when I was certain I would never work in the hotel industry again. Instead, I moved it from one drawer to another until it finally found a home in the bottom of the dresser in my *appart,* beneath a tumble of socks and a few bulky sweaters.

"Tour groups would be good," she said.

"I know, but we aren't big enough. Most bus tours are fifty people, and we're topped out at thirty-six guests."

"We have the attic," she said thoughtfully. "Maybe three or four rooms there."

"But no elevator up there," I told her. "One flight of stairs is charming and old-world, but the stairs to the attic are narrow and badly lit. Remember, some of these tours cater to seniors, and they'd have a hard enough time with the main staircase. To the attic? No way." I had a brief vision of a bent old lady plunging to her death while trying to get to her room.

"I suppose. But look at this room. I'd climb a few extra steps to sleep here." Claudine put her arm around my shoulders and gave me a squeeze. "I knew you were the right person for the job."

"*I* didn't know," I told her. "I almost left that first night. When my friend Julia gets here, you can thank her for talking me down."

"And now?"

"Now I can't imagine being anywhere else."

She dropped her arm. "That is good to hear. Now, let's finish cleaning this bathroom. And then we go across the hall. Yes?"

Yes.

In the weeks that I'd lived there, I had managed to give my tiny *appart* a bit of personality more in line with my old suite at The Fielding. There were two comfortable chairs now at the window, with a bookshelf displaying some of my favorite childhood reads in French, and a collection of objects found at the Saturday market and various thrift shops: a brass lamp worthy of Aladdin and his genie, a delicate footed silver bowl, mercury glass candlesticks, a copper pitcher. There were watercolors on the walls now, and a few copper pots hung from a rack over the tiny kitchen stove. I didn't cook much but had mastered the omelet, coq au vin, and the galette, the Breton crêpe cooked on its own shallow pan. I ate several times a week across the street, usually a large, somewhat late lunch.

Vera and I usually shared a glass of cider on the bench outside her front door. Karl often grabbed me as I was just opening my door, and I'd get an invitation for port. Colin's flat was crammed with several stringed instruments of varying age and size, and I could often hear him playing something on his favorite violin, the music drifting through the now always-open windows.

My life had settled into a pattern that I found easy and comforting. I knew that once the hotel officially opened, there would be a whole new normal, so I relished the predictability of my days and nights now.

Marie Claude and Eliot had the flat on my right, and although the walls were a foot thick and solid limestone, I heard them arguing more and more. Not words, just the loud and deep rumble of Eliot's voice, and the higher, more conciliatory notes as Marie Claude answered. Often, after these fights, I could hear the door slam and see Eliot walking across the courtyard and out the iron gates.

After one such evening, I could hear what could have only been Marie Claude sobbing. I closed my computer and stood. I did not want to know what was so obviously wrong between her and Eliot, but she'd been coming into the hotel late in the mornings, her eyes red and shadowed, tired and cross. That would not do once the Hotel Paradis opened. Whatever issues the couple had needed to be resolved by then.

I went out my door and stood in the courtyard, listening. Yes, she was crying. Poor Marie Claude.

I heard someone behind me and turned to find Colin leaning out of his doorway, shaking his head.

"They're at it again?" he asked.

I nodded. "I think so. He just left."

He motioned me toward him and held open the door of his flat.

I hadn't been inside, just had gotten a glimpse of what seemed to be a room filled with nothing but string instruments, and as I walked in, I saw that yes, there were violins and cellos everywhere, but there was also a long leather sofa and a small table with one chair.

"Have a seat," he said. "Wine?"

I shook my head and stayed standing. "I love hearing you play in the evenings," I told him.

He ducked his head and blushed. "Thank you. I sometimes wonder if it's annoying."

"I can't imagine it ever being annoying."

"Well," he said, making a face, "I'll probably have to stop once the hotel opens."

I shook my head. "Not at all. Why should you?"

He pushed his hands into the pockets of his khakis. "Won't it disturb the guests?"

"I don't think so. Only the front-facing rooms have a chance of hearing you, and most paying customers will think the live entertainment is a perk."

He smiled. "That's very kind. Please. Sit."

I did. I was unsure why he'd invited me in. He was a quiet and fairly private man, and after the first few whirlwind days of him being in on every conversation I'd had with Claudine, he'd stepped away and become a patient and helpful, but very reticent, addition to the painting crew. Claudine had been right. He loved the tedious and fiddly jobs like painting the front gate and the wrought iron chairs. I knew he taught music at the university in Rennes, he wasn't married or appeared to have any one person who was a constant in his life, and he was always drinking tea from a dingy white mug.

He picked the mug up now. "If not wine, then tea?"

I shook my head again. "What can I do for you, Colin?" I asked.

He looked flustered and sat down across from me on the single chair. "I know that we're all getting new locks once the hotel opens, and I'm fine with that, but I'm worried about our, well, personal space. We're going to have all sorts of people walking in and out of here, aren't we?"

I nodded. "I sure hope so."

"Yes. Yes, of course you'd want that. That's the whole point, isn't it? To have guests?"

"Yes, but the front courtyard will be more of a passage. Guests won't congregate there. We have plenty of public space adjacent to the hotel. I can't foresee guests dragging benches from the garden to sit right out in front."

"Yes. I suppose you're right. It's just . . ." He paused, then leaned forward, his elbows resting on his thighs. "We've all rather gotten used to the peace and quiet."

"I'm sure you have. But you knew that once the hotel opened, that would change."

"Yes. Yes, of course. But, well, none of us really ever imagined it *would* open."

I didn't know what I was supposed to say about that, so I said nothing.

He cleared his throat. Obviously, he thought it was my turn, so I searched for something to say other than "Well, in that case, we'll just shut everything down."

"Colin, Claudine is very aware of all of you. After all, you've been living here a very long time, and considering the rent you pay, well, let's just say she's been more than accommodating. And now, it's your turn. To be accommodating."

He grimaced. "We were afraid of that."

I shook my head. "All of you here have invested your time and, in some cases, your money into turning this place into a successful venture. I don't understand. What did you all expect?" I narrowed my eyes. "Who else is worried about this?"

"All of us. Vera and Karl. Bing . . . Well, it doesn't really affect Bing. Nothing seems to affect Bing. Marie Claude is just looking at her new job and what that means. Eliot is more outraged his wife is not following him to Lyon like she has every summer, but he doesn't want strange people wandering in and out of his flat."

I frowned. "Why would any of our guests be in his flat?"

"You know what I mean."

"No, I don't. Look, just because there's a wall around us doesn't mean this is *all* the hotel. Your private spaces will remain private. If we were just on a street somewhere, and a hotel was on the same street, it would be the same, right? Strangers coming and going past your door, right?"

He frowned, then nodded. "Yes. But the gates will be open during the day. Anyone can wander in."

"Which is why you will all have locks. And at night, the gates will be locked, and only guests will have access."

"Well, what if the guests are . . . you know." He made a very French gesture with his hands.

"Are you suggesting they might be criminals?"

"Maybe."

I sighed. "So, you're worried that people who are paying a fairly hefty price tag for a private room in a boutique hotel will actually be here just to break into your two-room *appartement* and rob you blind?"

He looked embarrassed. "When you put it that way, it sounds ridiculous."

"Because it is. I think if a criminal mastermind were planning a dangerous heist, this particular location would not be a top choice." I stood up. "Did you all draw straws to determine who was going to have this conversation with me?"

He looked sheepish. "Actually, yes."

"And you lost?"

"Oh yes." He stood and laughed.

"Why don't you just talk to Claudine?"

"She's been very good to all of us, and we don't want to seem ungrateful. I would hate for her to think, well, you know . . ." He shrugged. "You won't tell her?"

"Of course not, because it's not an issue. But tell me, who was worried about having all his valuables stolen by a master thief?"

"Karl, actually."

"And does Karl have anything worth stealing?"

He laughed. "Now that I think about it, probably not."

"Well. You can tell them all they'll be fine."

"Okay." He ducked his head. "Thank you for this."

"No problem." I went to the door. "Good night, Colin."

"Good night."

I went back outside. Marie Claude had stopped crying, and the courtyard was in shadows. I could hear the faint sound of traffic and the rustle of leaves. I had grown accustomed to the peace and quiet as well and knew that I was going to miss these tranquil nights.

But we would adjust. All of us.

We had worked out a schedule where either Marie Claude or I would be at the desk during the day and evening hours, and a third person, who would hopefully be fluent in English, would be hired to fill in the shifts we did not cover. Claudine was to be on call overnight.

Claudine refused to have a traditional phone system installed, and I didn't blame her. The cost was high, and she didn't want more wires running through the plaster walls. We had worked out a system where, upon check-in, the guest would enter our mobile phone into their cell phone and put us on speed dial, so that they could call a staff person at any time. The house phone would be carried by whoever was on duty, and Claudine would take it after eleven at night.

We hadn't hired the third person for the desk, but we had time. I wasn't looking forward to it, as I found that hiring in France was a much different situation from hiring in the US. The idea of everyone having a work contract was new to me. I had assumed that my own contract with Claudine was because of my position, but apparently, any full-time employee hired for any position signed a contract for work, based on a government-issued work code that was very specific and worker-friendly.

I had asked Claudine to do the hiring, because some of the guidelines were simply beyond my ability to grasp and understand. For example, an employee's schedule was fixed. At The Fielding, every manager's nightmare was the weekly schedule for hourly employees, trying to plug holes for vacation or callouts, moving employees around doctor appointments and kids soccer games. Here, the employee had a set schedule and they worked it, every day, week in, week out.

But on the flip side, there were a series of holidays and designated days off, long vacations, and the length of the contract—the minimum you could hire a person for was six months. If the employee didn't work out, then you didn't sign another contract. *But—*

"Claudine, what if the employee is a screwup?"

We were in the back office, looking through online applications. She frowned. "What do you mean?"

"What if the employee is, well, bad?"

"There are guidelines. You can fire someone for cause, of course."

"But front desk people need to be a certain type. Not just helpful. They need to be willing to go above and beyond for the guest. That's what's going to make our hotel different from others: our excellent customer service."

She shook her head. "You can't let a person go without cause. And an unwillingness to go above and beyond is not cause."

"What if they sleepwalk through the day? We can't have that."

"That is why it is very important to have a thorough interview process. It's the one chance you have to assess a person's personality." She tilted her head. "Surely, you've hired hundreds of people. You should be able to tell, what is that expression? The wheat from the chaff."

I held my tongue. Yes, I had hired hundreds of people. Well, maybe not hundreds, but enough that I had once been very confident in my hiring skills. I used to think I could read a person, know their strengths and weaknesses, in the first ten minutes of conversation.

But that was before the man I trusted above everyone else in my life, the man I'd thought was one of a kind, turned out to be a common crook.

Claudine watched me and seemed to home in on my thoughts even as I was trying to make sense of them. "You cannot spend the rest of your life doubting yourself because one person managed to make a fool of you."

"He didn't just 'make a fool' of me, Claudine. He—"

He what? Shattered my self-worth? Made me question my ability to read and understand people? Destroyed years of confidence built from experience, mistakes made and learned from, and careful observation of an industry that was still very much an old boys' club, despite a general outward acceptance and approval of my work?

She leaned forward. "I can't begin to imagine what damage your ego has suffered, but here, in this place, you have proven yourself a worthy and valued employee. Do not look backward, Lucy. Continue to look forward, because that is where your life is going. It will never go back."

I nodded. "Yes. But." I shook my head. "All these *conditions*."

She smiled. "We are a country that has never forgotten the workingman. In every sizable city or town, there is still the center, where the guillotine stood."

I had seen the place in Rennes, a circle of cobblestones, with a single white head in marble at the center.

"I will worry about the contracts," she said. "But you will hire, yes?"

So, I did the hiring, but Marie Claude, who I thought was a shoo-in, was digging in her heels. She did not look happy. In fact, she glared at me as though I suggested she walk out of the hotel, through the courtyard, and out into the street, naked.

"What do you mean, deliver towels?" she asked.

"Here's the thing," I explained. "Claudine is reluctant to hire too many people until we figure out the workflow. You can understand that, right? So, our housekeeping staff will only be here in the mornings, to make beds, clean the rooms, and tidy up all the public spaces. But it doesn't make sense to have someone here in the evenings, just sitting around, does it?"

She shook her head slowly. "No, I suppose not."

"Exactly. So, if you're on duty at the desk during the evenings and a guest needs towels, you can bring them up. Your contract says . . ." I scanned the page, one of many, until I found the spot. "'Will provide additional services as determined by the general manager.' That's me."

She huffed and set her jaw. "Are you going to deliver towels?" she asked.

"I will. I'll deliver towels. I'll rearrange flowers if I find any drooping. I'll straighten rugs that are askew. I'll pick up wineglasses that have been forgotten. I'll do whatever I need to do to make sure every guest that checks out of the Hotel Paradis goes home and tells all their friends and family what a great time they had."

She made a little face. "Well, then, I suppose I can deliver towels if I need to."

I smiled. "Thank you, Marie Claude."

She smiled back. "You're welcome, Lucy."

Chapter Eleven

I interviewed three people for the front desk position and hired a retired teacher, Celestine, thinking that having dealt with unruly children, she'd be perfect with demanding guests. She spoke excellent English, as well as Dutch and Russian. I had found that most of the people who applied for a job requiring English spoke at least one additional language as well as French. Marie Claude spoke excellent German, so we had pretty much the entire continent of Europe, as well as English-speaking countries, covered.

Our housekeeping staff consisted of two sisters, Ines and Rose, both attending university part-time. They were perfectly happy to clean rooms, change sheets, and work in the kitchen as needed. The commercial laundry equipment in the cellar didn't cause either of them to blink, which impressed me to no end, as I went into a mild panic that the huge machines would eat all my clothes every time I did my personal laundry.

Karl refused to be put on the payroll, although he had expanded his role beyond tending the garden to keeping the courtyard and patio free of debris, as well as attending to all the plants and planters inside and outside Hotel Paradis.

"How can I take money for doing what I love?" he asked me.

"I love my job, too, Karl," I said. "But I still need ready cash."

He shook his head. "I have a very good pension." He grinned. "I could explain it to you, but I think sometimes that maybe I explain too many things?"

I grinned back. "Sometimes."

"I have to pick some roses, then tend to the garden. We have many tomatoes." He grinned. "And I will not mention to Claudine that you wanted to put me on your payroll." He held his finger to his lips. "I swear, not a word."

"Thank you, Karl."

He bowed out of the office, and I checked another item off my list. I glanced at my phone. Stavros and I were meeting in a few minutes to talk about the new menu.

Stavros met me in the salon, looking excited, holding pieces of paper in various sizes and shapes. He spread them across the table in front of me.

"Here is the menu," he said proudly. "Josiane helped, of course. She likes this long and narrow shape. I prefer the traditional square. It's up to you."

The shape of the menus had not given me a jolt. It was the words on them. "Stavros, do you really mean to make chocolate chip pancakes?"

In France, breakfast was an inconsequential meal. The French did not eat pancakes. Or waffles, French toast, or eggs Benedict. Yet all those items were on his menu.

Stavros beamed proudly. "I have been practicing. I think they are very good."

"But—" How did I tell him that this menu was exactly what I did *not* want? "I thought we'd go with more traditionally French food for breakfast. You know, tartines and jam, soft-boiled eggs, fruit." I felt the hairs on the back of my neck stand on end as I read the description of the Sunday omelet: three eggs, bacon, brie, and avocado, served with home fries and rye toast. That was not French breakfast food. That was American diner food.

Stavros shook his head. "You are catering to Americans, yes? They will want to eat American food."

"But—" I stalled. "Not all our guests will be American. We need a more, ah, international menu."

He frowned. "Porridge?" Once again, a food not commonly found on the table in France before noon.

"No. I mean, okay, maybe. But our guests are coming here for a very traditional Breton experience. Our rooms are old-fashioned and charming. Our breakfast needs to be the same. We're getting baguettes and pastries from the boulangerie?" The bakery around the corner had bread that was, even for France, extraordinary, and they agreed to supply us every morning with loaves and pastries.

Stavros nodded. I could see a little of the enthusiasm leave his face.

"Well, then, let's keep it simple for now, okay? We can serve here what you'd serve across the street. That will make it much easier on everyone if there doesn't have to be a full staff in the kitchen."

His excitement vanished. "I see."

"So." I picked up the long and narrow menu. Stavros had three daughters who were working with him, and they all had a better idea of what I wanted than he did. "I like this one here. Josiane is right; it's a little different and very attractive." *Hotel Paradis* was printed across the top, and at the very bottom was our trademark fleur-di-lis. The font was classic and simple, and on her menu, there was not a chocolate chip or caramelized banana to be found. "Tell Josiane this is perfect. Can we run this off on our computer?" We could use card stock and change the menu on a whim, based on what fruit or specialty pastry we had available.

He sighed, clearly disappointed that he would not be flipping pancakes and frying bacon. "As you wish, Lucy. And I suppose it will be easier. I was going to have to hire someone for the kitchen to help."

I jumped on that. "Exactly. This way, Simone can come over, get things all set up, and we'll just put the food on a sideboard, and she'll serve drinks. The girls we just hired for housekeeping are willing to chip in as needed."

He looked crushed. "I was reading about barbecue."

"Excuse me?" I looked up from the menu. "Barbecue? For breakfast?"

He shook his head. "No. To have barbecue night at the restaurant for your guests."

I sat back, thinking. "That might be a very good idea, Stavros."

His expression brightened. "Really?"

"Yes. We could do it here. Just once a week. Maybe. What does French barbecue taste like?"

"I don't know. I'll experiment."

I smiled. "Make sure you bring some of your experiments over to me. After all, I worked for three years in Houston, Texas. I know barbecue."

He beamed, all his good humor restored. "Of course. And Simone knows a bluegrass band. We could have music."

"A bluegrass band? Really? The French like bluegrass?"

He gathered up his menus. "We have a bit of an obsession with bluegrass music."

"I'll run this by Claudine, but you do your research and see what you can cook up."

I watched him leave, and I glanced around the salon. There were more than enough tables for people to eat dinner, and then, of course, tables could go out to the patio. We could set up a long buffet, with barbecue and the fixings: corn on the cob, coleslaw . . . What was the French version of baked beans?

I stood up and walked out to the patio. As usual, it was very quiet and still, without so much as a leaf rustling. "Do you like music?" I called out softly.

I felt a slight breeze, but nothing else. "Is that a yes or a no?"

The breeze faded. I went back into Hotel Paradis.

Georges came into the back office, a cigarette behind one ear, his cap twisting in his hands.

"You want see me?" he said in his somewhat fractured English.

"Yes. Thanks for coming in. Please, sit down."

He perched on the edge of the chair and looked as though he could be off and back out the door at the sound of the gun.

I had been rehearsing this all morning. "First of all, I want to welcome you to the team," I said in French.

He relaxed a bit. "Thank you."

"Now, I've had magnetic signs made up for you to put on either side of your car." I had them ready on my desk and pulled one out of the large cardboard folder they had come in. "See?"

It was simple. An ivory background, with a peacock-blue fleur-de-lis in the center, and the words *Hotel Paradis* printed in the same font as our logo.

"You can just put them on the sides of the car when you're doing hotel business, and then take them off when you're not on duty."

In theory, he'd be on duty all the time. That was the deal, that our guests would be his priority. But he was also going to be ferrying around other passengers as an independent Uber, and Claudine had no problem with that.

He took the sign from my hands and looked at it closely. "Very nice."

"Yes, it is." I sat up a little straighter. Here was the tricky part. "But about your car, Georges. It needs . . ." What? A new paint job, the upholstery repaired, the air fresheners pulled off the rearview mirror, the smell of smoke scrubbed away. "Sprucing up."

He frowned, lowered the sign, and glared at me. "Marcel is perfect."

This confused me. "Marcel?"

"The Volvo."

"Ah." He'd named his car *Marcel*? "I'm sure it is. *He* is. But maybe we could look at it—I mean, *him*—together and see if any improvements can be made."

He put the sign, somewhat forcefully, back on the desktop. "No improvements. Marcel starts, and he goes. I have heat, and all the windows open and close."

Good heavens, what was the problem? "I'm sure. But can we just, you know, take a look?"

His mustache quivered, but he nodded. He stood abruptly and headed out the door.

I followed him out into the courtyard, where Marcel was parked by the entrance to the garden. Georges trotted ahead of me, presumably to do some quick cleanup to the car interior.

Or not. When he reached the driver's side of the car, he turned and faced me, arms folded across his chest, a sour expression on his face.

"Marcel is perfect," he repeated.

I opened the door to the back seat and peered inside.

It still smelled of cigarette smoke and cheese and faded pine. The air fresheners still dangled from the rearview mirror, and it didn't look as though they had been changed out or added to. There was a long split in the seam of the seat behind the passenger front seat. The floor was littered with scraps of dried leaves, receipts I recognized from Monoprix, six empty coffee to-go cups, presumably empty, and a withered orange.

I straightened and looked at Georges. "This is not acceptable. When was the last time you vacuumed?"

His mustache quivered again. "Vacuum?"

"Yes. There's so much stuff in the floor back here, there's no room for a passenger to put their feet." I pushed past him and opened the driver's-side door. Piled on the passenger seat was a cardboard box filled with old books, and on the floor were more coffee to-go cups, the hand-printed Hotel Paradis sign, and the bald head of a female mannequin. I didn't want to know.

"Georges, guests coming to Hotel Paradis from the train will be met by *you*. You are the first impression. And this—" I gestured with a hand. "This is not a good first impression." I looked at him. He was wearing crumpled khakis, a denim button-down shirt over a plain green T-shirt, and on his feet were scuffed boots. I looked him up and down. "*You* are not a good first impression."

His mouth opened to say something, it shut, then it opened again. "Marie Claude has blue hair," he sputtered.

I nodded. "Yes. But it's clean blue hair. And her uniform will be a white shirt and black pants or skirt. Maybe you should make that your uniform, too."

His eyes widened. "I would never wear a skirt."

I stopped both eyes midway through their roll. "No, Georges. You don't have to wear a skirt. But you have a white shirt, don't you? And a pair of black pants?"

He nodded, his eyes narrowed.

"Good. Now, about cleaning up the inside." I cast a quick eye over the body of the car, taking in the mud around the wheels and splashed up against the bumpers, the dusty windshield, the bits of unknown foliage trapped under the windshield wipers. "And outside. When was the last time you went to a car wash?"

"Car wash?" he repeated blankly. I closed my eyes. Were there car washes in France? There had to be. Surely, cleaning your car could not be exclusively an American obsession.

"We would pay for it, of course," I told him. "The hotel. We'd have Marcel cleaned inside and out, and maybe a little touch-up on the paint job." There were noticeable scratches along the front and sides of the hood. Not an especially reassuring sight for guests to see first thing.

He noticeably softened, and I realized it wasn't the actual cleaning he objected to but the paying for the cleaning that was the issue.

"You also," I said in English, "have to practice speaking English." I knew that he understood very well, but never spoke in English. "From now on, anytime you do work for us, you have to speak English. Understood?"

He frowned again. "What if the guest is French?"

I sighed. "Then, of course, you'll speak French."

"What about if they're Polish?"

"Then use your best judgment, Georges. Now, do you know a place that can clean your car? And do a bit of bodywork?"

"Yes. And I bring you the bill?"

"Yes."

"*D'accord.*"

I shook my head. "No. *Agreed.* Say it."

He finally smiled. "Agreed."

Claudine scowled. "What do you mean, dry run? What is a dry run?"

"We need for all our staff to perform in real time. With guests."

"And where do we get these guests?" she asked.

"Well, Colin, Karl, and Vera. Have Bing come down from his studio. Eliot. We can ask Stavros's daughters."

She narrowed her eyes. "Not Josiane."

I waved a hand. "Maybe not her kids. We can invite Raoul and his girlfriend. How about Georges? Is he married?"

"Three times," Claudine said absently, her eyes on the computer screen as she scrolled through our reservations.

"So, invite his ex-wives. We need people. We need to have check-ins and beds made and breakfast served and issues resolved."

She lifted her head. "What issues?"

"Exactly. We won't know until they happen, and we don't want to be unprepared if it happens to a guest."

"You want me to start paying people to work here so we can wait on the same people who *live* here?" She shook her head. "You seem to think I have money to spare."

"Claudine, I know you don't have money to spare, but this is necessary."

She drummed her fingernails against the desktop. "Really?"

"This is my job. Remember?"

She took a deep breath. "Fine. And I'll reach out to a few of my favorite old clients and see who wants a free stay for the weekend. Unless we can charge them?" She looked up at me hopefully. "Maybe half rate?"

"If you think you can get away with charging people to stay someplace that isn't officially open and with an untrained staff, go ahead."

She grinned. "I can get away with it," she said, and I had no doubt that she would.

I spent the evening walking to each flat and extending the invitation. Everyone was flattered and agreed, except Eliot, who balked and argued with Marie Claude, claiming he would not be able to enjoy himself knowing that his wife was working.

"Eliot, all we have to do is go to bed, wake up, and have breakfast," Marie Claude cajoled. "Then, do it again the next night. What is the problem?"

I left them. I had, at that point, no patience left for Eliot and his continuous objections to everything from the size of the new key card to the length of Marie Claude's skirt.

I headed back to the hotel and climbed the stairs to Bing's loft. We had officially finished painting six days before, and I had not seen much of him since. Claudine, Marie Claude, and I had finished off the last of the rooms, arranging furniture, hanging artwork, and fluffing pillows.

As I climbed the last flight of stairs, I could hear him talking. Did he have company? I didn't want to interrupt, but I had a sudden urge to see him. It was a sudden urge to see who he might have been entertaining in his studio.

"Bing?" I called.

"Come up," he boomed and continued his conversation.

As I reached the top of the stairs, I saw he was sitting at his worktable, phone in one hand, his laptop open. He glanced at me and waved me farther in.

"No, I can't. I told you that won't work. What about the third?" he said into the phone.

I walked in, circled behind him, and sank into one of the large, overstuffed chairs by the window. It was just getting dark, and the brilliant orange of the sunset cast the studio in a warm glow. I leaned my head back against the cushions and closed my eyes. In the almost four months I had been at Hotel Paradis, I felt like I had been living in an ongoing state of exhaustion, either from manual labor or the daylong expeditions into and around Rennes with Bing.

He was talking about a deadline. With his editor? I sometimes forgot that he had a whole other life, a very successful one at that, outside of Hotel Paradis, and that life involved writing and painting, business deals, and scheduled meetings.

I took a deep breath and felt myself slipping into something of a half sleep, when his voice jolted me back.

"Did you just come up here to nap?" he asked, laughing. "Or was there some ulterior motive?"

I shook myself back to wakefulness. "Sorry. It's been a busy kind of a day."

He was sitting across from me, his body stretched out, legs crossed in front of him. "Busy? Let me guess. Flower arranging? Towel folding? No, wait . . . how about lining up the silverware in the kitchen?"

I immediately felt my imaginary hackles rise, and I once again fought the urge to throw something at him for being so glib, condescending, patronizing, chauvinistic . . .

"Actually, Claudine and I carried eleven quilts out into the side alley and hung them to air out, then rearranged the tables in the salon—again—because Stavros wanted the buffet table closer to the kitchen, then went through our checklist in every single room, then—"

He held up both hands in front of him. "Okay. I give up." He lowered his hands and looked sheepish. "I did it again, didn't I?"

"Did what again? Assume that my work here wasn't important? Or stressful? Or tiring?"

"I'm sorry," he said quietly. "Now. What can I do for you?"

"Check into the hotel this Thursday and stay the weekend," I said.

He raised his eyebrows. "Check in? Here? Downstairs?"

I nodded. "Yes. Next Monday, we are officially open for business, but I'd like to have a dry run before the paying guests arrive. There are a million small things that can go wrong. I think I've accounted for all of them, but I need, well, the whole staff needs practice. So, I'd like you to pack a suitcase and arrive at the desk sometime on Thursday. I've created reservations for all our practice guests, and we're going to have a full staff all weekend, just to make sure nothing screws up."

He pursed his lips and nodded. "Yes, I suppose that makes sense. What should I do while I'm a guest here?"

I shrugged. "Do what you'd do if you didn't live upstairs. Come and go. Ask what there is to do and where to eat. Don't make your bed. Leave your towels on the floor. Leave your espresso cup in the garden. Complain about the Wi-Fi. You know, tourist stuff."

He grinned. "You know, I used to be a very demanding guest when I stayed at The Fielding. I once sent back my breakfast eggs for being overcooked."

I grinned back. "That was because Bernie was in the kitchen. He had a thing about raw eggs and was constantly ignoring sunny-side up. He was afraid the raw yolk would kill somebody. It was a bit of a problem for a while."

He chuckled. "That was my order! Sunny-side up!"

"And Marianne comped your breakfast and threw in a free drink."

"Yes." He narrowed his eyes. "The staff there was very well trained."

I shrugged. "Except in the kitchen. They were all prima donnas there. Thank God Stavros is a little more pliable."

"Then you talked him out of bananas foster French toast?"

"You knew about all that?"

He made a face. "He asked me about American breakfasts. If I had known he was planning to use the information for nefarious purposes, I would have lied."

I laughed. "Well, I won't hold it against you." I stood. "I can count on you? To play tourist?"

He stood as well. "You can count on me for anything you need, Lucia. I am at your service."

We were barely a foot apart, and once again, I felt like there were sparks flying in the air between us. I wondered if he felt it, too, or if I was just reacting to a very attractive man on a purely physical level, because I wanted more than anything to take one step closer and put my arms around his neck and draw his face down to mine . . .

"Lucia?" he said, very quietly, and leaned slightly toward me.

I gulped, stumbled back, and cleared my throat. "Good. Thanks."

Then I turned and practically ran down the stairs.

Mimi had a bruise on her cheek, and Cara's lip was doubled in size. I tried not to jump up screaming when I saw them both over Facebook video.

"What happened?" I asked lightly.

Please, I thought, *don't let there have been a car accident.*

And please, if there had been one, don't let it be Joe's fault.

And if it was his fault, oh, please don't let it be because he was drinking.

"Daddy bought us skateboards," Cara practically shouted. "And then he took us to a skateboard park. And we were taking lessons and we were getting really good, but then we both fell."

They were both grinning happily, and the relief felt like a thunderous wave slipping from a peaceful shore. "Skateboards? Really? Aren't you supposed to have padding for skateboards?"

Cara was already pushing her elbow, scraped and raw, at the computer screen. "We had kneepads and elbow pads, but the one on this arm slipped when I fell."

Mimi was nodding impatiently. "And I was right behind her, so I fell, too. There aren't any face pads."

I let out a long and relieved laugh. Now that I could see their actual faces rather than just the bruises, I realized they were both very pleased and proud of themselves. "No, I guess you're right. No face pads. Did it hurt a lot?"

They were both nodding enthusiastically.

"I cried," Cara said.

"Me, too," Mimi said. "Daddy was so scared, he forgot to yell at us."

I nodded, my heart going out to my baby brother, trying to imagine what he must have felt watching the two brightest bits of his life tumble down into a pile of arms and legs and cries of pain.

"He wanted to take us to the hospital, but the teacher at the skate park said we were fine 'cause of the helmets," Cara went on. "And she had Band-Aids and everything, and then we got to skate again."

I was grinning with them now. "Wow. You must have really liked it, then."

They both nodded.

"Daddy said we can go during the summer," Cara said.

I stepped back into caution. "Oh? Don't you go to camp in the summer?"

Mimi shook her head vigorously. "Not this summer. I mean, not sleepaway camp like last year. We're just going to day camp. Gramma's giving it to us for early birthday."

Gramma was Vivian, Sara's mother, who I knew was not really in the kind of financial position to afford even day camp for two. Which meant Joey . . .

"Is Daddy there? Can I talk to him?"

Of course he was there, and the girls blew kisses as they scrambled away, yelling for their daddy. He shuffled into view and repositioned the laptop screen.

"Hey, sis. What's up?" He looked very tired. And old. He had such an old face. As a young man, he had been killer handsome, with thick dark hair and deep, smiling eyes. Now, his hair was buzz-cut short and gray, his eyes half-drooping and sad. There were deep lines around his mouth, drawing down the sides of his face in a perpetual frown.

"Just checking in. The girls sound like they had a blast." I had learned long ago that, sober or not, Joe did not take well to questions or criticisms, and those tough conversations were better when started with a positive note.

He half smiled. "They scared the shit outta me. But they're tough, man. They got right back up and went back at it."

"They get that from you," I said. And it was true. Joe was an alcoholic, and for the rest of his life, he would teeter on the brink of another perilous decision. But he was fearless in his choices, the good and the bad, and had been his entire life.

"Yeah, I guess you're right there. I got plenty of faults, but I've also got plenty of guts. How are you doing over there? Mom and Dad don't say much."

"I'm good. Working hard. It's not what I'd expected, but I think it's going to all work out." I spoke carefully. "The girls say that Vivian is paying for camp?"

He nodded, rubbing his hand across his cheek. "Yeah. I didn't ask, but I have to replace the transmission on the car, and she just kinda offered."

"That was good of her."

He shrugged. "She feels guilty. She wasn't much help around here when Sara was dying."

I took another slow breath. "It was her *daughter*, Joey. Her daughter was dying."

"Yeah." He stared down for a long minute. "Listen, I gotta go."

"Okay. Next week, then, okay?"

He reached to hit a button on the keyboard, and the screen went blank.

Raoul checked in first, a scruffy duffel bag over one shoulder, holding the hand of a very pretty girl who looked much younger than he. She gazed around the lobby in wonder, pointing excitedly at the chandelier, the marble floors, the elegant chairs clustered by the window. Raoul puffed up a bit, and I couldn't blame him. After all, a large part of the hotel's success depended on the physical condition of the property itself, and he was responsible for most of that.

I stood at the end of the mahogany counter, watching Marie Claude. We had a set welcome speech that she had practiced, and as Raoul approached, she gave him a dazzling smile.

"Welcome to Hotel Paradis. Do you have a reservation?"

He winked at his girlfriend. "Yes. As a matter of fact, I do. And I requested a king-size bed?"

The truth was, antique beds were not built for king-size mattresses, but I had convinced Claudine that we needed to improvise, and so we'd found a few sets of twin-size headboards and footboards and had Colin bolt them together.

Marie Claude nodded. "Certainly." She shuffled through the reservations, each printed on a separate sheet of Hotel Paradis stationery. She handed Raoul his reservation.

"Please make sure this information is correct, and may I have your credit card?"

His face fell, and he looked past her at me. I held up a hand.

"We need the practice, Raoul. That's all. We won't charge you, I promise."

He looked relieved, dug into his wallet, and handed Marie Claude the card. She smiled, swiped it, and handed it back.

"Please sign right here," she said, pointed, and handed him the plastic key card.

"We don't have in-house telephones," she began, and dove into her prepared speech. "So, if you would enter this phone number into your cell phone and put us on speed dial, you will be able to reach a member of our staff at any time."

Raoul nodded. "That was a good idea," he said. "Much better than trying to run phone wire through this place."

Marie Claude, undeterred by the interruption, plowed on bravely. "Our salon is open for your relaxation twenty-four hours a day. You may feel free to bring your own wine out onto our patio in the evenings."

Raoul drew back in mock horror. "What? Drink with a ghost? I don't think so."

Marie Claude didn't flinch. "Breakfast is served from six in the morning until eleven."

Raoul laughed. "Six in the morning? Who wants to get up that early? This is a holiday, no? We have better things to do in the early morning."

"Through the salon, we have our library, if you'd like some quiet time or if you need a private space to do some work," she continued. We had decided that *library* was a more resort-friendly word than *office*. "There is a printer for your use and a copy machine. You can also access our garden from there."

Raoul put his arm around his girlfriend and gave her a quick kiss on the cheek. "We need the private space, but not for work."

Marie Claude blushed. "The front gate is open until ten o'clock every evening. After that time, you can use your key card to unlock the gate. It will automatically close behind you."

That little bit of engineering had cost Claudine a pretty penny, I knew.

"If there is anything I can help you with, please feel free to ask," Marie Claude concluded.

"Thank you," the girl said quietly. Then she giggled, and she and Raoul turned and practically ran up the stairs.

Marie Claude turned to me. "Did you know he was a sex maniac?" she asked.

I shook my head and tried not to laugh. "No. He always seemed to be a very reserved young man. You did well. You're going to come across all sorts of people. Keeping a straight face is the hardest part."

She grimaced. "Believe me, I know. Working at the bank? Some very crazy people came in there, let me tell you. And some scary people. Even the managers did not want to deal with them."

"Well, if anyone gives you even the slightest hint of a scary vibe, go back into the office, lock the door, and call me. Or Claudine. One of us will always be here. Understand?"

She nodded and leaned her elbows on the counter, resting her chin on her cupped hands. "I think I will like doing this very much."

I looked at her. "You love this place, don't you?"

She nodded. "My mother knew Claudine and asked her if I could stay here. I was from the north, a very small village outside

Nancy, and I wanted to go to university as far away from home as possible. I came to Rennes, and I stayed here, and it was like . . ." She paused, and her eyes got cloudy. "It was so different from home. Home was not so good sometimes. But here, I could breathe." She gave herself a little shake. "Claudine was very kind. Everyone here welcomed me."

I thought I might as well take the dive. "And you met Philippe."

She straightened abruptly. "I have not seen him in five years. I don't know what to do, Lucy. I don't know how I feel about seeing him again. Eliot is very upset that I will not be going away with him, but what else can I do? I must stay here and work." She took a deep breath. "Eliot is jealous. What should I do?"

I mentally took a step back. "Marie Claude, I am the very last person in the world you should be asking for advice about love. Or any kind of personal relationship. I used to think I had great instincts about people, but I was proven very wrong. At this point in my life, I don't even trust myself with Napoléon there." The white cat, who had been curled up under a potted palm, lifted his head at the sound of his name, yawned, then tucked his head back down.

The young woman sighed. "I hope there will be no drama. I have very much liked my life with Eliot. It has been calm and quiet. It is what I wanted. Philippe wanted to travel the world, go from one place to the next. I wanted a home. Eliot has given me that, and I am very grateful to him. But now, we are fighting. We never fought before."

I knew they'd been fighting. I heard it more and more. But the last thing I wanted was to involve myself in some sort of love triangle between people I barely knew. I took a further step back. "Surely you have a close friend you can talk to?"

She shrugged. "Yes." She looked up and smiled briefly. "Of course."

"I'm going to be in the back," I told her and brushed past her on the way to the office, ignoring the look she gave me.

I sat down at my desk. She was a young woman, troubled, and she needed a bit of help. Why had I felt so trapped? I liked Marie Claude and would have wanted to help her, but something had locked up inside me and pulled away. Why?

I had felt myself relaxing here, had grown comfortable with the people in and around the Hotel Paradis. I thought it meant that I was growing surer of myself, of my ability to relate to and connect with people. After months of feeling a knot of anger and mistrust at my own judgment, I thought I was finally seeing a way through.

Obviously not.

Vera checked in with a brightly colored tote bag over one arm, pulling a midsize suitcase. I knew she had come from work, looking a bit tired, but she knew exactly how a guest at a boutique hotel should behave and gave it her all.

She listened to Marie Claude's speech, nodding in all the right places, and dutifully entered the hotel phone number into her cell. Then she looked past Marie Claude to me.

"You might want to take my number as well. That way, when I do call down, my name and room number will show up on your caller ID. It will be an extra touch if you already know who I am."

I raised an eyebrow. "Great idea, Vera. Thank you. Marie Claude, can you do that?"

The girl nodded.

Vera took her key card. "Will there be someone to help with my suitcase?" she asked.

Marie Claude never blinked. "I will be happy to assist you. Follow me to the elevator, right through here." She went to the front of the desk, grabbed the handle, and went off, Vera trailing behind.

"Is there fresh water in my room?" Vera called over her shoulder.

"There will be," I answered. "We'll bring it up shortly." I sent a quick text to Ines in housekeeping. Both the sisters were on for the weekend even though we would only have a total of fourteen guests, with only ten rooms to be attended to each day. As Marie Claude came down the stairs, Ines appeared from the kitchen, carrying a silver tray with one of Claudine's crystal pitchers on it and two small glasses.

Marie Claude grinned. "I love Vera very much, but I bet she will be our most demanding guest."

"No," said Bing, coming down the stairs right behind her. "*I* will be your most demanding." He was carrying a small bag of beautifully worn black leather and a very distinctive set of initials embossed on the front. "I will want fresh flowers daily, a continuous supply of ice for my whiskey, and a daily massage from a Swede named Bjorn."

I laughed. "I think you are mistaking exactly what kind of hotel this really is."

"What?" he said, dropping his bag with a flourish and winking at Marie Claude. "This is *not* the kind of hotel that allows Swedish massages?"

Marie kept a professional air, although I could see her shoulders trembling with laughter. "Your name, sir?"

"David Graham Bingham, artist and illustrator extraordinaire. I believe I reserved a room overlooking your famous haunted patio?"

Marie Claude nodded. "Yes, indeed you did. If you could just verify the information here and sign at the bottom."

"And when," Bing asked, signing with a flourish, "can I expect your ghost to make an appearance?"

"Between midnight and three in the morning," Marie Claude answered promptly. "Unless otherwise provoked." She then went into her prepared welcoming speech, taking Bing's phone number and entering it into the hotel's cell phone, not once cracking a smile.

She finally took a deep breath. "And if there's anything else you need, please let one of our staff know."

Bing grinned at her, then switched his eyes to me. "Excellent customer service you have here, Lucia."

I braced for the dig, but instead, he bowed briefly.

"Kudos to you." Then he picked his bag back up and headed to the stairs, whistling.

Chapter Twelve

The first official guests of Hotel Paradis were a couple from Paris, who, after checking in, informed us that although they had only reserved for three days, if they had found Rennes worthy, they would, of course, extend their stay. Marie Claude did not let on that we had vacant rooms going through to the whole of the next week. Instead, she frowned at the computer, made a few discreet noises as she clicked, then assured the couple that, yes, we could squeeze them in if necessary.

Claudine, who had been lurking in the lobby, pretending to be totally disinterested in the process, practically threw kisses at Marie Claude after the couple left the lobby. I grinned at Claudine. Our girl knew her stuff.

The next check-ins were three women from Germany, traveling together but each in their own room. They made appropriate noises of awe and delight, seemed appreciative of Marie Claude speaking German, and chattered happily up the stairs, waving the street guide to Rennes in their fluttering hands.

Then I got a text from Julia.

On my way. Your driver is delightful, and the car has a certain vintage charm. Can't wait to see you.

Wait. Georges delightful? And Marcel had . . . charm?

I ran out into the courtyard. Could it be that she had gotten into the wrong vehicle and was being brought from the train station in a random Uber?

But no. It was indeed Marcel who finally turned into the courtyard, pulling up directly in front of the doors. I reached down to open the door for Julia, and she floated out in a cloud of pale linen and Chanel No. 5.

I hugged her for too long, but she hugged me back, rubbing her palms along my shoulders until I finally stepped back, blinking away tears.

"Oh, Julia, it is so good to see you," I gushed.

She smiled. Julia never gushed. "Likewise. Oh, Lucy, you look just marvelous. You really do. Your hair is so long, but it suits you. And you look happy!" She turned as Georges went by, carrying a Louis Vuitton suitcase in each hand, with a makeup bag slung over his shoulder. "Oh, Georges, that's so kind of you. Thank you so much." She leaned closer as he went through the door. "What a lovely man. How lucky you are to have him. Is all your staff so accommodating?"

I stared after Georges, then leaned down to peek inside Marcel. The back seats were covered in what looked like dark green velvet seat covers. The floor was spotless, and there was the faint scent of lavender instead of the evergreen/cheese/smoke combo of before.

Way to go, Georges.

I straightened, and Julia put her arm through mine, then turned, looking back at the cobblestone courtyard and the black iron arch.

"This is just fabulous. And that building there? The old stable? Why, it's pretty, Lucy. I half expected peeling barnyard-red paint and rusty hinges on the doorways. As soon as I'm settled, you have to show me *your* place."

Georges came back out, and Julia held out a hand, slipping a folded something into his. "I'll be sure to let you know when I can take that tour, Georges. Thanks again."

I narrowed my eyes at Georges as he nodded and got into the front seat.

"Tour?" I asked Julia as he drove away.

"Yes. A tour of the Old City, he said. You know, churches and ramparts, those sorts of things. It sounded very interesting."

She saw the expression on my face and laughed. "Oh, this is not a hotel-sponsored tour? Well, you should come with me, then. I bet you have no idea how many churches there even *are* here in Rennes."

We went into the hotel together.

"You're right there," I told her. "I haven't spent much time sight-seeing. Although I do know certain bars and restaurants that are outstanding."

She leaned against the front counter and pulled her reading glasses out of her bright orange Birkin bag. "And yes, we are going to Paris, so don't argue." She turned to Marie Claude with a dazzling smile. "What, dear? Oh yes, let me see." She quickly read her reservation and signed at the bottom. Marie Claude gave her speech, Julia nodded and murmured, then took her key card.

"What, no strapping young valet to carry my suitcases?"

I shook my head. "No. I'll take them. The lift is right here."

"*Lift?* Really? My, you *are* becoming a native."

Luckily, both of Julia's suitcases were on wheels, and there was just enough room in the elevator for the both of us and the luggage. On the second floor, she stepped out, rounded the corner, then stopped and clapped both hands together in delight.

"Lucy, look at this place! I was expecting something from that castle in Frankenstein. The original one with Boris Karloff, all black and white with shadows and cobwebs."

I laughed, dragging her suitcases down the broad corridor, the sconces gleaming softly, a gallery of portraits hung from an ivory-painted picture rail, scattered console tables and fragile-looking chairs pushed against the walls. She opened her door and stepped in, paused, then clapped again.

"Splendid. Just splendid. And is this your haunted patio?" She crossed the room and threw open the glass doors. "Oh, I'm going to sleep with these windows open every night so I'll be able to hear her when she comes."

I guided her suitcases to the foot of the elaborate bed. This one was a four-poster, with rosewood carvings and intricate hangings.

"And that bed," she said appreciatively. "Too bad Doug couldn't come. That bed is made for some serious sex."

I laughed. "Maybe he can just fly over for the weekend," I joked.

She shook her head. "No. This weekend, we're going to Paris."

I shook my head. "I can't go to Paris," I told her.

She raised an eyebrow. "And why not?"

"This is opening week."

"So? I thought you had staff."

"I do."

"And are they well trained?"

"Yes, of course they are. But—"

"And aren't you supposed to only work so many hours a week? I still can't understand this entire work contract thing they have over here, even though you did explain it to me many times, but I assume your own contract allows you time off. Am I right?"

Yes, she was. My contract required me to work thirty-seven and a half hours every week, although I had pretty much worked 24–7 since arriving.

I thought. "Paris?"

She opened a suitcase and began shaking out clothes, already on hangers, all very chic and expensive. "I actually got us an Airbnb in Le Marais. Just a little two-bedroom place, but it's close to a metro stop, so we can go wherever we want. For Friday and Saturday, because things are closed here on Sundays. What do you think?"

Our dry run of last week went without a hitch. It had been useful for finding overlooked details, and there were no major mishaps. I had all week to watch and see what was happening, and I wasn't scheduled for the weekend, anyway . . .

"I'll tell Claudine," I said.

"Good. Now, let me unpack. And I need a quick bath. Then you can show me around and introduce me to everyone. I feel like I know them already." She gave me a look. "Especially Bing."

I soothed out a tiny bump in the toile quilt. "Bing has a bunch of meetings this week. He has another book coming out."

"I'm sure he would love to join us for a glass of wine. Or dinner?"

"Maybe."

She looked at me shrewdly. "What?"

"Nothing." I shook my head.

I had worked with Bing daily for months, painting, cleaning, arranging furniture. We talked about everything during those times. Or we talked about nothing, just listened to whatever selection of music he had on his phone. We had become, I thought, friends. The attraction I had first felt had faded to an easy familiarity, although I felt a definite tug of something stronger at odd times. But once I had stopped seeing him every day, I found myself looking for him, and that tug was stronger than ever.

But—so what? He had been kind and attentive, but that was all. If there were any tugs going on with him, he certainly didn't let it show. And I still had a strong distrust of my own judgment and was convinced that, at any moment, he would be exposed as a notorious serial killer.

I stood. "Really. Nothing. Come down whenever you're ready. I'll give you the grand tour."

In the first three days of her visit, Julia managed to charm every living creature at the Hotel Paradis: staff, residents, guests, and Napoléon.

She remembered everyone's name and was very careful to ask if she was pronouncing it correctly. That was a trick I had learned after years of observing good versus bad customer service. For her, it was just an innate ability to find interest and worth in everyone she encountered.

She took Georges's tour of Rennes and, upon returning, convinced three other guests who happened to be lounging in the salon to take it as well.

Ines cut open her finger during breakfast, while slicing a melon, and Julia not only staunched the flow of blood with a linen napkin, but she also finished preparing the fruit salad and advised Ines how to get out the bloodstains.

She prevented Karl from doing bodily harm to a guest who began picking unripe eggplant from the garden. Karl, seeing a stranger pillaging his carefully tended crop, blustered up to the guest, arms waving. Julia, who happened to be sitting in the sun chatting with one of the German guests, intervened. She successfully calmed down Karl and solicited a sincere apology from the guest. She then offered Karl a few suggestions on what to do with unripe eggplant, as well as taking him into the library, where they printed out several signs that read *Please do not pick the vegetables* in four different languages.

She came back from one of her jaunts into the Old City with four small pots of live catnip and, with Karl's permission, discreetly tucked them into a few of the large urns that stood in front of the hotel. I don't know how Napoléon knew it was she, but he spent every moment not rubbing against the catnip following her around, wrapping himself around her ankles, and purring loudly.

Bing, after sitting with us on the patio over wine and, of course, cheese, watched her leave to go back to her room with a wry smile.

"You are very lucky to have a friend like her," he muttered.

"I know. Isn't she just the best?"

He raised an eyebrow. "Her husband?"

"Doug? He's a very nice man. He's the owner of a cyber-security firm. Very successful. He works pretty much around the clock most of the year, then takes off a whole month to take her anywhere she wants to go. This year, I believe he's renting a yacht in Tahiti."

He laughed. "They must have a very happy marriage, then."

"Yes," I agreed. "They do. They have two sons, both grown, both a bit of a problem, but they are a very devoted couple."

He finished his wine. "I've found that a bit of distance makes for a much happier relationship."

"Really?"

He nodded. "These people who work together, then go home together . . . How does one appreciate the truly golden moments if you spend all your moments together?"

"You and Claudine seem to get along just fine," I said.

He shrugged. "That is different. We're not in love anymore. We share a son; that is a connection that will stay strong forever. But that's not the kind of relationship I'm talking about." He shifted his body until he was facing me. "I'm talking about two people who are together or finding their way *toward* together. There's a tension that you feel when you're not around each other. And then, when you are together, there's a bit of a rush, an exhilaration. A surprise of joy. And even though the time in each other's company may be perfect, it's the waiting that is really telling. The wanting."

It was getting dark, and I could barely see his face in the faint light coming from inside the hotel. But I could feel him, scant inches away, and as I set my wineglass down, my body moved forward, toward him, so that our knees were touching and my arm brushed against his, and talk about *wanting* . . .

"I never thought of it that way," I said softly, proud of myself for keeping my voice steady even though my heart was racing. "Tony and I were one of those couples who were attached at the hip. For years. I thought that was safety. I thought that was commitment.

And I was fine with it, even though it was all proved false. But you're right. There were no surprises. No . . . joy."

He reached out very gently and stroked my cheek. "I'm so sorry. You deserve joy."

If I turned my head just a fraction, his fingers would be in my hair. If I moved in the other direction, my lips would have grazed the palm of his hand. I could hear words in my head . . . *Do it . . . Do it . . . Kiss his palm, then turn his hand over and gently bite each long and graceful finger, push back the rough linen of his shirt to taste the sweet skin of his strong wrists . . .*

The near-empty plate of cheese clattered suddenly to the ground, sounding loud and harsh as it hit the slate. We both jumped back from each other.

I bent and picked up the plate, unbroken. "Good night," I mumbled, hurrying back into the hotel.

In the kitchen, I placed the plate in the dishwasher and stared out to the salon as Bing walked past.

Damn ghost, I thought. Of all the times to make an appearance, why then?

Claudine didn't even blink when I told her I was going to Paris. "You must go. You've worked like a dog for months with just an occasional afternoon off. We are running smoothly. Go. Enjoy." She busied herself with some paperwork on her desk before adding, "Bing said he wanted to go to Paris. Ask him to go with you. He can help with the trains."

And so it was that the three of us took the first fast train to Paris, coming into Gare du Nord just as the city was waking up. Bing took us into Le Marais on the metro and walked us to the Airbnb that Julia had booked. She had planned for us to leave our luggage there, so we wandered the narrow streets, Bing acting as guide. We took the trolley up to Sacré-Coeur, and there, spread below us, was the whole of Paris.

"Oh," I said softly. "My."

Julia looped her arm through mine. "I know."

"It's glorious," I breathed.

"Yes," Bing said, smiling. "Wait until you meet her close up."

"We only have two days," Julia said. "We're going to avoid all the obvious tourist spots." She had been here several times before with Doug. "We have to see Shakespeare and Company, of course, and the Victor Hugo Museum. And we should take one of the boats down the Seine."

Bing laughed. "Isn't that an obvious tourist thing?"

"Yes. But it's also unforgettable." She looked at him. She had been very careful about curbing her interest all week, but she had decided it was time to get curious. "And what will you be doing? An assignation with an ambassador's wife? Burrowing into the archives at the Louvre? Buying a wine so rare as to be priceless?"

He stared at her for a moment, then threw back his head, laughter echoing out across open air. "Julia, I'm not an international spy. I'm an artist. And I write children's books. I'm meeting with someone about a gallery opening."

She sighed. "Oh. How disappointing." She looked over at him again. "Will you be able to join us for any late-night dinners?"

He shook his head. "Afraid not. And I have to get back to Rennes in the morning for a conference call."

I felt a small bite of disappointment. Of course, being with my best friend in one of the most beautiful cities in the world was nothing short of marvelous, but I had been hoping . . .

Bing said goodbye at Shakespeare and Company, which was fine, because once I walked through its doors, I was completely unaware of anything but the rows and shelves of books before me. There were few things that evoked memories for me more than scent. Tomato and garlic brought back Sunday dinners in my mother's kitchen. Coffee took me to my first job in a hotel, waiting tables for the breakfast crowd at the local Holiday Inn. One whiff of exhaust and I tumbled back to Manhattan, racing across Fifth Avenue, dodging taxicabs and buses. And the smell of old books? My work-study job in the library at Rutgers University, the only non-hotel-related work I'd ever done, going back into the stacks for odd reference books and journals. I'd loved that job: the quiet, the sense of calm, the feeling that so many of life's questions could be answered just by opening a book.

"Remember," Julia murmured after finding me hunched in a corner, a small stack at my feet, "you have to carry all of them across Paris."

I ended up with a copy of *The Wind in the Willows,* in French, and a slim volume of *Leaves of Grass.* We walked along the river, looking at the bookstalls and artists, just talking.

"You seem so much more relaxed," Julia said at last. "And I think you're happy."

I nodded. We had finally settled at a café, wine in small glasses before us. "I feel an incredible sense of relief," I said slowly. "I really didn't know if I could pull this off."

She tut-tutted. "Lucy, you have always been one of the best at what you did. You gave speeches at conferences. You got awards. I never understood how falling in love with the wrong man had anything to do with your ability to do the work."

"Falling in love with the wrong man changed everything," I told her. "How I saw myself. What I valued about myself. I know now, looking back, that I should not have let what happened with Tony overwhelm everything else in my life, but when it was happening . . ." I trailed off. "But I think I am getting better. I mean, that hotel is pretty damn special, isn't it?"

She grinned. "Yes, it is. So, what about Bing?"

I sat back. "What?"

"Bing. That perfectly attractive and charming man who would probably fall at your feet if you gave him even the slightest bit of encouragement."

"First of all," I said, getting my thoughts together, "he's not exactly the type to fall at anyone's feet. And you make it sound like he's the sort I couldn't help but fall for. Believe me, he's not so perfect." I felt myself warming up to my argument. "He tends to question every single thing I do because he thinks he knows better, and you know how I just *love* people who don't think I know what I'm doing. And when he's not hovering around, waiting to criticize, he's wrapped up in his own work, and I don't exchange a word with him for days. And I just—" I stared down at my wine. "Having the hotel be a success has patched up a huge hole in my psyche. But it didn't do anything about restoring my willingness to let people get too close."

She rolled her eyes. "I've been here long enough to see how everyone involved in the hotel thinks you're the next-best thing to sliced bread. These people, all of them, like you, Luce. And I've seen you with them. These are your friends. Or at least, they could be." She tilted her head. "You were never good at that, were you? I mean, in college, you were always in a group of people, but I'm the only one who lasted. Why, do you think?"

I threw her a smile. "After you became my friend, why would I need any more?" Then I sobered. "You're right, though. It was always hard for me to let people into my life. I was always on guard against my family. I think that was part of it. If I couldn't trust *them* to be on my side, well, what could I expect from strangers?"

"And Bing?"

I made a face. "I think he may be trying to work his way in."

"And you don't want him? Well." She waved a hand. "If nothing else, I bet he'd be good in the sack."

Luckily, I'd swallowed my wine, or I would have probably choked on it. "Jules."

"What? Like it hasn't crossed your mind?"

Yes, it had. Every time I felt the heat of his body as he passed, saw the muscles in his forearms flex, caught the twist of his mouth in a smile. Just last night, as he waved and the long curve of his back turned away from me, I felt my insides turn to jelly. "You know I was never like that," I mumbled. "Even in college."

She made a face. "True. I was the one who was into mindless sex. You always held out for *feelings*." She looked around. "Should we just get some supper here? Or head back and get something closer to the apartment?"

I looked at my empty wineglass. "Let's go. We can walk, and maybe something marvelous will just pop into view."

And something did, and we grabbed the last table on the sidewalk of a quiet café. I had sole in delicate wine sauce and fresh peas and baby potatoes that melted in my mouth. I had finally stopped being amazed at how wonderful the food was in France, but this was extraordinary. Then we went back up to the flat and drank more wine and talked and remembered.

The next day, we saw the Musée d'Orsay, and I spent almost an hour gazing at the Renoirs, and I'd give up an hour every day of my life to do it again. We took a leisurely boat ride down the Seine under a striped canopy, sipping wine. I was a perfect tourist, thrilled to see every familiar landmark.

"I love the oldness here." I sighed. "New York is beautiful, but it's all so *new*. There are no ghosts."

"I agree," she said, leaning her head back. "I could easily live here."

I looked at her. "Really? Because I would give you a job in a heartbeat. You have managed to charm the entire staff, not to mention every guest you've come across at the hotel. You're a natural."

She laughed. "Yes, but if I were paid to be charming, I wouldn't last a week."

I reached over and grabbed her hand, giving it a gentle tug. "I'm so glad you're here. And I'm so happy I saw Paris with you."

She was usually not the sentimental type, but I saw real tears in her eyes. "You're one of the best people I know, Lucy. I would do anything for you. You know that. And being here this week has been a real gift."

We got off the boat and walked some more, then went back to Le Marais, got our luggage, and took the train back to Rennes. Georges was waiting for us, and we got back quite late. The hotel was dark, and we were both tired. She went up to her room, and I slipped gratefully into bed. The next morning, Georges was there to take her and all her luggage to the train station, where she would go back to Paris and the airport and then on to New York, and as I gave her one last hug, I felt as though a bit of bedrock that had been shoring me up all during the week had slipped, just a little.

Marie Claude came to stand beside me. "One day," she said softly, "when I am old, I hope I have a friend like that, who remembers me as I was, not just as I am." Her voice shook just a bit, and she seemed suddenly very young and fragile.

"You have plenty of friends, Marie Claude," I told her.

She shrugged. "It is one thing to have a friend who you can go out with and laugh with and drink with. I'm talking about the kind of friend who knows your secrets but loves you anyway."

I looked down at her. "You have secrets, Marie Claude?"

She shrugged. "We all have secrets, Lucy. And if we're lucky, we can share them. Sharing eases the burden." She looked at me, the corners of her mouth drooping. "Eliot and I are not getting along very well right now."

I nodded. "Yes. I know. We all know."

She sighed. "He is worried about Philippe."

"You married *him*."

Her shoulders made a small movement. "But how do I know

what to do or say to reassure him if I don't know myself how I will feel when I see Philippe again? What we had . . . it was unlike anything I had ever felt before. Or since."

On the one hand, my heart went out to her. She was obviously hurting and in need of a shoulder to cry on and maybe some gentle words of wisdom. But I was not the person for her to seek out. "Marie Claude, I am the last person in the world to give advice. I divorced my husband because he finally told me he wanted a real home. I thought my career was more important. For years, I drifted from one place to another, one short-term relationship to another because I didn't want to put in the time or the energy for anything long term. And when I finally did decide that I was ready and thought I had found the perfect person, it all turned out to be a lie." I sighed. "All the things that you say you want in your life are things I never cared about."

She shrugged. "Eliot is leaving for Lyon as planned. He does not even want to hear about maybe going later. He does not want me to be here when Philippe arrives, but he refuses to change his plans. He just wants me to change mine."

"Eliot has always struck me as being very set in his ways."

"Yes. But you would think that if there were a good enough reason, he'd be willing to bend. Just a little."

I scrambled for something, anything to sound reassuring. "Surely he trusts you?"

"Yes," she said faintly, then gave another shrug and walked back into the office.

"We're learning archery," Cara crowed. "Like Robin Hood."

"At camp? Wow, that's exciting, huh?"

Mimi was nodding her head vigorously. "Yes. And to swim. This camp is way cooler."

"I thought you liked sleeping away?" I asked them.

Cara rolled her eyes. "There were bugs," she said. "Everywhere."

"That's because you were in the woods instead of the city," I explained.

She looked at me steadily across thousands of miles. "There were bugs, and they were disgusting."

"Ah."

"And," she continued, "we're swimming in a pool and not a lake, so it's not even dirty."

I would have argued that point with an adult, knowing a little bit about the cleanliness of municipal pools, but chose to stay silent. "But no boats."

Mimi sighed. "No boats. But lots of arts and crafts, and we can bring our skateboards next Wednesday, and they will take us to the skate park."

"That will be fun."

Cara rolled her eyes again. "It's gonna be all boys and then us."

"Don't like boys much?" I teased, just a bit.

Cara looked at me with something akin to pity. "What, exactly, is there to like? They're stupid."

Touché. "Yes. They are. Are PopPop's tomatoes ripe yet?" My father's garden faithfully produced delicious beefsteaks, and the favored sandwich of summer was sliced tomato on white bread with mayonnaise.

"Not yet," Cara told me. "He said eight days." His uncanny ability to accurately predict the ripeness of his crops was something of a marvel.

"I miss those tomatoes," I told them. "Everything in France is really delicious, but nothing beats PopPop's tomatoes."

"We could mail you some," Mimi offered.

"I don't think so, but thanks for the offer. When do you go back to school?"

"Three weeks," Cara said. "Next week is our last week at camp, and then we're staying with Nana and PopPop, then school."

"Are you excited?"

They both shrugged. "It's school," Cara said.

"I love you two."

They beamed. "We love you," they said, together.

The screen went blank. "Love you more," I whispered.

Chapter Thirteen

Marie Claude and I were going over the next week's reservations, assigning rooms, when I heard the front door open. I paused, waiting to hear a guest call out. Silence. Good.

I nodded to Marie Claude. "Okay, are we good, then? This Swedish couple asked for a balcony and a garden view and the ground floor. How do they expect a balcony on the ground floor?"

She flashed a smile. "I thought bank patrons were crazy, but they had nothing on these guests. They want the moon *and* the sun."

"Yes, well, welcome to the hospitality industry," I said.

"Hello?" a voice called.

"I'll go—" I stopped.

Marie Claude turned white as a sheet and rocked back in her chair.

"Are you okay?" I asked, concerned.

She put one hand over her mouth and, with the other, gestured me out of the office.

I hurried to the door, glanced back at her, and went to the front desk.

There was a young man standing there, tall and impossibly handsome. His face was all sharp angles, and his dark hair was swept off his forehead in a way that seemed familiar. He was dressed in jeans and a T-shirt, his body slim and wiry. He had a bulging backpack over one shoulder, and there were two suitcases on the floor beside him.

"Hello," I said, my mind racing. We didn't have any arrivals booked for today and only one room available for part of the week. "Are you looking for a room?"

He grinned. His English was perfect, without a trace of an accent. "You must be Lucy." He stretched his hand over the counter. "I'm Philippe."

Of course he was. As I took his hand, I saw Bing as he must have looked thirty years ago, young and reckless, ready to take on the world.

"Do they know you're here?" I asked. "Claudine didn't say anything."

He dropped his hand and shook his head. "I wanted to surprise them. Unless they're both off to London. Then the surprise would be on me."

"No," I said, grinning. "Your father is in his studio. Claudine is in the garden, I believe. Karl is harvesting zucchini at an alarming rate."

He waggled a finger at me. "Your American is showing," he said with a laugh. "Not zucchini. Courgette."

"Yes." I nodded. "Courgette. By the bushel."

He clapped his hands. "Excellent. That means ratatouille. Not from my mother's kitchen, of course. Unless her cooking has improved?"

I shook my head, laughing now. "Sadly, no." He made a face, and I think I fell just a little in love with this charming, charismatic man.

He picked up his suitcases. "I'll put these away and go and find her. You won't give me away, will you?"

I put my hand over my heart. "Never."

I watched as he made his way across the lobby, disappearing into the corridor behind the staircase.

I let out a slow breath and walked back into the office. Marie Claude sat very still, the color still drained from her cheeks. She looked up at me in the doorway.

"Where is he?"

"He's putting away his luggage. Then he's going into the garden to find Claudine."

She stood up abruptly. "Are we done?"

Technically, this was her shift until seven that evening, but I nodded. "We're good. You're going?"

"Yes. He can't see me."

"Marie Claude," I said gently, "how can you possibly imagine that he's not going to see you? He's going to be here for what, three weeks? You must work. You can't spend the whole time behind the door of your *appart*."

She wrung her hands. "I didn't think I would . . . I mean, I thought . . ." She stared at me, her eyes wide. "What should I do?"

"Go out and say hello to him. Now. Go out to the lobby and wait for him and greet him as though he were just another guest."

"But he's not," she whispered. "Look at me. I feel like I can't even breathe, and that's just after hearing his voice." She gulped. "What about Eliot? He can't see me like this. He will be crazy. He is already so jealous and angry."

"Marie Claude," I said as I walked over to her. "I told you. Don't ask me for advice here. I am the last one to tell you what to do about love. I'm a failure at relationships."

"But who else is there? I can't talk to Claudine. This is her son." She covered her face with her hands. "Everyone I know, they were glad he left. They all told me we would have been so unhappy. No one will understand what just happened now."

I crouched in front of her. "What do you mean? What just happened?"

Her eyes filled with tears. "I heard his voice and I wanted to run to him. To throw my arms around him and tell him how much I missed him. How much I love him."

"Marie Claude," I said, shocked. "What?"

"I can't help it, Lucy. I am overwhelmed. The feeling just came over me like . . . like . . . a burst of wind. I couldn't stop it if I tried."

I sat across from her as I watched her. Tears were streaming down her face. "What should I do?" she whispered again.

My heart lurched. "Oh, honey, I'm so sorry. But I have no idea what you should do."

And that was the truth. I'd often, in the past two years, wondered how I would feel if I suddenly saw Tony again. I had loved him so fiercely. Would I be able to forget how much he'd hurt me? The anguish he had caused me and the many people I felt responsible for? Or would the mere sound of his voice send me right back to a place Marie Claude now occupied, at the mercy of an ungovernable heart?

I grabbed both her hands and squeezed. "Look at me," I said quietly.

She took a deep breath and looked into my eyes.

"Now. You're going to breathe in very slowly."

She nodded and took a long, shaky breath.

"Again," I said.

She did.

"Now, you are going to tell me three amazing things about Eliot."

She stared.

Hmm. This was not going as well as I'd hoped. "Okay . . . tell me three reasons you married him."

She nodded. "He had a good job. His family wasn't around to bother us. And he liked living in Rennes."

Wow. This was not going well at *all*. "Now, tell me three things he does that make you happy."

She chewed her lip. "Ah, um." She scrunched up her forehead, thinking hard. "He is a good cook."

I wasn't going to give up just yet. "Go on."

Her face crumpled. "Philippe made me laugh. He believed in all my dreams. He would dance with me in the middle of the room, singing to me. He would put a flower on my bed in the middle of the day. He—"

"Marie Claude, stop." I squeezed her hands. "You chose Eliot. He's your husband now."

She jerked her hands away. "And I have just been reminded of what a stupid choice I made." She lurched out of her chair and ran. I dropped my head and heard the front door slam shut.

I'd *told* her I wasn't any good at this.

I knew that Marie Claude was scheduled the next morning. I woke early, puttered around until a decent hour, then made my way over to the hotel, pretending that I was just doing a normal walk-through rather than satisfying an intense curiosity to see the two of them together.

Claudine usually sat in the salon from eight-ish until the last of the guests had finished their breakfast. She chatted to those who motioned her over, cleared empty tables of their white cups and saucers, made sure there were enough croissants. This morning, however, she was sitting apart from the guests, Philippe across from her, Bing lounging at his son's side. They were all laughing together at something Philippe was saying. Seeing him with Bing, I saw how much alike they were, not only in looks but in mannerisms as well. Philippe had the same way of leaning in when explaining something; he had the same tilt of the head, flash of smile. I got myself a cup of espresso and was standing with one of our American guests, when Marie Claude suddenly appeared in the doorway.

Looking white but determined. I could see her swallow hard and square her shoulders as she approached the three of them at the far end of the room.

"Claudine," she said, somewhat loudly. "I just heard from the council about the new meeting date. Next Thursday. You said you wanted to know right away." Then, with a slow turn of her head, she looked down. "Hello, Philippe. You're looking well."

He was staring ahead, out into the sunlit patio, and at the sound of her voice did not move. Then he pushed his chair back so that he could better look up at her. "And you, Marie Claude, are as beautiful as ever. I've missed you."

I wanted to march over and smack him upside the head. *Wrong, Philippe. You're supposed to just smile in acknowledgment.* Maybe comment on how it had been a long time. How about congratulating her on her marriage to Eliot? Anything but telling her she was beautiful. Anything but saying he missed her. What the hell was wrong with him?

There was something shimmering in the air between them. She suddenly relaxed, and a smile broke across her face that was warm and lovely and only for him. He did not stand but shifted his body just enough to allow her space in his world, at the same time shutting the rest of us out. His face was bright as he spoke to her, and I could not hear the words, but saw the look that went between Bing and Claudine. Then Marie Claude laughed, a clear, silvery sound I had not heard before.

And then it struck me. He had no interest in trying to make her comfortable. He didn't want her to feel he was not a threat. Because he was. I suddenly felt very sorry for Eliot, because I saw, in real time, what the two of them were to each other. Eliot had every reason in the world to be jealous.

Simone, coming beside me with a basket of fresh berries, leaned toward me. "Poor Eliot," she whispered. "He doesn't stand a chance."

And standing there, watching Marie Claude and Philippe weave together a web of what seemed like spun joy, I had to agree.

Eliot left for Lyon. I heard him slamming the door early one morning, muttering as he passed by my window. I wanted to jump out of bed and follow him out, urging him to stay. I wanted to remind him that his wife was feeling a bit off-center and that his staying with her would show love and support. I wanted to remind him that of all the men she could have chosen, she had married him.

What I really wanted to tell him was that he was a stubborn, arrogant fool to leave his wife with a charming, handsome man who was still in love with her, especially since he'd been acting like a complete bear for weeks.

I just stood by the window as he trundled past, thinking that there were two sides to every story, and maybe I didn't fully understand his. Maybe I never would. But it was not my job. That was Marie Claude's job.

I was burning with curiosity, so I waited until Philippe and Claudine were settled in for breakfast before slipping up the attic stairs to Bing's studio.

"Hello?" I called up.

"Come," he answered.

He emerged from the bathroom as I walked up, dressed in linen drawstring trousers and nothing else. His chest was broad and covered by a mat of gray hair, and his skin was almost golden. I could see the ripple of muscle across his shoulders as he scrubbed his hair with a towel.

"Lucia? Everything okay?" he asked.

I let out a slow breath. *Everything is fine,* I wanted to tell him. Just perfect. *Can I just sit here for a bit? Look at your naked torso? Imagine those strong hands entangled in something more interesting than a towel?*

"Lucia?"

"Morning. I'm sorry, I didn't mean to disturb you."

He waved a hand. "No, it's fine. Just let me put on a shirt."

Really? Do you have to?

He narrowed his eyes. "Excuse me?"

Oh my God. Had I said that out loud? "I mean, you don't have to. I've seen naked men before. Well, not that *you're* naked, but . . . Never mind."

He grinned. "I'll be right back."

He disappeared behind a large screen on the other side of his bed. *How French,* I thought. That's where I would go, to peel off one article of clothing at a time, flipping them up in the air and over the screen until there was a small pile of clothes on the floor, and then I'd step out in all my shining glory . . .

"Lucia?"

I cleared my throat. "Eliot left this morning," I blurted.

Bing made a face. "I tried to tell him that was not such a good idea," he muttered. "I like Eliot. He is a decent man. I think he took advantage of Marie Claude. When he met her, she was still in a bad place because of Philippe, and I think Eliot saw an opening he wouldn't have had otherwise. Not that I blame him. She is a delight, that girl. Any man would be lucky to have her. But once they married, he became very complacent. And that was a dangerous thing to do. Women, even the most independent women, need to be shown they are loved. Valued." He looked at me. "Letting a woman know how important she is to a man is a most valuable weapon."

"You make it sound like love is a war," I said lightly.

He crossed to me and stood close. "Not a war. I prefer to think of it as . . . a constant engagement."

"Oh?"

He reached out and brushed a stray curl from my cheek, his fingers scorching my skin. "Falling in love with a person, *being* in love with a person, is not passive. It is work. It takes time and energy."

His hand drew back, and he leaned forward so that our eyes were perfectly level. "Especially if one of the parties needs a bit more convincing than the other."

"And how do you know?" I whispered. "That one party needs more convincing?"

"Usually," he said, a smile playing across his lips, "I can tell by how fast they run in the opposite direction every time they see me coming."

I had been leaning forward, I could feel myself being drawn closer and closer, to the clean scent of his skin, the damp curl of his hair around his ears, the crinkle around his eyes. I wanted to slip my arms around his neck, feel the cool damp in my fingers as my hands crept through his hair. I wanted to know how those lips would taste, if they would be soft against my own. He lifted a hand, and I felt him lightly touch the curve of my waist, and I took an abrupt step back.

No.

No.

I cleared my throat. "I need to go to work."

"Of course," he said softly, still smiling.

I turned and carefully made my way down the steps. I was proud of myself for not running.

Henry Spicutto was something of a legend in the travel business. He started giving small, personal tours of his hometown in Italy, then moved into larger groups in all of Italy, and finally became king of the European bus tour, catering mainly to wealthy senior married couples who didn't mind walking around when they were sightseeing, but didn't want to worry about finding the next meal. When he retired, he turned over the bulk of his business to his sons but kept his thumb in the pie by going back to small, intimate tours, personal and expensive. I'd met him on several occasions while at The Fielding, as he was very active in several hospitality groups. We liked each other. And after the scandal broke, he was one of the few industry people who reached out to me right away, offering support. He'd sent me flowers on the day it was announced that the FBI was dropping its case against me.

He was a very sweet old man and one of the few professional contacts I hadn't purged from my phone. So, when his number came up as calling in, I was surprised and delighted.

"Henry? Hello! Oh, it's so good to hear from you!"

"Lucy, honey, I should have called you sooner, but, you know . . ." I could picture him shrugging, a short, wiry man in his seventies, with a halo of gray hair and twinkling dark eyes.

"Yes, I do know. Life. Gets in the way, doesn't it?"

He chuckled. "Yes. It does, but it goes on, and that's why I'm calling. I have a trip in four weeks. Not big. Fifteen couples. We were going to do Paris and vineyards, but this group, they keep telling me they don't want to walk outside in the sun and dirt just to see a bunch of grapevines. So, I thought maybe we'd do Brittany instead. Rennes, Dinan, Saint-Malo, the whole English Channel thing. What do you think?"

"I think that's great," I said. Then, jokingly, "Do you need a few rooms?"

"Why do you think I called?" he asked. "I've been keeping tabs, you know? Your place looks pretty good. So, can you do fifteen doubles for eight days? We'd come in on a bus, of course, and maybe do a few overnights, but we'd use the Hotel Paradis for a home base. What do you think?"

I'd been at the front desk but hurried to the back office and sat behind my computer. "When?"

"Arriving September 3. Departing the eleventh."

We had the rooms. Of course we did. September marked the end of vacation season in Europe, and on the last day of August, we went from a full house to almost empty.

"Our elevator is tiny and ancient," I told him.

"My guys are spry, and they can use the exercise. Can we all be together?"

"You can have the whole second floor," I told him. "And we can put tables and chairs in the hallway so your clients can sit and talk together. We only do breakfast."

"Yeah. I know. Your website is very nice."

I felt a glow. "Thanks, Henry."

"How are you liking it over there? Must be very different."

"You have no idea."

"Are you right there? At the desk, I mean. These folks don't speak French."

"I'm everywhere, Henry, and if I'm not around, I will make sure Marie Claude is available. She speaks excellent English."

"Good."

"So, to confirm, we have fifteen double rooms. Email me the names. We will comp another room for you. And David?"

David Garcia had been Henry's business partner and companion for as long as I'd known him. Twenty years younger than Henry, he was a charming dynamo of a man whose main talent was tempering Henry's enthusiasm with common sense.

"Of course."

"Perfect. How would you feel about a barbecue buffet one evening for your guests?" I had been stalling Stavros all summer, but with a tour, it was the perfect chance to get a set number of diners in one place at one time.

"Barbecue as prepared by a French chef? That sounds just great, Lucy. Great."

I wasn't sure if Stavros was a chef, but in the months I'd been eating his food, I'd never had a bad meal. That pretty much went for every place I ate in Rennes, but Stavros, I thought, had a certain touch. "Okay, then. That gives you the entire second floor. Some of these rooms have balconies, some don't. Is that an issue?"

"Nah, they're pretty chill about that. But I'll take a balcony."

I smiled. Henry always treated himself very well. "I really appreciate this, Henry. September was going to be a slow month for us." And October. And November.

"I'll talk to some people. Let them know there's a classy, American-friendly hotel with good rates and a central location."

"That would be very generous of you, Henry."

He was quiet for a moment. "I knew Tony a long time."

"Yes. I know you did."

"You didn't deserve any of the bullcrap."

"No, I don't think I did. Thank you for supporting me, Henry. You did from the very beginning." I felt my throat start to close up, and unexpected tears filled my eyes.

"I don't know why everyone believed him instead of you. You were the one left behind. He was the one who ran." That had been my argument as well. If I had been a partner in crime, wouldn't I have disappeared as well? But the FBI had dug in their heels.

"Yes. Well."

He was silent again. "I gotta go, Lucy. I'll give a few folks a call and see if we can send some business your way."

"Thanks again, Henry."

I hung up and stared at the computer screen. We had one more booking for the week that Henry would arrive and three bookings for the following week. Thanks to Henry, we would maybe make payroll for the month.

I got up to find Claudine and give her the good news. She lit up when I told her.

"This group, you know the owner?"

I nodded. "He does a small, very personalized tour. Usually only ten or fifteen couples, which is perfect for us. You know we couldn't accommodate larger groups."

"But he could send more groups our way?"

"Yes, but we talked about this, Claudine. We don't have the rooms for larger groups."

She tapped her fingers against the tabletop. "I know that attic rooms are out, but where else could we expand?"

I stared. "Claudine, it's going to be a very slow fall and winter. There won't be much money for anything as extravagant as expanding. And where would we go?"

She shrugged. "We could do something with the other stable block. I mean, we don't need as much storage anymore, and we have room in the cellar." She wrinkled her brow, thinking. "We'd need to install bathrooms, of course."

"And heat. We could replace all the existing wooden doors with *portes-fenêtres*," I said, my mind kicking into high gear. "Maybe create private patios in front of each unit with planters. A table and some chairs, right in the courtyard? We could get in the ten more units we'd need. It's a lot of space there."

Claudine grinned. "Yes. I would be happy to sacrifice Karl's toolshed for ten more units."

"But money, Claudine."

She made a vague gesture. "Maybe I can find another investor somewhere," she said.

I left, thinking that if anyone could materialize a source of money out of thin air, it was Claudine.

Philippe was making his case.

There were flowers left at the desk when Marie Claude was on. Nothing obvious, often just a single bloom wrapped in a piece of ribbon. The flowers were not from Karl's garden, so Philippe had to venture out in the very early morning on the days when Marie Claude arrived at seven. She would pick up the offering and pin it to her lapel, or tuck it behind her ear, fluffing her blue hair around it.

He had breakfast every morning with his mother, and if Claudine was aware of his subtle campaign, she never said anything.

Philippe spent most of his time up in Bing's studio, working, but he would come down at some point in the day just to lean against the counter and talk to Marie Claude. She always lit up when she saw him. He always left her laughing.

I don't think he ever visited her in her *appartement*. At least, I didn't hear anything through the thick walls. In the evenings, when she was not on duty, they would walk together out through the iron gates, returning late. Always laughing.

One morning, when I was at the desk, Philippe came down, his hands smudged with color, the smell of oil paint on his skin.

"Marie Claude isn't on until this evening," I told him.

He nodded. "Yes. I know. I just wanted to say hello. And I was wondering if I could spend a little time with you? My mother has told me you are the one I should be learning from."

I raised an eyebrow, surprised. "Learning what?"

He shrugged. "This business. Apparently, Hotel Paradis is not only up and running but making money. And since I am the sole heir to the family fortune, I should at least know how things work."

"Well, Philippe, I would be happy to show you how things work. But first"—I looked him up and down—"you need to change. Black pants, white shirt. And as pretty as that particular shade of blue is, you can't wear it."

He grinned. "My father is right. You are the consummate professional."

I felt a glow. Bing had said that about me? After spending weeks—no, months—questioning just about everything I did and said? "I'm good at what I do. And I've been doing it for a very long time. So, we can start this morning, once you've showered and changed."

He grinned. God, he was beautiful, and he had his mother's

warmth and charm. He would make an excellent innkeeper, I thought, in the truest, most old-fashioned sense of the word.

A few minutes later, Claudine came out, as she always did, to check reservations.

"We are full?" was always her first question.

"Three empty rooms. But we'll be full by the weekend," I told her. "Philippe is coming down later this morning. He says he wants to learn about the hotel."

She nodded and gave me a grateful smile. "Yes, I think he is coming to terms with his place here. Luckily, Bing has made it clear that you can be a successful artist and be something else. With Philippe, it was always all or nothing."

"He was young," I said.

"Yes. Very young. Being away has done him a world of good."

"And Marie Claude?"

She looked thoughtful. "Marie Claude always had her feet firmly on the ground. Firmly here. I think Philippe sees that 'here' is not a bad place to be."

"But, Claudine," I said, thinking carefully before I spoke, "she is married to another man."

She sighed. "I know. I have grown to love Eliot. He is an honorable young man. But this is my son. He has never stopped loving her. And he will try to win her back." She shrugged. "I cannot tell him not to follow his heart."

"Even if he breaks up her marriage?"

She looked at me. "Things that are whole cannot be broken, Lucy. Only things that are weak or already have cracks. And only Marie Claude can decide what her marriage is worth."

I sighed. "If I believed in true love, I suppose I would find this all very romantic."

She snorted. "You don't believe in true love? Bah. You know you do."

I laughed. "Oh, really? And how do you know?"

"Because when people see true love before them, they react. They move, either toward it or away. They either open themselves up, or they close themselves off." She looked smug. "They may think they are being very cool, and no one can notice, but"—she smiled—"but the world always knows."

"Oh," I said, feeling the heat rise in my cheeks.

"Look," she said suddenly. "Here comes Philippe. Darling, I will leave you to our good Lucy here. She will teach you everything you need to know."

He waggled both eyebrows. "Everything? My, I thought I was just getting a lesson in how to run a hotel."

She laughed delightedly, and I had to join her.

Philippe, in slim black pants and a fitted starched white shirt looked handsome and very efficient. "I am ready for anything," he announced.

Yes, I thought. He probably was.

Eliot returned from Lyon five days sooner than expected. I was in the back office when he suddenly burst in, looking disheveled and a bit angry. "Where is she?" he demanded.

I looked up from my work. "She won't be on until this afternoon. I think she and Vera went into the Old City."

"Why?"

"I have no idea. Shopping?"

"And where is he?" Eliot asked, his eyes darting around the office.

"Where is who?" I asked, refusing to play his game.

"Philippe," he snapped. "Has he left yet?"

I shook my head. "No. And I don't think he is leaving. I think he's going to stay."

Eliot froze, and his eyes narrowed to ugly slits. "Why?"

"Because this is his home?" I suggested. "Because both of his parents are here? Because someday, this hotel will be his?"

He turned and stomped out.

I sought out Claudine. "Eliot is back. Early. You may have to cover a bit of Marie Claude's shift. I don't think it's going to be a very joyful reunion."

She shook her head. "I was afraid of this. Yes, of course I can cover."

As I made my way across the courtyard, I could hear their voices. The doors to their *appartement* were closed, but I could hear the rise and fall of Eliot's deep voice and the faint replies. As I opened the door to my *appart,* Vera popped her head out and motioned me to her door.

"Eliot?" she asked in a hushed voice.

"Yes." I sighed.

She sat on the bench outside her doorway, and I sat beside her.

"She has been very happy the past few weeks," she said.

I nodded. "Yes. I noticed."

"Eliot has been a good husband, but he never made her laugh." She ran her hands through her cropped hair and shook her head, her earrings clinking faintly together. "I, for one, never understood why she married him in the first place. I watched the whole courtship and would have never expected her to say yes."

"He should have stayed," I said. "He should have fought for her."

"And why should a husband 'fight' for his wife to remain faithful?" she asked.

"I don't think she has cheated on him with Philippe," I said slowly.

"I'm quite certain she hasn't," Vera agreed. "Not physically, anyway. But you've seen them together?"

I nodded. "Oh yes."

"And? Do you really think if Eliot had stayed, she would not have fallen again under Philippe's spell?"

"I guess," I said. "I'm angry because Eliot didn't even try. He didn't care enough to stay with her, to remind her every day what their marriage was. To show her how much he loved her. He just ran away."

"Or maybe," Vera said, "he stepped aside so she could make a decision without undue pressure."

I stared at her. "Like, what, giving her permission?"

She gave a look that suggested I go back to the drawing board. "Of course not. But it takes two people to be happy, or unhappy, in a relationship. And I don't think Eliot was ever as happy as he thought he had a right to be."

We sat in the afternoon sun, just enjoying the breeze and the faint sound of traffic.

"Those roses Karl planted are beautiful," she said.

"Yes. I bet next year they will be really something."

"The hotel is doing well, I take it? Lots of folks going in and out."

"Yes, we're doing pretty well. Does it bother you? To have all these strangers walking through?"

She looked thoughtful. "It's not as big a deal as I'd thought it would be. They leave me alone. They're curious, of course. After all, how often do you see people living in an old stable? I sometimes think I could charge the more curious ones a few euros for a peek inside."

I laughed. "Karl was thinking about selling some of his produce to the guests. Everyone here is trying to figure out a side hustle."

"I'm just happy for Claudine. She finally has her hotel and her son, and she deserves all her happiness. She's a very special person. She was lucky to have found you."

I didn't argue, as I might have a few months or even weeks before. Not just anyone could have done what I'd done with Hotel Paradis. I had settled into that truth, and it felt good. This relic had needed a special touch, a different vision, and I had been the one to bring it all together. But I also knew that I, too, had been lucky. I doubted I could have found any other place as healing.

Vera and I watched as Marie Claude hurried out of her *appart*, running across the courtyard and into the hotel, getting to where she belonged. And a few days later, Vera and I watched again as Eliot, grim-faced and silent, stuffed a duffel bag and two large suitcases into the back of Georges's Volvo. Eliot got in beside Georges and didn't even turn to wave as the car slid out of the courtyard and away.

Chapter Fourteen

The bus pulled in later than expected, and it was almost five in the evening before I heard the faint whine of a motor coach in the courtyard. I was in my *appartement,* and Marie Claude had sent me a quick text they were arriving, but I was already on my way to greet them.

Henry came out of the bus first and spread his arms wide when he saw me.

"Lucy! Darlin', you look gorgeous!" he exclaimed as he wrapped me in a bear hug.

His arms felt so good around me, and I felt a quick start of tears that took me by surprise. As he stepped away, I brushed them with the back of my hand, but he saw.

"Oh, Lucy," he said. "Don't. I know how hard it was, but it's all good now, right?"

I nodded and moved aside as David stepped out. He grinned and gave me a quick kiss on the cheek. "So good to see you," he said, then held out a hand as the first of Henry's tourists came off the bus.

They were all older, all well dressed, and seemed genuinely excited to be checking in to an honest-to-god château dating back to the 1700s. They oohed and aahed in the courtyard, pointed to the stable *appartements,* grinned over the cobblestones, and, with Henry's enthusiastic encouragement, told me how much they loved the place before they even got into the lobby.

Henry sure had primed them right.

David and Henry already had the room assignments and were carrying up the luggage from the bus as the guests waited to check in. They all seemed perfectly content to carry their tote bags and duffel bags. I knew that Henry only allowed one suitcase per person, and it had to be small enough to qualify as an airline carry-on, so the suitcases were all parked outside of the rooms by the time everyone was checked in. Claudine swept in and, in halting English, welcomed them all to her family's hotel and wished them all a pleasant stay. There was actual applause when she was done, and as I watched them all start up the grand staircase, I leaned over to Marie Claude.

"These may be the best-behaved guests we've ever had," I murmured to her.

She nodded. "You may be right. I'm starting to appreciate American guests more and more."

"They're awed by the history. France is a very old country. This hotel may be the oldest building some of these people have ever slept in."

She nodded. "Philippe says the same thing about Canada," she said.

"And how are you two getting along?" I asked, trying to sound totally disinterested.

She sighed. "I don't know. I feel very sad about Eliot. I wish he would have stayed. I thought he loved me more than that."

I watched her face. Her eyes were full of tears, but she smiled bravely. "After he left, I thought, *Now there is nothing to stand between Philippe and me. Now, we can be together.* But then, I feel sad again." She took a deep breath. "Love is very confusing sometimes."

I nodded. "You're right there, Marie Claude." I had not seen much of Philippe, or Bing, for that matter. They spent most of the daylight hours on the third floor, only coming down at night to sit in the garden after going into town for dinner. Every morning, Philippe had breakfast with Claudine in the salon, where she had taken to having her espresso and croissant with the guests.

But after a few days, some of the more outgoing members of Henry's tour group took notice of the father and son.

After the very successful Frenchified southern barbecue, Evelyn Butterworth detached herself from her husband and asked if that "rugged older Frenchman" lived at the hotel. Marie Claude had managed to put her off by pretending to not understand the question, sending the determined and obviously not-all-that-happily-married Evelyn after me.

"Lucy, dear," she said, lowering her voice and leaning over the counter. "That older gentleman, with his son? The ones that sit out in that lovely garden of yours every night? Does he live here? I mean, are he and Claudine . . . ?" She raised her eyebrows, giving me a very significant look.

"He has his own suite," I told her. Then I lowered my voice and added, quite suggestively, "As do I."

"Oh." She pulled back, looking disappointed. "Really?"

I nodded. "Really."

"Oh. Well . . ." She sighed and looked back at the stoop-shouldered Mr. Butterworth. "How disappointing."

Talk about jungle drums. The next morning, as they were boarding the bus for a day trip to Saint-Malo, Henry motioned to me.

"Is it true? About you and that delicious artist chap?"

I pulled back and stared. "Chap? You mean Bing? Henry, are you kidding me? Is that your Cary Grant imitation? And where did you hear that?"

He shrugged. "Every tour is the same. As soon as they run out of historical trivia to talk about, they zero in on each other. Or the staff. And Evelyn has already developed quite the reputation."

"For what?" I asked, fascinated.

He raised his eyebrows. "You should have seen her in Paris. With a waiter. Of course, now that I know her husband a bit, I completely understand, but for a woman her age, well, you'd at least expect a certain amount of discretion."

I stared after her, slight and smiling, vaguely pretty with snow-white hair and pale blue eyes. "Oh my."

"She had zeroed in on—what did you say his name was? Bing?—immediately. And she is apparently very disappointed that he's not readily available because of his involvement with you," Henry confided.

"Well, as long as it doesn't affect our Yelp rating," I murmured back, waving to the libidinous senior as she climbed aboard the bus. "But no, we're not involved."

"Well, if I were you, I'd keep the fantasy alive, for his sake. And it will keep Jonathan away," Henry continued.

"Jonathan of the gray goatee?" I asked.

"Yes. Twice he's asked me if you've been known to, I believe the expression he used was, 'shtup the clientele.'"

I drew back. "Really? How old is he, anyway? Seventy? Isn't he a bit old for shtupping?"

Henry grinned. "Men are never too old," he said. "And I've seen the inside of his carry-on. He packed enough Viagra to service every whore in Marseilles."

I thought back. Yes, Jonathan had flirted, but not just with me. Marie Claude mentioned something, as had Simone after yesterday's breakfast, and the maid Ines. "What a dirty old man," I muttered. "Has he never heard of sexual harassment? Doesn't he know he can't do stuff like that anymore?"

Henry laughed. "Men like him think they can do whatever they like. And you can't blame him for trying. You're still quite a looker, you know."

I poked him in the ribs with my elbow. "Henry, don't ever change."

"Not if I can help it, darlin'." He waved his arms. "Let's hurry this up, folks. It's a beautiful morning. We don't want to waste it."

I watched them go with a twinge of envy. I had made the trip to Saint-Malo myself, in late May. There had been a break in the work because Raoul had fallen behind, and I had a day with nothing to do. I had wanted to spend it in bed, napping and reading, but Claudine had mentioned Saint-Malo, an ancient pirate strong-hold, and talked up its high stone fortifications and sandy beach. It was a day trip, quick but lovely, and I walked along the same water that lapped the coast of England, miles and miles across the channel.

I waved as the bus turned out of the courtyard. They would be there for six more days but had an overnight in Nantes planned for the next day, giving us all a bit of a breather. They had been, all in all, a delightful group, patient and easy to please. I knew that some tour groups could be a real horror show, but Hotel Paradis had made it through the summer crush with flying colors.

Claudine was behind the desk as I came back into the lobby.

"Are they gone for the day?" she asked.

I nodded.

"We could use another tour like that one," she said. "We could use several."

"I'll work on it," I told her. "These tours are booked months in advance. No one is going to call us up and reserve for next week. But Henry will get the word out. How about your connections?"

She made a face. "What connections?"

I rolled my eyes. "Gee, Claudine, wasn't that the minister of—wait—*tourism* that sat here a few weeks ago, knocking back hundred-year-old wine and looking smug?"

"Oh. Him." She made a face. "Yes, I suppose I can give him a call."

I glanced around at the empty lobby. "I'm going to run up to Bing's for a second. I'll be right back down."

She shrugged and gave me an unreadable look. "Take all the time you need."

Up in Bing's studio, he was not at his easel but at his laptop, Philippe looking over his shoulder.

"Sorry," I called when I saw them. "I'm interrupting. I'll come back."

Philippe straightened and waved. "No, I'm the one who should be going." He put a hand on his father's shoulder. "I'll see you later."

He went past and down the steps. I watched as Bing closed his laptop.

"I've come to warn you," I said. "Evelyn Butterworth has got you in her sights."

He looked delighted. "Really? And which one is she? That tall one with the improbable red hair?"

I shook my head, smiling. "No."

He managed to look disappointed. "Oh. The gray pixie cut? She looks like there's a bit of life left in her."

I shook my head again. "Nope. White hair. Blue eyes. Her husband is the short, bald gentleman with the stoop."

"Her husband?" He threw back his head and laughed. "Should I be flattered or worried for my life?"

"You're safe for now, I think. I insinuated that you and I were, well, an item?"

He sat back, one arm draped across the back of his chair. "Aren't we?"

I was struck dumb.

He cocked his head. "Well, aren't we? Let's face it, Lucia, even though we tend to circle each other like cats when we're together, there's also a certain attraction. You don't really think I've been trying to improve my behavior just because I've finally recognized the error of my ways, do you?"

"Improve your behavior?" I blurted. "What improvement is that?"

He looked hurt. "You haven't noticed? I have been making a concerted effort to not nitpick and criticize your work."

"Maybe I haven't noticed because you're never around anymore while I'm actually *doing* any work."

He stood. "Well, forgive me if I've stopped painting walls to actually paint something else. This is how I make my living, you know."

"Yes, I know. But I haven't seen any improvement in your behavior. You still think you're always the smartest person in the room."

He took a step closer. "Sometimes I am," he pointed out. "Like right now. I know that you and I have something going on between us. Let's face it, when we're alone in a room together, there are sparks. When are we going to act on them?"

"Sexual attraction does not make us an item."

"Ah, so you admit to the attraction?" He was even closer now, and I swear I could feel the heat of him from a foot away. "What are we going to do about it?"

"Nothing," I snapped. "I'm not going to fall into bed with you just because I think it will feel good."

"I don't blame you. But what about the rest? You know it would not be just about sex."

I did know, and that was what kept me away. Yes, he drove me crazy sometimes, but he also legitimately challenged me, made me think, made me look at the world through a different lens, made me laugh . . .

"I made up the story to Evelyn so she would leave you alone. That's all."

His face softened. "Lucia, aren't you even going to try?" he whispered. He reached out both hands and gently took hold of my arms, pulling me toward him. I felt the rough linen of his shirt as my arms went around him and felt the cool brush of his lips against mine, and a hundred different feelings sprang to life at once, all glowing and shouting, *Yes!*

"I can't," I said hoarsely. "I don't, I can't . . ." I stepped away from him, my face burning with heat and want and determination.

He backed away. "Whenever you're ready," he said quietly.

I walked down the narrow steps with my hand pressed against my lips, as if to hold the coolness there forever. And when Claudine saw me, if she noticed my flaming cheeks or heard the pounding of blood in my chest, she didn't say a word. She just sniffed, handed me the reservations list, and smiled.

"You're right about dear Guillaume," she said. "I will give him a call. I think the minister of tourism for the entire country of France may have a bit of influence. Now that I see we can handle this, I will see what he can do for us."

I was grateful for the distraction. "Did you really doubt that we could take care of a tour group? Claudine, I'm disappointed in your lack of faith."

She grinned. "I always have faith, Lucy. But I am a practical woman. Now, after the past few months, I have seen what we can do. So, my faith is much stronger."

I felt a surge of pride. Yes, we had done a great job throughout the summer. Yes, we could handle a group. We could handle anything.

The only thing I knew for certain I couldn't handle was Bing.

When the call came, I just stared at my phone. I knew the number. It was Darren Whitman, the federal agent who had been in charge of the case against me. He had been a calm, determined man who, even after the government failed to find any evidence of my involvement in the theft of millions of dollars that Tony Fielding had engineered, pointed a finger in my face and whispered, "I know."

He didn't know squat. What could he possibly want now?

I took a breath and steadied my voice. "Agent Whitman. What the hell do you want with me now?"

"Ah. Ms. Gianetti. Still charming as ever, I see. How's France?"

"Fine." Full stop. If he wanted to chat, he'd have to work for it.

"Ms. Gianetti?"

"Still here."

"I have some information you might find interesting."

"Oh?" I had grown to hate the sound of this man's voice, so smooth and sure, even when he had nothing of substance to say. I heard him breathing. Was he waiting for me to say something else? Ask about the weather? Inquire about the kids? Sorry, Agent Whitman. You made the call.

Finally. "We've found Tony Fielding."

The words hit like a physical blow. I'd been leaning against the counter in the lobby of the Hotel Paradis. It was midafternoon here, meaning it was early morning in the States. I put my hand out against the smooth mahogany to steady myself.

"What?"

"We found Fielding. He's been living in a village in Wales. Someone in the local pub recognized him and called the local authorities, who notified us. He's being held and will be extradited in the next few days."

In Wales. A few hours from France. Just across the channel. I cleared my throat and tried to sound like the news meant nothing, hoping he couldn't hear the pounding of my heart across the Atlantic. "That's good," I said, pleased that my voice didn't crack.

"He's made a statement. He has claimed all responsibility for the theft. He swears you were not involved."

"But you knew that already, didn't you? By the complete lack of any evidence against me?"

"It's good to get verification," he said, without a hint of embarrassment in his voice. Or apology. He had dogged me for months, prying into every single facet of my life. I knew I was innocent, but he always made me feel that the one little thing he needed to put me in prison for the rest of my life was just at his fingertips.

"We also have the money," he said.

I blinked, and my mouth went dry. "The money?"

"Yes. He had it stashed in accounts all over the UK, and in Switzerland, but he's given all the necessary information, and we should be able to recover about ninety percent of what he took."

"And you'll give it back?" I asked.

I heard him snort. "Can't wait to get your hands on all that cash?"

I felt a rise of anger that I hadn't experienced since the last time I'd talked to this totally unsympathetic and arrogant man. "That pension fund represented years of savings for hundreds of employees who were counting on that money for their retirement. I'd only been there eight years, but some of those people had started with Tony ten years before that *and* had put the whole of their trust in him. They were devastated by the loss. And the investors? They believed in him. He *made* them believe. It's not just about me, Agent Whitman. It was *never* just about me, despite what you thought."

He was silent.

So was I. I needed to absorb this. Tony, living in a village in Wales. He'd talked about that, of going somewhere away from everything, a quieter, simpler life. A life without having to make countless decisions every day. No television or cell phone, no distractions at all. Where he could just *be*.

I had laughed when he'd described it. He had reveled in the spotlight, loved dropping the names of the rich and famous, took every photo op that came his way. I could never reconcile the man he so obviously was with the man he claimed he wanted to be.

"It will take a judge months to decide who gets how much money and when," Agent Whitman continued. "I just wanted you to know. If you come back to the States, I can probably arrange for you to see him."

"And why would I want to do that?" The words fell out of my mouth without my having to think about them. Whatever my heart may have still held for Tony, my head knew exactly the right thing to say.

"He asked about you. That was one of the first things he wanted, to talk to you. He wanted to ask your forgiveness."

"Well, he'd be wasting his time." I felt my heart start to race. "What he did was unforgivable."

"Oh." For the first time since I'd known him, Whitman sounded surprised. "I just thought, well . . ."

"You really shouldn't do that, Agent Whitman. Think, I mean. Especially when it comes to thinking about what I might know or say or do. Haven't you learned that by now?"

More silence. "Have a good life, Ms. Gianetti."

"You, too, Agent Whitman." I turned off the phone and set it, very gently, down on the smooth wooden counter.

Tony would go to prison, maybe for years, or maybe not. He was a smart, rich, well-known white man. That breed didn't usually spend time behind bars. Not that it mattered to me. Now that the initial shock was over and I readjusted my thinking around the fact that, for the first time in over two years, I knew where Tony was and what he was doing, I felt a calm detachment.

It didn't matter.

He didn't matter. Whatever thread I had been unconsciously clinging to for all those months had snapped, and I had a feeling of sudden and complete freedom. There was nothing left. Nothing holding me back. Now, for the first time, I could see my way toward another path.

I looked around the empty lobby. I could hear Marie Claude back in the office, her nails clicking on the computer. I needed to talk to someone. Anyone. My mind was racing, and I felt so many different emotions all at once: anger, sorrow, relief, sadness, regret . . .

I went upstairs to the attic.

To Bing.

I could hear music as I went up the last flight of stairs. Bluegrass music. A fiddle and a banjo and . . . what was that? A mandolin?

I stood at the foot of the stairs and called up, but with the music, I knew he couldn't hear me, so I climbed to the top of the stairs.

He was working. He stood at the bank of windows, his back to me, his brush flying across a large canvas full of soft pinks and greens. Was he painting from memory? No, I saw a large photograph pinned to the side of the canvas.

I watched him work. He nodded in time to the dancing fiddle. Then he stepped back, tilted his head, and set down his palette. He stepped back even farther, ran his hands through his hair, and nodded.

"Bing?" I called.

He turned sharply, and his eyebrows flew up. "Lucia? Is anything wrong?"

"They found Tony," I blurted.

He fumbled for a remote control and the music stopped. We stared at each other.

"Tell me," he said.

I crossed to the windows. I tried to stop my hands from twisting together. "He was in Wales. He's being extradited. And they found most of the money."

Bing grabbed my clenched fists and led me to one of the over-stuffed chairs. I sat, and he sat on the low table in front of me. "That's all good."

I nodded. "Yes. It is. And he apparently made a statement ex-onerating me."

He still held my hands, and he squeezed them. "That's very good."

I was still nodding. "Yes, I guess it is. I just—" I took a breath. "I don't know what to do with this. It's so much. After all this time. I don't know what I'm supposed to think."

His hands were warm and rough. There was oil paint smeared across one of his forearms, and I stared at the brilliant blue against his skin.

"He wanted me to forgive him," I said quietly.

Bing's eyes were steady. "And? Would you?"

"No. It wasn't just me that he betrayed. There were people who had worked for him for over twenty years. Who had helped him at the very beginning. Who had put all their faith in him. What he did to me was nothing compared to what he did to all of them."

"What he did to them was different," Bing said. "It was money. Sure, it was trust, but it wasn't about love. If he wanted you to for-give him, it was because of love."

"He never loved me," I said. "He never could have done what he did if he loved me."

"People make terrible mistakes all the time with the people they love," Bing insisted.

"Why are you trying to make him a better man than he was?" I asked.

Bing squeezed my hands again. "Because of him, you don't trust yourself anymore. Because you chose to love him, you think you will never be able to make any real decisions about who you let into your life. And I want you to be able to love again."

"Why?" I didn't realize I was holding my breath until he smiled.

"Because I think you could love me."

The room was very quiet. I could hear the faint sound of birds coming in through the open window and the sound of my own pounding heart, but that was all. Bing was still, sitting across from me, smiling gently, still holding my hands.

"You drive me crazy," I finally said.

"I'm sure I do," he conceded. "I can be a terrible pain in the ass at times."

"Why is that?" I was genuinely curious, but also playing for time. Here was something else I didn't know what to do with.

He shrugged. "It's just my nature, I suppose. I grew up in a house where no one wanted to make decisions. If I wanted anything, I had to kind of bully my way forward. Unfortunately, when I became an adult, not many people pushed back." His smile broadened. "I actually enjoy it when you push back."

"So, because I don't take your crap, you think I could love you?"

"No. But I know you're attracted to me. I know I'm attracted to you. I think we get along. We're a good team. We have the same values, and we enjoy each other's company. That's a good beginning, don't you think?"

I nodded. As I looked at him, I felt myself falling forward, into the deep kindness of his eyes, and I wanted more than anything to kiss him. "How can we know for sure?" I whispered.

"We can't know for sure. That's the point. You have to go on faith, and you lost yours."

"So, you want me to believe that loving Tony was the right thing to do because then I can love you?"

"Yes."

"How should we start?" I asked.

"I'll leave that up to you."

I leaned forward then and kissed him, and once our lips touched, it was like a dam burst, and weeks of circling and sparring and glances and glares tumbled together into a wave of wish and want that blocked out everything else. I felt like I was drinking him in, and once I began, I could not get enough.

We stood, our mouths never separating, and I could feel my hands against the smooth cotton of his shirt and then the smoother silk of his skin, and fingers fumbled as clothes dropped away.

Our lips parted only to speak, breathless fragments.

"Are you sure?"

"Don't stop."

"Oh my God."

"Is that good?"

"I have condoms . . . Wait . . ."

"Can I?"

"Should we?"

We somehow made it across the room and fell behind the wall of lace that surrounded the bed.

We were too rushed. I knew as we came together that we should have taken more time. We fumbled and panted like teenagers. What I would have wanted was to explore, experiment, ask more questions. But he must have felt the same way as I did because in the minutes after we were done—much too quickly—he laughed.

"That was not as successful as I would have liked." He rolled over on his side, looked down at me, and laughed again. "I usually don't apologize to women afterward, but . . ."

I snorted. The only satisfaction I felt was a feeling of *finally*. I nodded. "Yeah. I think that we probably could have done this better."

He let out a deep breath. "Thank God it wasn't just me," he said and laughed again. He fell back and reached for my hand, holding it tightly and bringing it to his lips. "I had envisioned a much subtler seduction."

"Oh? Did you really think you'd have to *seduce* me?"

"I wasn't sure. But I had planned on candlelight and soft music. Wine, of course. And possibly peeling grapes."

I giggled. "Peeling grapes? Very old-school, don't you think?"

He rubbed the back of my hand against his lips. "I am actually a very old-school kind of guy. When I proposed to my wife, I got down on one knee. And I sent flowers the day we divorced."

"Good to know. At least I have something now to look forward to."

We lay side by side in silence, and the afternoon sun was almost gone, casting shadows on the bed.

"If I were twenty years younger," he said at last, "I'd reach over, and we'd start all over again, much more slowly. But as it is, would you like to walk? We could get some dinner and exchange our favorite sex horror stories."

"Do you have many?" I asked.

"Not as many as I probably should for a man who's been unattached for most of his adult life. I sometimes think I was too cautious about sex." He rolled over on his side again to look at me. "What about you?"

"I probably have too many," I said with a grimace. "Lots of very attractive men come and go when you work in the hotel industry, and I was single for most of my career."

"How refreshing," he said and kissed me gently. "But no slut-shaming. I promise."

"I would hope not. This is the twenty-first century, after all. And France."

"Yes. And France." He stared down at me, and his mouth began to twitch. Then he started laughing, and I joined him.

It was a very good beginning.

Chapter Fifteen

*P*hilippe was spending his time behind the desk of Hotel Paradis with Marie Claude. I may have been the expert, but once Eliot left, Philippe must have figured that all bets were off and threw himself at the young woman with full force.

I didn't care. Leaving the two of them alone meant that I had more spare time, and that time was spent with Bing.

Had we been twenty years younger, we would have spent most of our time in bed. As it was, we sat and talked, walked the quiet streets in the evenings, laughed a great deal. When we were together, usually in his large attic bed, surrounded by wide windows letting in the evening stars, we were slow and patient, exploring, asking questions and learning all we could about our bodies and what they needed. Like everything else I felt with Bing, it was new and different and totally real.

We had two small tour groups come through, one from Spain and one from Italy. They were enough to get us through a small quiet spell, and then bookings picked up as the fall drew on. The weather was cooler, and older couples checked in—retired folks not dependent on summer shutdowns.

Karl's garden turned dry and golden, and I awoke one morning to see Philippe walking quietly away from Marie Claude's front door. I sighed and drew my robe up around my shoulders and looked back at Bing, snoring peacefully in my bed.

The hotel was suddenly busy. We had several return guests. The business types, who would have normally stayed closer to the city center, checked in more frequently now, praising the quiet and efficient service, grateful to be away from the noise and crowds.

Claudine raised an eyebrow. "I love my old clients," she said. "They have helped spread the word. Now, we need more rooms, Lucy."

I shook my head. "Ever hear of physics, Claudine? You can't create space from nothing. And you can't renovate existing space without money."

She threw me a look. "That last bit? What scientific principle is that?"

"Lucy's law," I said, and she laughed.

On my days off, I no longer looked for something else to do at the hotel. Bing and I would set off, sometimes just walking the old streets of Rennes. We'd take a train on a whim: Saint-Malo, Nantes, Dinan.

"The girls would love this," I told him, watching the boats glide gently down the river. "They love boats. They learned to kayak at camp a few years ago, and they've been fascinated ever since."

"Well, when they come to visit, we will rent a sailboat and take to the open sea."

I stared at him. "You sail?"

He shrugged. "I am a man of many hidden talents."

I laughed. "Yes, that you are."

He waggled his eyebrows at me. "I'm glad to have found such an appreciative audience."

I felt myself slowly slipping into a place of comfort, of safety. I let myself believe, a little bit each day, that this man would not hurt me, that he would, in fact, be there for me anytime I needed him.

And in letting Bing in, I found everyone else slipping through as well. Marie Claude, in a haze of her own, filed for divorce. Since she had not been married in a church, it was a simple civil affair, more paperwork than anything else.

Claudine and I became closer. She had never been one to hold back, but now we were even more relaxed around each other. She knew about Bing and me. Of course she did. And when I asked if she minded, she rolled her eyes.

"Oh, Lucy, I will never get over him. Bing will always be the man who saved my hotel by giving me a son. And he was also the man who saved me from my marriage. But that was long ago. I am happy for you both. Now, maybe it will be my turn?"

"Saved you from your marriage?"

She made a face. "When I first married, I thought every couple was the same. That all men treated women the same way. And then I met Bing, and he treated me completely differently." She settled in her chair. "Every year for my birthday, Hubert would throw an elaborate party, invite all his friends and family, and at the very end, he would present me with a very expensive gift. He would always say the same thing. 'Claudine,' he would say, 'you are worth every penny for putting up with me all year long.' Well, after one year with Bing, I looked at him and said, 'Thank you, but maybe next year, skip the gift and just not be such an asshole.'"

I burst out laughing. "You didn't!"

She shrugged. "Yes, I did. It's funny how you can be going along, perfectly content, thinking that this is what your life is supposed to be, and then suddenly, someone comes around that makes you look in another direction. Suddenly, everything is new. Because of Bing, I knew I would never settle for mundane again."

That was happening to me. I began to look past what I thought I knew as true, and the possibilities were endless.

I was happy. I had every bit of confidence back. The world was suddenly perfect.

Until it wasn't.

Until my father called me, early one morning, to tell me that Joey had been driving drunk, sped headlong into a tree, and had been killed.

I had stepped away from Bing's bed to take the call and now stood, cell phone in hand, staring out the broad expanse of windows into the morning light.

"Lucia?" Bing called, his voice thick with sleep.

"Joey's dead," I croaked. I cleared my throat and said it louder. "Joey is dead."

I heard the bed creak and seconds later felt Bing's arms around me, leading me away from the windows and back to the edge of the bed. He peered into my face, his hands holding mine.

"What happened?" His voice was quiet.

"Car accident."

"His girls?"

I shook my head. "Not in the car."

He exhaled. "Thank God. I will find a flight for you. Newark?"

I shook my head, still trying to process the words I'd just heard, my mother's voice cracked and shrill. "The quickest."

"Of course."

He was watching me, waiting, I knew, for some reaction beside a blank, unfocused stare, but that was what I felt: unmoved, without a single, coherent thought.

Then . . . "I'm their guardian."

"What?"

"The girls. Joey made me their legal guardian after his wife died. They're mine now."

"How lucky," he said softly, "you will be to have them."

I met his eyes and nodded. "Yes. We'll have each other."

"Let me tell Claudine," he said.

I nodded. "Yes."

"And then we'll find a flight. Rennes to Paris to New York."

I nodded again. "Yes."

He still waited, crouched down in front of me, watching my face.

"You can go," I finally said. "I'm not going to cry."

He took a deep breath, stood, and moved away.

No, I was not going to cry.

Not then, anyway.

I arrived at the Newark airport and walked through the endless lines in a daze. I hadn't slept and spent the entire plane ride with my jaw clenched and an ache in my chest to keep from crying. I finally saw, right beside the luggage claim area for my flight, Julia, looking calm and steady in a long black leather trench coat. She crossed the hard tile floor in a heartbeat, sweeping me into her arms. Then I let the tears come.

I managed to pull myself together quickly. "I'm getting tears and snot all over your coat," I muttered.

"Yes, well, I can always get another. Do we have to wait for your suitcase?"

I shook my head.

"Smart girl. I'll get the car." She took out her phone, sent a brief text, then walked through the banks of glass doors and stood in the cold autumn air.

"I spoke to your mother this morning," Julia said, her voice dry. "Sophia sounded fine, but said your dad is not taking this well."

"Dad is a fixer," I said. "He probably can't believe he couldn't fix his son."

"She also said that Frank was taking charge of things." Her arm, high around my shoulders, tightened. "Is he still a douchebag?"

I nodded and sniffed. "Yes. I guess I should be grateful that he's finally stepping up. He ignored Joe and all his problems for years."

"It's easy to be gracious to the dead," Julia said.

A sleek black Mercedes pulled up to the curb, and the trunk popped open as a young man in a dark suit jumped out. He opened the door for us, threw my carry-on into the trunk, and was back and driving the car away from the curb before I had my seat belt fastened. The interior of the car was quiet luxury, and I let my head fall against the seat back.

"Thank you again for picking me up," I said.

She had her phone out, checking something, but she slid it back into her purse. "Don't be silly. I couldn't let you get off a seven-hour flight and then climb into some Uber. Besides, Douglas insisted. You know how much he likes you."

"That's because I'm the only one of your friends who knew you way back when and doesn't hold it against your current status as queen of the roost."

She cracked a smile. "You're right there. You have always kept my secrets." She glanced at me. "Have you talked to the girls?"

"Just for a minute. Mimi just cried. Cara wanted to make sure I was coming." My throat filled up again.

She grabbed both of my hands and tugged at them. I looked at her, and her eyes were big and very serious.

"This is going to be harder than you think, Lucy. You are the one who was named to care for those two, but everyone will second-guess every decision you're going to make."

I took a deep breath. "I know."

"You lost a lot of confidence in yourself. I know that. But seeing you in Rennes, I think you got some of it back. You're going to need to trust your instincts again, Luce. You know what's best. You must believe that. Not just for them but for *you*." She squeezed my hands again. "You're going to have to be that tough-as-nails, take-no-prisoners Lucy that once owned the world. Families are impossible to deal with in the best of circumstances. You have to decide what you want to do and then stand by it, no matter what."

I was nodding. "I know. Mom and Dad are going to want me to stay with them. Like, for the rest of my life."

"And how do you feel about that?"

I closed my eyes and thought about the hotel, the work there, the success I had made from nothing. I thought about Marie Claude and Philippe, sitting on either side of me in one café or another, laughing and planning and asking my advice. I thought about Claudine and the trust she had placed in me with her family's legacy. I saw Karl's face, patiently explaining the different grape varietals. And Bing. Something new caught in my throat. Bing, who had once challenged my every move, but who had become my champion.

"I have another life," I said quietly. "I have a life that I love."

"Then hold to that, Lucy," Julia said. "Don't let anyone make you forget that life and how you feel about right now, at this moment. Promise me?"

I opened my eyes and stared out of the darkened window. The lights of the cars on Route 78 blurred and dimmed. "Mom and Dad have a point. This is what they know. This is what the girls are used to. How can I take them away from their home?"

"Their home was never with your parents. It was never with Joe, either. He moved, what, three times after Sara died? Four times? He went in and out of rehab, leaving them to bounce between grandparents. The last home those girls knew was with both of their parents, and that was years ago."

"This is impossible, Jules," I moaned.

"No. It isn't. It's easy, when you think about it. Mimi and Cara have been waiting for something, or someone, to save them. That's you. They'll go anywhere with you. You know it."

"Joey tried," I said, my voice breaking.

She dropped my hands to put both arms around me. "I know he did, Luce. He was crazy about his daughters. Anyone could see that. Hell, even *I* could see it, and I'm the biggest cynic in the world."

We sat together in the back seat of her quiet car, and I ran through every single scenario in my head. Having Julia right there beside me gave me a certain courage, but I knew that the weight of family was going to come crashing down on me, the years of guilt, the years of unhappiness, the million little pinpricks of hurt.

"You do what's best for you," Julia whispered. "Because if you are having a happy and satisfying life, then Cara and Mimi will have the same. If you feel trapped or unhappy, they will know. And they will blame themselves."

"Thanks," I said wryly. "Something else I hadn't thought of."

She sniffed. "Well, if your best friend can't rain down more smoke and ashes on your worst day, who can?" She looked over. "I will be happy to stay right by your side. For as long as it takes. You know that I have nothing else to do with my life."

"Nonsense," I said. "You have two sons, both of whom need constant supervision, despite their supposed elevation to adulthood. You have a very good job where people rely on you for every little thing. Remember, I've seen you at work. And you have a very loving husband who has all the patience in the world, but really just wants you there to cater to his every whim."

"I suppose when you lay it all out like that, I'm the most talented multitasker in the five boroughs. But I will be happy to remain at your side. No matter what."

The car slowed to a halt. The lights of my parents' neat little house shone through the front windows.

"What, they didn't even leave the front porch light on?" Julia muttered.

I got out of the car and took my small bag from the silent driver. I peered into the car at Julia. "I may send up a flare."

"I'll be ready. I love you, Luce."

"Thank God. I love you, too, Jules."

I shut the car door, squared my shoulders, and walked up the four steps and into my parents' house.

Chapter Sixteen

The service was short and simple. I was surprised at the number of people who had come to pay their respects, but then saw that most of them were from the neighborhood, there for Sophia and Bruno, because no parent should ever have to bury a child. No one came up to say they knew Joe from work, or from a meeting, or from the girls' school. My brother had been a charming, gregarious young man, but alcohol and grief had made him closed and isolated and without friends. His family mourned him. The rest of the world barely blinked.

At the house, surrounded by murmuring neighbors and second cousins, Frank suddenly became the loving brother racked with sorrow, accepting the handshakes and hugs from whoever came within touching distance. I sat with Mimi and Cara, both quiet in their dark blue dresses, looking around with red-rimmed eyes. I finally whispered that they could go back up to their room, the room that had been theirs since the death of their mother, the one room that had remained unchanged for them. They fled silently up the stairs.

My other two nieces, Heather and her younger sister, Brianne, slipped in on either side.

Heather put her arms around me. "This is just awful," she whispered. "What are you going to do?"

I leaned against her. "I have no idea."

"Are you going to Florida with Nana and PopPop?" Brianne asked.

I looked at her. "What?"

Heather glanced around. "Didn't they tell you? They bought a condo in Clearwater. They're moving as soon as they can get a buyer for the house."

I shook my head slowly. "No idea."

Heather rolled her eyes. "I heard Mom saying that you should buy this house so the twins can have some continuity. And you know Mom, she's all about showing her deep concern as long as it doesn't inconvenience her."

I eyed my niece. "Heather, that's not a very nice thing to say about your mother."

Brianne snorted. "Have you *met* our mother?"

I choked back a laugh. "This is all news to me. They already bought a place?"

Heather nodded. "Mom convinced them the best thing to do would be to tell you once it was all a done deal: the closing down in Florida, selling this place. Then when Uncle Joey died, she decided you needed to stay here and care for the girls."

"Oh. I see. And did she have any idea how I was going to live here? Without a job and all?"

Brianne tracked her mother on the other side of the room. "You know Mom isn't about the details."

"And yet, no one has said a word to me about any of this," I said. "How interesting."

Heather sighed. "Daddy didn't think it was such a good idea, but you know."

Yes, I did know. My brother Frank had long ago ceded any and all authority to his wife, Elena, making it easy for him to shuffle off blame or guilt.

Vivian made a brief appearance. She had not been at the funeral parlor for the service, nor at the cemetery. She just appeared in my mother's kitchen, carrying a tray of chocolate chip cookies, saying how sorry she was. She did not ask about her granddaughters. I spoke to her briefly; she was going back to California, she said. To live with her sister.

We did not kiss goodbye.

Then the house was empty. Some unseen and unheard signal had swept through the mourners, and they slipped away in a slow stream of black-clothed good wishes. I stood in the dining room and watched as Elena and Mom cleared half-empty plates off the table.

"Mom?" I asked. "This move to Florida. When exactly were you going to tell me?"

Elena put down a bowl of pasta salad. "Lucy, your mother—"

"You know what, Elena? This is a conversation I'm having with Mom, not you," I said, very quietly. "Why don't you give us some privacy?"

Heather and Brianne had been loading the dishwasher in the kitchen, and at the sound of my words, the faint clatter stopped. Frank, sitting in the living room with Dad, rose slowly. I saw him out of the corner of my eye as he approached.

"You know, Lucy, Elena only—" he began.

"I don't care what Elena only," I said. "Dad," I called, "were you in on this?"

He shuffled in, his face drawn and weary. "Please, Lucy, Elena just—"

"I'm tired of Elena. I want to know why you and Mom didn't tell me you were planning to move. I only spoke with you every week."

Mom glanced at Elena and gave a slight shake of her head. "Lucy, honey," she said, "we didn't want to give you anything else to worry about."

"What was I worried about, Mom? I was successful, doing good work, making money. Where was the worry?"

She tried a different tack. "We didn't want you to think you had to leave France and come all the way over to help us with anything."

"Why would you need my help? You bought a place without my help; you would easily list the house and sell it quickly. The only thing I could possibly help you with was what to get rid of in my old bedroom."

"It doesn't matter now," Dad said quietly. "We haven't listed the house, and Elena thinks you should keep it. Let the girls live some-place that feels like home to them. We would just sell to you. Elena, well, it was her idea, but your mother and I think it could work."

I pulled out a dining room chair and sank into it, resting my elbows of the table, my chin on clenched fists. "Joey died on Tuesday. I flew over the very next day. And now it's Friday. When did Elena tell you this great idea of hers? And why wasn't I in on the conversation? After all, I was right here." I took a deep breath. "I don't have any money saved. How was I going to buy this house? I don't have a job in this country. How was I going to live? Did you even ask the girls what they wanted? Do you think they want to live in this crumbling house, surrounded by old people and narrow streets and crappy schools?" I stared at Elena. "Well?"

She looked uncomfortable. "Joey made you the guardian, but I don't think he thought about what might happen after you left for France. So, it was up to us to figure out what was best for Cara and Mimi."

"No, Elena. It was not up to you. It was *never* up to you. It's up to me." I took a deep breath, my eyes never leaving her face. "You've been leading my brother around by his balls for years now, Elena. You make every decision for him, so I get it. I really do. But I can't imagine why you thought my parents were going to be so easily led. Or me."

I could feel Frank behind me, shuffling his feet. "Don't talk to her that way, Lucy. You have no right to say anything like that."

I stood. "Yes, I do, Frank. Because it's the truth." I looked at my father. "Tell me, Dad. Did you want to move?"

He shrugged. "I'm getting old, honey. I hate the cold. I hate shoveling snow. It made sense. And your mother, well, we have friends down there, from the church. She misses her bingo nights. And her card parties."

I nodded. "That makes sense. Okay, so go to Florida. Be warm, Daddy." I felt a hitch in my throat. "It's just as easy to fly from France to Miami as it is to fly from France to Newark."

"What do you mean, France?" Elena asked. "You wouldn't take the girls all the way to France, would you?"

I sighed. I was so tired. "I need to go upstairs. I'm still feeling a little jet-lagged, and I need to sort things out." I stood and walked away quietly, up the steps, and turned down the hallway toward my old room.

I passed the bedroom that my two brothers had shared as kids. Mimi and Cara were in there, huddled together on one of the twin beds, watching something on a small tablet. I went in and sat at the foot of the bed.

"This was a sad day, girls. How are you doing?"

Cara immediately started to cry and crept across the bed and into my arms. Mimi stared, dry-eyed. "Where are we going to live now?"

"With me," I said, stroking Cara's head. "You know that your aunt Elena wants me to buy this house, so we can all live here. How do you feel about that?"

Cara, her face in the crook of my neck, shook her head. "This is a sad house, Aunt Lucy."

She was right. This was a house that people left as soon as they could and did not return unless something bad happened. Like a young mother slowly dying. Like losing a job and being threatened with prison. Being so blind drunk that days were forgotten, or going back into rehab, or waiting to find another apartment because you were evicted from the last one.

I held Cara for a few more minutes, rocking her gently, until she pulled away and edged back next to her sister. "I'm glad we're going to live with you instead of Aunt Elena," she whispered.

I had to smile. "Me, too. I'll be right next door if you need me, okay? Are you hungry?"

They both shook their heads.

"Okay, then, you just go to sleep when you want to, and I'll see you in the morning. Okay?"

I left them and continued down the hall to my own old room.

I had left my cell phone on the dresser when I left for the service and saw I had three voice messages. The first was from Julia. She had been to the service but had not come back to the house. Her message was brief, just saying she was thinking of me and to call if I needed anything.

The second was from Bing. I wanted to wait until I'd changed and gotten safe and comfortable in bed before calling him back.

The third call was a shocker.

"Hello? Is this Lucy Gianetti? This is Fred Paloma."

I stared at the phone. Fred Paloma was the regional manager for Carlton Enterprises, one of the biggest hotel chains on the East Coast.

"Anyway," he continued, "I heard all about Tony being taken into custody. I heard he got you off the hook. I always believed you were innocent, but, well, you know."

I did know. If there was the tiniest sliver of scandal hanging over my head, I was a pariah.

"So, anyway, we're looking at our Newark airport property and wanting to make a change. A big change. And we think you're the person to do it. I don't know about this crazy time thing—you're in Europe, right? But call me. We could talk."

I stared at the phone.

The Newark airport property? Close to three hundred rooms, I knew.

A big change? That usually meant renovations, new personnel, a change in services.

They thought I was the right person to do it?

I was the perfect person. And what would a job like that pay? So much money . . .

I stared out the window into the growing darkness. Across the highway, I could see the airport, the lights of the towers blinking, and heard the faint roar of a plane's engines as it circled to land.

I shut the phone off and lay down and was asleep in minutes.

"Lucia," Bing said gently. "How did everything go?"

In the morning, the sun was shining, and Frank and Elena were gone. Cara, Mimi, and I took my dad's Subaru to the IHOP, loaded up on pancakes and bacon, then went out to their favorite park. I was huddled on a bench, watching them climb a fantasy structure of turrets and waving flags.

"It was fine," I told him. "Awful. I mean, you know."

"We miss you," he said. "But I know you have a lot to square up over there."

"You know that Joey named me the guardian. For the twins."

There was a long silence. "Yes, and that certainly complicates things," he said at last. "I imagine they would want to stay close to what they know. Your parents. Their other grandmother."

"My parents are moving to Florida," I said. "And Vivian is moving to California. And since I am apparently no longer persona non grata in the hotel world, someone reached out to me about a property."

"There?"

"About half an hour from where I'm sitting right now."

Silence. Then, "I imagine it's a tempting offer?"

"I haven't called back, but it's a huge property. They probably want a soup-to-nuts change: rooms, services, everything."

I could hear him let out a long breath. "Well, I could certainly understand why you'd want to take on a project like that."

I gripped the phone tighter. *Please,* I thought, *give me a reason to say no. Any reason, really, but tell me that you'd miss me. Tell me that you don't want me across a wide ocean. Tell me you want me back in France. If you care even a little bit . . .*

"I suppose I could always move back," he said.

Wait. "What do you mean?"

"To the States. Maybe a place in Connecticut? No, you're in Jersey, so . . . well, are there places in New Jersey with rolling hills? If I did move, I'd need a big barn or something as a studio. I don't think I'd want to be in a city; it would never be the same as living here."

"Bing, what are you talking about?" I asked him, totally confused.

"Well, I don't think I'd want a long-distance relationship. Would you?"

Something swelled inside me, lovely and aching and unfamiliar. "No," I croaked, then louder. "No. You'd leave Rennes? You love it there."

"Something has changed in the past week. I love it a little less. I'd much rather be with you."

"Oh," I breathed.

"What did you think?" he asked, his voice rough. "Let's face it, the sex is nice. But it's not the reason I want to be with you, Lucia. I think I'm falling in love. And I certainly want the chance to find out if it's real. I can't do that if you're all the way over there and I'm here. So, maybe you could find a little bit of countryside?"

"What about Philippe?"

"What about him?"

"He's finally settled into the hotel. He's not traveling all over the world anymore."

"And it's a good thing, because Claudine is already worried that you're not coming back. In fact, I've had to convince her not to call you every day since you left. At least with him there, she won't get too crazy."

"If you leave, she will."

He laughed. "Yes. That may very well be true. But she'd get over it." He was quiet. "I don't think I'd get over you."

I stared at the twins, running and shouting now, chasing each other around the swings. "I haven't even talked to him. Fred. About the job."

"Well, let me know what he says. I know what it would mean to you, to be back in the high life, so to speak. Call me as soon as you've said yes. I have a lot of packing up to do."

"Okay. I will. As soon as I decide."

He laughed. "What do you mean, decide? They'd be idiots not to offer it to you. And you'd be perfect for the job. Goodbye, Lucia."

"Goodbye," I said faintly and hung up.

Bing thought he was in love with me.

I watched the girls, on the swings now.

He thought I'd be perfect for the job.

He was right, of course. Know-it-all. If they did offer me a project like that, I could grab it in my teeth and run with it.

Which meant long days and nights in an office somewhere. Would I have a suite on-site? So, Cara and Mimi would be living in a hotel? In the middle of the Newark airport? Were there swings in the Newark airport?

I remembered Julia, in the back seat of her car, driving from the airport. She said if I had a happy life, then the girls would, too. Would I have a happy life, neck deep in turning around a hotel that would require most of my time and energy for years? Maybe once, yes. But I was older now, and I had started to realize that time and energy could be spent on other things. Long walks down quiet streets. Train rides to a pirate hideaway. Meals lasting into the night with good food and laughter. Working every day surrounded by people who valued me. Looked up to me for guidance.

Loved me.

I called Claudine. "I have a question," I said.

"The answer is yes," she said.

I choked on a laugh. "You don't even know what it is."

"If it is any condition you have that will mean you'll be coming back, the answer is yes. We need you back."

"No, you don't."

"All right. I want you back."

I took a breath. "I'm the legal guardian of my two nieces. If I come back, they'd have to come with me. Live with me. At the hotel. I know that you haven't exactly embraced the idea of kids at your hotel. Would that be a problem?"

"I don't like the idea of *strange* kids at my hotel," she said. There was a long silence, then a sweet, clear laugh. "But twin girls? I'd finally have little *girls*? That I could dress up and have tea with? That I could take to dancing lessons?"

I watched as Cara hung, upside down, from her knees. "To be honest, these two like skateboards and archery."

"I can work with that." She was quiet. "You belong here now, Lucy. So, of course you may bring those little angels. We will all welcome them."

I hung up the phone, feeling so many things at once I was sure I was going to burst wide open. I waved my arms and yelled. The girls came running over, panting like little puppies, sweaty and red-faced.

I wrapped my arms around the both of them and held them close. "How would you two feel about moving to France?"

Chapter Seventeen

The girls slept their way through the entire flight, for which I was grateful. But I also knew they would wake up hungry, grumpy, and, in Mimi's case, complaining about everything. They were not morning people, these two, and even though Paris time was past noon, their morning unpleasantness would not be avoided. I spent the last hour of the flight running over various scenarios as to how I was going to get them some food, wrangle the luggage, make it down to the metro, then out into the vast, loud, confusing train station while trying to find the fast train to Rennes, then probably more food . . .

When we landed, I felt hopelessly overwhelmed and just wanted to cry.

We trundled off the plane and through endless corridors, past gates and barriers, asking and answering questions, until I finally had them going up the escalator to the luggage claim. *One hurdle down,* I thought, *fifty more to go.* And then I saw, leaning against a smooth tiled pillar, arms folded across his chest—

"Bing," I whispered.

He straightened when he saw us, and he readjusted the long

strap of his satchel and began to walk toward us. I had slowed, and felt Cara's impatient tug on my hand, then she followed my gaze.

"Who is *that*?" she asked.

He stopped in front of us and squatted down. "I know one of you is Cara, and one of you is Mimi," he said slowly. "But how in the world can I tell which one of you is which?"

Mimi stepped up to the challenge. "I'm almost an inch taller, and I have pierced ears. Cara didn't want pierced ears because she was afraid they would hurt."

"Ah." Bing said, nodding. "Well, that's a very easy distinction to make, thank you very much. And did they? Hurt?"

She shook her head vigorously. "No. Well, at first, but not anymore. I'm Mimi."

He held out a hand, and she shook it. "I'm Bing."

Cara gasped. "You're Bing Davis? The writer? Boodily and Flap?"

He held out his hand to her, and she grabbed it tightly. "The same. I hear you two young ladies have read my books?"

Cara gushed, her cranky whine gone. "We have all of them. Well, we did. We had to leave all our books home because they were too heavy, but we love your books."

He straightened. "Glad to hear it. It's always a pleasure to meet a fan. And as for books, well, I have extra copies lying around. You can read them whenever you like. How does that sound?"

Mimi glared up at me accusingly. "You told us you *knew* him," she said. "You didn't tell us you were *friends*."

I met his eyes. All I could do was nod. He reached into his satchel and handed Cara a brown bag. "I have some very special doughnuts in there for you, just in case you're hungry. You can sit on that bench right over there while I say hello to your aunt."

Mimi grabbed the bag, and they scampered off. He watched them as they sat, then he turned to me and opened his arms.

I fell into them as falling into a quiet, safe harbor. My arms went around him and I buried my face into the crook of his shoulder, and he just held me, his hands soft in my hair, his lips against my cheek.

"Thank you," I managed at last. "Thank you. I have been dreading this, trying to get the luggage and then the metro and the train . . ." My voice caught, and I gulped. "I was so afraid I'd just lose them in the depths of Paris, and I'd never see them again."

He brushed a few tears away with a rough thumb. "Nonsense. In fact, the only reason I'm here at all is because I had to be in Paris yesterday and thought I'd meet you, you know, just in case. You'd have figured it all out, Lucia. Don't you always?"

I fought a smile. "And what has suddenly convinced you I was capable of handling any situation more complicated than making toast?"

He tilted his head at me. "And when have you even considered thanking me for anything other than a decent roll in the hay?"

I laughed out loud then, and the girls looked up from their serious eating to smile at me.

We collected luggage. The girls were fascinated by the metro.

"So clean," Mimi whispered in awe. At the train station, Bing wrangled more food, this time sandwiches and french fries.

"Better than McDonald's," Cara declared. While we waited, Bing reached into his satchel and pulled out a tablet and began showing the girls the new sketches for Marnie and Pug.

"They're a secret," he said in a hushed voice. "You must swear never to tell anyone you saw them."

The girls crossed their heart repeatedly, obviously thrilled to be included in such a vast conspiracy of silence.

They sat together on the train, quieter now, and Bing held my hand while I told him what had happened. He didn't say anything, just watched me and nodded a few times. And when I was done, he let out a long, slow breath.

"You are a person of courage, Lucia. Their father made the right choice. And so did you. Bringing them here is best for us all. And can I tell you, the entire hotel is waiting for them."

I exhaled slowly. "It's going to be tough going for a while. I don't know what the sleeping arrangements are going to be. We're going to be awfully crowded."

He chuckled. "Not really. Philippe and Marie Claude decided to take over the extra rooms in the attic. And since that meant the *appartement* next to yours was empty, Raoul broke through the wall. So now you have—how can I put this? A duplex? The girls have their own space, with a bedroom and bath and sitting room, and you can pull out your kitchen, if you'd like, and put a bit of an office space back there. Marie Claude and Eliot had a very nice kitchen fitted in just last year. We already have two beds, and a long table and some chairs, and a dresser for each of the girls—wait, please, you're not crying *again,* are you?"

Georges met us at the station, frowned at all the luggage, and began to grumble, but Cara took one peek inside the Volvo and turned to him with an excited grin.

"Your car is beautiful," she said.

Georges froze, then a smile crept over his face. "His name," he told her slowly, "is Marcel."

Mimi nodded her approval. "That is a great name for a car," she said. "My daddy's car was named Leon."

"That is also a great name," Georges said. "But not as good as Marcel."

He drove quickly, not the tourist route, as it was obvious the girls were fading fast, but as we went through Place Sainte-Anne, both girls gasped. "It's prettier than Disney World," Cara said. Bing laughed.

We went through the iron gates, the lights in the hotel gleaming, the breeze rustling the leaves, and the fading sunlight casting shadows in every corner of the courtyard. We stumbled into my *appart* and through the newly hewn archway.

The kitchen in the adjoining flat was indeed a step up from mine. There was a full-size refrigerator, a stove that could fit more than two pots, and lots of built-in cabinets. A long table had been set by the window, with four chairs.

Cara and Mimi went through the next doorway, and I heard the squeals. I glanced at Bing, who was grinning.

"Apparently, Vera also always wanted girls," he said.

The room was painted the palest of pinks, with twin white iron beds draped in soft pink quilts and piled high with pillows. Ruffled drapes hung from the ceiling over each bed, creating canopies any princess would envy. Two white dressers were adorned with painted roses and ivy. A tall gold-framed mirror worthy of Cinderella herself was propped next to the bathroom door.

Cara dumped her little carry-on with a flourish. "This bed is mine," she declared. "Do I get a whole dresser to myself?"

I nodded, then cleared my throat. "Well, there are two dressers there, so I guess so." I noticed that there was an actual closet built in by the window, obviously newly constructed.

I glared at Bing. "Why didn't I get a real closet?"

He was still grinning, watching the girls with obvious delight. "Because you're not nine and adorable."

Georges had dropped all the luggage outside the front door, and Bing and I carried them in.

"Girls, you can unpack tomorrow." I could feel the lack of sleep creeping in, and I knew it would hit hard soon. "We all need to sleep, and in the morning, you'll get a breakfast and a tour and meet everyone. How does that sound?"

Mimi crinkled her nose. I knew they were both tired and over-whelmed by the whole trip. I also knew they could dig in their heels and be royal pains, and it looked like Mimi was headed in that direction when I heard a quiet thump of light feet landing on the stone floor.

Napoléon strutted in, tail high, ears perked, looking totally in control. He jumped up on the dresser closest to the door, sat, and observed.

"This is Napoléon Bonaparte," I said. "He sleeps here, but he's not my cat. He belongs to everyone. And if you ignore him completely, he may allow you to pet him."

Mimi's face changed, and I watched as she fell in love. "Okay, Aunt Lucy," she whispered. "If we get in bed right now, do you think he'll sleep with us?"

"Gee." I sighed. "I don't know. But let's give it a shot."

They were washed and in bed a few minutes later. Napoléon did his part, sitting patiently and watching. As I backed out of their room and turned off the light, he shot me a look, suggesting what a martyr must do for love and country.

Bing had been sitting in my little living room, reading something on his phone. He looked up when I finally sat down across from him.

"Claudine said to wait until the morning," he said. "Do you want me to stay tonight?"

I shook my head. "No. Well. Yes, I do, but chances are the girls will wake up at least once. Your being here would only add another layer of strangeness."

"Of course." He reached out a hand, and I grabbed it. "You need to tell me how to do this," he said carefully. "We had barely figured out the two of us. And now, there are four of us."

"Yeah. How about that." I watched his face as I spoke. "I know this is so much more than you ever could have bargained for. So, I will understand if you want to create, ah, a little distance."

He shook his head. "I admit to being old and overbearing. I'm trying very hard to not be such a pompous know-it-all. I will fail spectacularly, and often, but I will continue to try. If you can put up with that, I can manage a beautiful, strong woman and two little girls."

"You're not all that pompous," I muttered. "And sometimes you're very on point. I tend to be oversensitive about certain things."

He raised his eyebrows but managed to keep a straight face. "Really?"

I swallowed hard. "I love you," I said, very softly.

"Ah," he said, smiling gently. "How lovely. Because I love you, too. Very much." He leaned over and kissed me lightly on the lips, then drew back, eyes dancing. "Such declarations should be followed by opening fine wine and making long and delicious love. Sadly, we are both too tired."

I felt a giggle ripple out. "True that. One glass of wine and I'd be fast asleep."

He stood. "We will have to find a quiet afternoon, sometime quite soon, for us to mark this occasion. After all, it isn't often two people such as us can find something so joyous to celebrate."

He slipped out, and I peeled off my clothes and crawled into bed. Mimi cried out once in the night, and as I watched her, she thrashed about for a few moments, but didn't wake. Cara had her faded stuffed monkey clenched in her little fist, and she never let go even as she stretched and turned. I watched them for a few more minutes, then went back to bed, and Napoléon curled at my feet and was there in the morning.

It was cool when I awoke, the kind of cool that whispered that fall was coming. The girls and I crossed the courtyard and went into the hotel. Celestine was behind the desk on the phone, but she waved and smiled as we passed. In the salon, there were a few guests by the window. I steered the girls toward the long table, and they eyed the fruit and pastries.

"Can we have anything?" Cara whispered.

"Yes," I said. "And this is Claudine. This is her hotel. Claudine, this is Mimi, and this is Cara."

She had a handful of starched white napkins, which she put down on the table. She smiled down at them. "Welcome to my hotel," she said in slow English. "I don't speak English very well, but I'll try harder, and you will learn French, and soon we'll be good friends. Okay?"

The girls nodded.

"Just sit, girls," I told them. "I'll bring over some fruit. And bread and jam. Give me a minute, okay?"

They found a table in the farthest corner.

To my surprise, Stavros poked his head out of the kitchen. "I can make them an American breakfast," he said. "To say welcome. Eggs and bacon?"

I felt a rush of gratitude. "That would be so lovely, thank you."

He nodded. "And waffles and hash browns?"

I fought down a laugh. "No, but thank you. Just eggs and bacon."

He withdrew to the kitchen with a grin.

Claudine watched the girls. "They are beautiful," she said. "I have found them a school."

"Already? I thought, well, I mean—"

"I know what you thought, but you know nothing about schools here in France. You probably have your own ideas about how the girls should be taught, but trust me on this one. It's a very progressive school with children from all over the world attending. The girls will learn French, of course, but will not be taught in French, so they will never feel left behind." She shot me a look. "I know the headmaster."

"Yes, I'm sure you do," I said wryly. "Is it close?"

"They can walk. Or rather, you can walk them."

"Thank you."

"I'll bring you some coffee. Orange juice for the girls?"

I nodded and she hurried back into the kitchen.

I sat.

"She doesn't speak English very well, does she?" Cara asked.

"She's getting better every day. She can understand, but English is a very hard language to learn."

Mimi was not convinced. "But everyone speaks English."

I shook my head. "Nope. Sorry."

"Are we going to have to learn French?" Cara asked.

"Yes. You won't have to wait for middle school, either. Don't worry. Claudine has found a school that we can walk to every day. You can spend the afternoons right here in the hotel, if you'd like, or back in the *appart*."

Claudine set down a tray with café crème and two small glasses of orange juice. Cara looked up and said, very loudly, "Mercy."

Claudine grinned. "Very good," she said, then backed off.

"What's *appart*?" Mimi asked.

"The apartment. Where we live. Over here, it's called an *appart*."

"That's our home now?" Mimi looked up. "The *appart*?"

I nodded. "Yes. It's not very big, I know, but you two are used to sharing a room, and we have a nice kitchen where I can cook dinner and we can sit together every night." As the words fell out of my mouth, I tried not to cringe. Dinner? Every night? As in, me cooking it? But then I remembered. "Or Bing can cook for us. He's a much better cook than I."

Cara narrowed her eyes at me. "Is he your boyfriend?"

"Yes."

She made a face. "Are you in love?"

"Yes," I said again.

Mimi looked completely at a loss. "But you said that boys were stupid."

"Yes, they are. But men aren't. Not some men, anyway."

At that moment, Stavros hurried to the table, a plate in each hand, and he set them down with a flourish.

"Welcome, ladies. I have made this very special breakfast to say hello. Enjoy." He bowed and smiled, then vanished.

The girls looked at their plates.

"Bacon and eggs are special?" Mimi asked, carefully picking up a piece of bacon.

"Here, yes. Stavros went out of his way."

Mimi sighed. "Grown-ups are weird," she muttered.

"Yes, Mimi, we are. Now. Try that juice. It's the best orange juice you will ever taste."

We finished breakfast, and I carried our dishes back into the kitchen, stopping to speak to Simone and asking she thank her father for us. When I went back out to the salon, the girls were out in the patio, holding hands, looking around. I walked through the doors. Cara was smiling faintly, and Mimi nodded at something.

"Girls?" I called.

They dropped hands and skipped over.

"Did you see her?" Mimi asked.

I opened my mouth to say, "See who?" then changed my mind. "No. I never have. But you did?"

Cara nodded. "Yes. She's very pretty. She smiled at us."

"Well, then, that's a very good sign. If she likes you, then I think you'll fit right in."

They hurried inside. As ever, the patio was completely still. No wind ruffled the leaves piled in the corners, no sound of traffic.

"Thank you," I whispered and went inside.

Two days later, they walked to school. They loved the uniforms. They loved the new backpacks. They were fearless as we walked up the wide stone steps, and why wouldn't they be? They had agreed to a brand-new life, and I knew how determined they could be. They had already survived the worst. They and I knew only better days were coming.

I climbed the stairs to Bing's studio, and he put down his paints and played a little Bach while we drank cool white wine and spent the afternoon exploring each other. We both remembered patience and the value of slow kisses, light fingertips on skin, whispered words, and quiet sighs. Then he walked with me back to the school and met Cara and Mimi, and we talked about their first day as we walked beneath leaves changing green to gold, Bing with his hands behind his back, asking questions and nodding wisely.

"You have them wrapped around your little finger," I told him later.

He just shook his head. "No. Actually, it's the other way around."

I helped Marie Claude and Philippe with their new rooms. I watched her carefully as she said to me, "You did such a wonderful job; would you mind helping us? Eliot was, well, he was a minimalist. We had nothing of warmth or color. And Philippe, well, he wants everything all at once, all the books and all the paintings . . . It's too much for me."

"This is a big step, Marie Claude," I said cautiously. "I so appreciate your giving up your *appart,* but are you sure?"

She looked down at her hands, then up at me. "I have told him that the hotel is my home and that I cannot be with him if it is not his home also. He says he is done with wandering and that he is ready to build a life with me. He even thinks he might learn the hotel business." She glanced up. "But even if he doesn't, I know enough. Our children will someday own this place, and I will be able to teach them."

"Okay, then," I said. "Whatever furniture was left was trundled up to the attic, so at least we won't have to worry about moving it too far. And I know Claudine stashed a few treasures in that little room behind her study."

Their rooms were on the other side of the attic, away from Bing's studio, up another narrow stairway tucked in yet another forgotten corner. There were no wide windows, so Philippe decided to continue to work with Bing, but the three small rooms quickly became overstuffed with plush chairs and layered rugs, lamps draped in red silk scarves, piles of books and small framed artwork leaning against every surface. The one bathroom had been for the servants, of course, narrow, windowless, and cold. Marie Claude just lifted an eyebrow at Philippe.

"I refuse," she said mildly, "to have sex in that shower."

Philippe looked stricken, threw me a wicked grin, and got down on both knees in front of her. "I promise, you'll have a beautiful new shower with no ugly black grout," he said.

She looked unimpressed as she took a small pile of folded towels from me. "Maybe."

He grabbed the towels from her hands. "A claw-foot tub?" he teased.

She pulled the towels back. "Maybe."

"With a chandelier?"

She looked very serious, then nodded. "Yes. With lots of tiny crystals. But you must promise me that I will never have to clean it. I am responsible for the chandelier in the lobby, and that is as much of a burden as I can bear."

Philippe stood and grabbed her, bending her backward, towels and all, and gave her a long kiss. When she finally returned upright, she seemed unruffled.

"Yes, well. But still no sex in that shower until it is fixed. Understood?" Finally, a crack of a smile.

He beamed back. "But we can have sex everywhere else?"

"Of course," she said lightly, and I laughed with them, because of course they were in love, of course they were perfect for each other.

Of course. This had been worth the long and lonely time away.

⁓

It felt odd that Thanksgiving was not celebrated in France, but when the day came, I made a turkey and Bing did the rest—stuffing and roasted carrots, creamed onions and fresh cranberries cooked down with orange and sugar and a splash of wine. Philippe and Marie Claude brought stuffed mushrooms, and Vera made an apple tart. Karl had a box of perfect little chocolates. Claudine had arrived with long baguettes and a crock of honey. Colin brought the hard cider and played music for us, the girls listening as if to a pop star.

It was a lovely holiday. We FaceTimed Mom and Dad, and even my niece Heather got in a call, promising her cousins that she would visit next year.

"Can I visit, Aunt Lucy?" she asked. "I know Mom and Dad will throw a fit, but I have money saved."

"Of course you can," I told her.

It was the following week that another phone call came from Agent Whitman, this time telling me that the money that Tony Fielding had stolen had been placed in an escrow account, and he would be sending me the paperwork necessary to have it returned to me. I gripped the phone as he told me.

"Did you hear what I just said, Miss Gianetti?" he asked after a very long pause in the conversation.

"Yes. Yes, I heard. That's . . . that is amazing news. Thank you for telling me."

"Everyone else got a nice, formal registered letter, but I wanted to break the news to you myself," he said.

"I appreciate that," I said, and I meant it.

I had been in the *appartement,* of course, but after I hung up, I walked out and looked across the courtyard, swept clean of all the leaves that had fallen and looking quite empty.

The stable block across from me was the same length as the *appartement* block, so I knew what the interior space looked like. We could put bathrooms across the back, and individual heating units.

I squinted. Maybe we could build a pergola across the front, create small individual patios with iron chairs and potted palms. We could replace the heavy wooden doors with *portes-fenêtres,* lightly draped with soft linen, the inside rooms painted soft cream with dark, stained floors and thick-hewn beams. Ten more rooms. We could fit two double beds in each unit, bringing our occupancy numbers up to over fifty guests. The magic number. We would be able to accommodate tour groups.

If we began now, the rooms would be ready by the start of the season. Maybe sooner.

As I walked back into the hotel, my mind started doing the math. With more rooms, we'd need more help, someone else in housekeeping for sure. Maybe we could hire someone to help Karl and act as a bellman, toting luggage up the grand staircase. But the additional income . . . We could charge more for the outside units, of course. . . . What would we call them? Not suites, exactly. Carriage house rooms? Guesthouse rooms?

Claudine and Philippe were together in the office as I went back in.

She looked up, a broad smile on her face. "We are starting to get reservations for the Christmas markets. They're very popular here in Rennes. People come from all over. We'll fill up fast. And Philippe would like to learn more about them."

I stopped, delighted. "And does this mean we may have some extra help back here?"

He rolled his eyes. "Between Marie Claude and my mother, it would appear that I am doomed to take up the reins here sooner or later. I have decided to stop trying to turn the tide."

"That's great. Really. And I'm glad you're both here, because I need to ask you both—is there a word in French for the rooms we can make out there in the stables? Once we renovate them, I mean. I was thinking *carriage house,* but that's not quite right."

Claudine raised an eyebrow. "I thought we didn't have any money to do that. I believe *you* told me that?"

I sat. "Well, here's the thing, Claudine. I think I have found you a new investor."

She sat down across from me, folded her hands, and leaned in.

"Tell me," she said.

So I did.

Acknowledgments

As ever, my thanks to Lynn Seligman for always being a believer.

Thanks also to Alice Pfeifer at St. Martin's for being my head cheerleader and having infinite patience and grace.

And to Olga Grlic, Jen Edwards, Gail Friedman, Chrisinda Lynch, Sara Ensey, Marissa Sangiacomo, Alyssa Gammello, Anne Marie Tallberg, and all of those who worked behind the scenes, who I never met and maybe never will, but who have helped make this book the best it can be—my heartfelt thanks and appreciation for all your hard work.

About the Author

3 Chicks That Click

Dee Ernst began her career as a writer in Morristown, New Jersey, in the fourth grade, equipped with a spiral-bound notebook and a blue Bic pen. Her dreams of being a writer persisted through several college majors, multiple career choices, and many, *many* years. She self-published her first book in 2010. *Lucy Checks In* is her second book with St. Martin's Griffin, proving that dreams do, in fact, come true if you're willing to keep on trying. She lives in northern New Jersey with her husband, two spoiled cats, and a very lucky terrier mix, working, as always, on the next book.